Picking u[p]
of his new gu[n]
when a hard knock on his door shook him out of his reverie.

A man planted his feet and stood akimbo in the doorway, a man who presented an intimidating impression with his rugged good looks, his burnt mahogany hair and eyes. He announced in a firm voice with an English accent, "My name is Jonas McDever, and I am the captain of the *Scarlet Lion*. I have come to get the new weapon you are working on."

Reid looked up from his worktable as an uneasiness settled over him. He recognized the captain's name, and his ship, the *Scarlet Lion,* was one reputed to attack and destroy any other ship unfortunate enough to get within spyglass range. This McDever was a pirate of the worst sort, and proud to be one.

"I dinna ken what ye're talking about. I have no new weapon to show ye."

McDever took a step forward and pressed his fists into his hips, using his height and stance to assert his power and control. "I'm not here to argue with you."

Praise for Susan Leigh Furlong

STEADFAST WILL I BE:
"A certain hit for those who love highland historical romances!"

~Juliette Hyland

BY PROMISE MADE:
Finalist in N.N. Heaven's Book for Best Book of 2020
"*BY PROMISE MADE* is a historical romance I couldn't put down. The descriptive narration is so well done, I sniffed the air and heard the sounds of everything going on."

~N.N. Light

BY PROMISE MADE:
"The Scotsman Hugh Cullane—His skills are many, his attraction irresistible."

~Kat Doran

KEEPER OF MY DREAMS:
"Once again Furlong has given us a beautifully written historical novel that combines intrigue, adventure, and romance. She weaves the actual history of the time throughout the book. Another captivating novel written by this talented author!"

~Claudia Rogers

Keeper of My Dreams

by

Susan Leigh Furlong

This is a work of fiction. Names, characters, places, and incidents are either the product of the author's imagination or are used fictitiously, and any resemblance to actual persons living or dead, business establishments, events, or locales, is entirely coincidental.

Keeper of My Dreams

COPYRIGHT © 2021 by Susan Leigh Furlong

All rights reserved. No part of this book may be used or reproduced in any manner whatsoever without written permission of the author or The Wild Rose Press, Inc. except in the case of brief quotations embodied in critical articles or reviews.
Contact Information: info@thewildrosepress.com

Cover Art by *Abigail Owen*

The Wild Rose Press, Inc.
PO Box 708
Adams Basin, NY 14410-0708
Visit us at www.thewildrosepress.com

Publishing History
First Edition, 2021
Trade Paperback ISBN 978-1-5092-3713-5
Digital ISBN 978-1-5092-3714-2

Published in the United States of America

Dedication

I dedicate this to all the people who say "Wow!"
when I tell them I'm a writer.
They say being a writer is something special,
but I think they are the special ones.

Chapter One

Stirling, Scotland, 1586, during the reigns of King James VI of Scotland and Queen Elizabeth I of England

The door to the inn had barely shut behind her when a horse trotted by on the rain-soaked street, splattering her with gobbets of mud from the waist down.

"Oh, Losh! Crivvens!" she cried out.

Two men, pulling up their collars against the drizzle from last night's late summer downpour, passed by, laughing aloud. "Serves ye right," one said. "Ye're a country lass? Have ye no' been on a street afore?"

Leena turned a cold eye in the men's direction. Even if she were a country lass from her family's estate in the southern Highlands and proud of it and even if this were her first time in a city, he had no right to point it out. She wanted to shout back at him with a string of curses far worse than "losh" and "crivvens," using words her older brothers had taught her, but she thought better of it, especially since they weren't around to defend her. The men walked away still laughing.

While shaking her skirt to get the mud off as best she could, she crinkled her nose. *What was that nasty smell?* A rotten, garbage-filled trench ran down the middle of the road, and the stench made her eyes water. How could the townspeople live with that filthy channel of refuse right under their noses? Her home at Makgullane in the Highlands, just like anywhere else, accumulated trash and garbage, but no one would think to throw it in an open trough. They disposed of it properly!

Nevertheless, she had a mission to reach the wardrobe mercer's shop across the road to buy cloth and notions. It was one of the reasons she and her brothers had come to this awful city, so she tugged her shawl over her head and took her first tentative steps. Horses, wagons, and people heading in all directions at a fast pace darted around her in a confusing dance unknown to Leena.

She was nearly across to the mercer's shop when disaster struck.

Two young girls, herding a gaggle of geese across the muddy, rut-riddled street, arrived at the same spot as three men carrying bales of fleece coming from the opposite direction. Before Leena could cry out a warning, a chaotic mess of feathers, fleece, shouting men, and squawking geese surrounded her. Stumbling, she fell facedown over a bale of fleece now sitting ruined in the mud. She righted herself just as the geese tangled in her legs again, honking and nipping at her. One of the fleece-carrying men grabbed her arm, but instead of helping her up, he pushed her away while trying to keep his own bale from falling into the garbage-filled drain.

Knowing that if she ended up in that trough, it would be the worst day she'd ever had in her life, she closed her eyes and prepared to land on her backside.

Suddenly strong arms wrapped around her waist, lifting her up. Those arms carried her safely the rest of the way across the street to the wardrobe mercer's front door where, pressed against a tall, muscular man wearing a leather apron, she eventually found her footing.

"Oh, my stars," she said in a breathless voice. When at last she stood upright and balanced, those arms released her.

Turning around to see her rescuer, she looked up into his most enchanting pair of eyes. Sparkling flecks of white light bounced off bright blue centers, although blue wasn't the right word to describe them.

Azure, maybe.

Bluebell. Nay, too ordinary to describe these eyes.

Incredible, aye, incredible like the sky on a cloudless day in the middle of summer at noon on the happiest day of the year.

"Are ye all right?" he asked. "Ye're out of the road now. Can ye stand on yer own?" His mellow voice floated around her, but the words were meaningless. Those eyes held her spellbound.

When she didn't answer, he put his callused hands on her arms. "Let me help ye to the bench so ye can catch yer breath."

She let him lead her to a wooden bench outside the gunsmith shop next door. Backing her up to the seat, he gently pushed her to sit. "There, that's better. Take a few minutes to gather yerself."

She could not stop looking at him. His thick hair, a smoky gray with splashes of white, fell carelessly around a chiseled face. He needed a shave, and his generous eyebrows matched the black in his beard. Even the thin rays of crow's feet at his temples suited the look of him perfectly.

"I'll get yer shawl out of the mud," he said as he stepped back into the street, shooed some geese out of the way, and picked up her knitted woolen shawl. Holding the mud-soaked garment well out in front of him, he opened the door to the mercer's shop and called in, "Ethel! Ethel, can ye help me here?"

A pretty young woman with ginger hair twisted into a bun at the nape of her neck appeared in the doorway. "Master Haliburton, what is it ye want?"

"Can ye clean off this shawl for this woman? She nearly fell into the mud, but the shawl got the worst of it. Can ye help her?"

"For ye, I can." Scrunching up her nose, she took the filthy shawl, held it with two fingers, and vanished into the shop.

"Ethel's a good lass. She'll do the best she can."

But Leena couldn't look away from this man. Every detail about him intrigued her, including a slight tear at the shoulder of his sark. Knowing she could stitch it closed in no time at all, she reached up to touch it, but she quickly pulled her hand down.

Words began to form in her head. They turned out to be ridiculous words.

"How old are ye?" Leena asked.

His forehead furrowed and his lip curled, telling her she had embarrassed herself beyond all social acceptability, first by stumbling in the street like a colt learning to trot, and again with her rude question.

"I am thirty-nine," he said, quickly adding, "How old are ye?"

Leena swallowed hard as a blush rose in her cheeks. "A lady ne'er reveals her age."

His eyebrows shot up. "Well, this one better, or I'll

put ye back where I found ye about to land on yer arse in the puddle." The stern expression on his face said he meant it.

"I...I...am thirty-two."

"For sooth?"

"Do ye think me a liar?"

"Nay, mistress. 'Tis that I would have guessed younger."

Leena's blush rose higher. "My brothers say I look like an old hag, eighty-five at least. They're no' a kind bunch."

"Brothers rarely are."

An awkward silence passed between them before he said, "If ye're all right, I'm on an errand, and I'm late as it is. So if ye're feeling like yerself again, I will leave ye to yer own errands."

He turned away, but she put her hand on his wrist. She couldn't let him leave thinking she was a mannerless fool!

"Please, forgive me," she said, talking faster with each word. "The near fall must have shaken all my manners clear out of my head. I'm here with my brothers to buy things we canna find in the Highlands. Please, dinna think me an ignorant bumpkin, but I've ne'er been to a town this big before, ne'er had to cross a street so crowded. I apologize for my clumsiness. I made myself look like a fool, and now I'm chattering on and on like a sparrow in the tree. I do that when I'm flustered."

She took a deep breath to calm herself. "Forgive me. I am usually no' as rude as my brothers. Thank ye for rescuing me."

"I would hardly call it a rescue, more like a

gentlemanly kindness, and there's no need to apologize. The geese and the fleece should have been looking where they were going. Courtesy would have avoided all of this."

With a wave of his hand, he silenced one of the fleece men, who had flung a muddy bale of fleece over his shoulder and glared at Leena before walking away.

"And I ne'er would have guessed ye were one of yer brothers. Good day."

"Wait, sir, what is yer name? I am Leena Cullane Adair." Her words came out in a rush again. "My parents named me 'Kathleen,' but my three-year-old twin brothers couldna say it right, so it came out 'Leena.' And I've been 'Leena' ever since. Look, I'm rambling again." Taking another deep breath and, speaking slowly, she said, "My name is Leena Adair."

He turned back in her direction with an amused look on his face. "My name is Reid, Reid Haliburton. I'm the gunsmith, and my shop is right here." He pointed behind the bench. "Good day, again."

He left Leena thinking wicked thoughts about him, thoughts she hadn't had about a man in eight years, not since her husband, Johnnie, had died. *He does look fine walking away!*

Leena couldn't push the tall gunsmith out of her mind until the moment she stepped through the door of the shop and became mesmerized by the stacks of colorful cloth on the tables and on shelves from floor to ceiling. She stared at the rolls of material in every color she could imagine. The shop in the town nearest to her home of Makgullane never carried more than twelve bolts of plain cloth, mostly sturdy linen, but here were silk, and satin, and the finest imported woven cotton.

"Here, mistress," said a voice behind her.

Leena jumped, knocking several ells of green linen to the floor. "I didn't see you."

"Aye, mistress," said Ethel, picking up the dropped cloth and setting it back on the table before holding out Leena's shawl. "Just as Reid asked, a cleaner shawl."

Unfolding it, Leena said, "Ye did a fine job getting the mud off. Once it dries, I'll be able to wear it again. Thank ye so much."

Ethel rolled her pale hazel eyes and spoke in a monotone. "May I show ye something in the shop, mistress?" After only a brief pause, she repeated, "May I help ye find something, mistress, anything? If no' I have work to do."

Leena and her older twin brothers, Taran and Dillon, had planned this trip to Stirling for weeks, and everyone understood how important it was to the family estate. They had managed quite well in recent years with abundant harvests and good prices at livestock sales, and now they had enough coin to purchase brand new tools to ease the endless need to repair the old ones. This was a once-in-a-lifetime trip.

All the hands on the estate had begged to go, now that the biggest part of the harvest had been completed, but Taran and Dillon could buy anything they needed, and their older brother, Bran, and their father, Robin, would pick up the slack in their workload left by their absence. The twins would return with two new ploughshares, leather enough to redo reins and straps, two metal flails for threshing, and scythes along with other assorted tools, maybe even a new saddle. What a celebration the day of their return would be!

As for Leena, she had come to buy cloth and

notions for new work clothes for nearly everyone living on the estate. Mending and patching were the custom, so all the women and girls were giddy about getting something new. Leena had to admit that being able to choose fabrics and patterns would be as thrilling for her as purchasing new tools would be for her brothers.

Leena had promised her mother and her younger sister, Meara, that she would also look for something special for them. Her mother, Suannoch, might be satisfied with the same sturdy cloth as the maids, but Leena insisted on something fancier for her. Meara, on the other hand, did love pretty things and insisted that Leena look for only the best and newest fashion for her. *Green or yellow, please!*

Leena, pulling herself out of her anticipation of actually running her hands over the beautiful fabrics, said, "I am looking for durable cloth to make work clothes. Do ye carry that?"

"We carry a large selection of working-class fabrics," said Ethel, "but 'tis in the back of the shop. This way."

Leena followed the younger woman past the rows and rows of fine fabric down a hallway to a room that was much less tidy. Here the sturdy, less elegant material hung on racks or sat haphazardly on tables. The colors were fewer, mostly dull reds and shades of brown with the occasional gray or blue.

"Look through what we have, and call me after ye've made yer selection," said Ethel quickly as the door clattered shut behind her.

"Well!" muttered Leena. Could the reason for Ethel's rudeness have to do with Reid Haliburton? Did Ethel fancy him? He was certainly a handsome man, and he probably caught the eye of many women in Stirling, but 'twas of no matter to Leena. She would only be here for a sennight, and she had a job to do.

It didn't take long to make her choices. She decided on bolts of dark brown to make trews for all the men and dark blue for overdresses for the women. Some dorneck linen in a light beige would do for sarks and blouses. Then a serviceable, but nice-looking broadcloth for waistcoats for the men, and surprisingly, she spotted a bright yellow for aprons for the women. She also noticed balls of lemister wool in the corner that would do nicely to make knitted caps.

After carrying everything to an empty table near the door, she went to find Ethel in the front of the shop. "I left the material I want on the table," she said to her.

"We'll wrap it up and prepare your charges. If ye will wait by the window, I will get it ready for ye."

Leena's brothers carried all the money they had brought with them from Makgullane, hiding it in pouches under their sarks and vests. Leena had only a few coins, so whatever she purchased she would have to ask the proprietor to keep on hold until her brothers returned to pay for it. This arrangement annoyed her, as if she couldn't be responsible with money because she was a woman, but she did agree it was safer. Pickpockets and thieves were everywhere in a town the size of Stirling, and as a woman, she would be an easy target.

"Please, put it on account, and I'll return to pay in full this evening or tomorrow morning at the latest."

Ethel scowled and stuck out her chin. "Mistress, we dinna put large orders on account for strangers. Master Haliburton may be a friend of the shop, but even he canna vouch for yer credit."

Without looking at Ethel, Leena fingered some expensive dark blue caffa damask on a nearby table. "In that case, I will purchase all my cloth needs for my twenty workers and for myself, my sister, and my mother elsewhere. I am certain another shop will carry even lovelier caffa and, perhaps, some sarcenet and taffeta for our gowns. We also have need of wool for cloaks, but since I canna put anything on account here, I will order elsewhere, including what we need for comfortable undergarments and the necessary thread, needles, and other notions…since ye canna accommodate me." She paused and for her trouble received the response she expected.

"In that case, mistress, I am certain the master of this shop will be glad to open an account for ye. What kind of gowns do ye have in mind?"

A rich green satin for Meara drew her eye. "My sister is verra particular. May I take this bolt out into the sunlight to check the color accurately?"

"Of course," said Ethel. Lifting the roll, she followed Leena to the door and out onto the street.

Leena draped a length of cloth over her arm, admiring how the sunlight, which had suddenly appeared out of the clouds, glistened over the cloth. She imagined how the gown would look on Meara against her curly black hair and green eyes. Out of the corner of her eye, she noticed three lads sitting on the bench in front of the gunsmith shop.

"Do ye like this color?" she said to them.

The youngest one on the end of the bench looked over and said, " 'Tis verra pretty, mistress, but I like blue better."

"Oh," said Leena. To the clerk she said, "Could you bring me a bolt in blue to compare?" Ethel left the green cloth with Leena and scurried back inside.

"How are ye lads this morning?" she asked as she walked closer to the bench.

The oldest one said, "We're fine, mistress. We're waiting for our father. He's taking us to our lessons."

Leena knew right away who this lad's father was. He looked just like him, with lighter hair that would darken as he got older, but the same brilliant blue eyes and strong jaw.

"Ye're Reid Haliburton's sons."

The lads nodded. "Aye, mistress," said the older one.

"I'm glad to hear ye're taking lessons. An education is a fine thing." Noticing the small chapbook in his hand, she asked, "What are ye reading?"

The lad quickly folded the few dog-eared pages and tucked it into his sark. " 'Tis naught. Our teacher, Mistress Waltham, says we shouldna read such drivel."

"Is it an exciting story?" she asked.

The middle lad jumped up. " 'Tis one about a brave woman named Lyra. She was named after the stars, and she goes on many adventures."

Leena smiled, knowing that her husband, Johnnie Adair, now dead for eight years, had written that chapbook and made her the heroine in it. A small line at the end of *The Star of Lyra* read "My Lyra came out of the stars and into my arms."

Just then Ethel returned with a smaller bolt of the same fabric in a rich midnight blue. Holding it up beside the green, she said, "We have less of this blue left. What do ye think, mistress?"

As Leena compared the colors, Reid Haliburton strode past them. Stopping briefly in front of the bench, he said in a tone that demanded immediate obedience, "Off ye go. I'll follow to make certain ye get to yer class."

The lads jumped off the bench at once and ran up the street. Reid started after them, but stopped and turned back, fixing Leena with his incredible sapphire-colored eyes. "The blue complements yer coloring better. Choose it," he said before leaving to follow his sons.

After he was out of earshot, Ethel tipped her head close to Leena. "Their mum used to walk the lads to classes every morn, so Reid could work on his guns, but she died a few years ago, and now their da takes them and picks them up after class every day. They wait here every morning while he does his daily errand. Reid is quite clever, always making his weapons better than anyone else's. Many people come to his shop, but he doesna sell to everyone, only the ones who use the guns for a proper purpose, no' to kill people. He willna sell to soldiers."

"A noble purpose, but no' always possible to do."

"He's raising his sons alone. They're well-mannered lads and friendly."

"Mr. Haliburton is setting a fine example for them. He rescued me from landing in the mud in the street today, and I am most grateful."

In a scolding tone, Ethel said, "Dinna be getting thoughts about him."

Leena didn't answer. *'Tis too late for that.*

"Many unmarried women in Stirling wouldna mind helping him raise those lads, myself included, but he has no time for anything besides working on his guns. He makes fine ones, he does. He is well-known and well respected in Stirling."

"Where does he go every morning?"

"As I said, 'Dinna be getting thoughts about him.' How do ye like the blue?"

"I'll take the green for my sister." She smiled and let her eyes follow the handsome gunsmith striding away. "And I will take the blue for myself."

Chapter Two

After taking his lads to their lessons, Reid came back to the shop and, propping open the door to let fresh air in, sat at his worktable. Looking over the pieces of his newest innovation, he smiled proudly. This gun would contribute improvements to all future weapons. Previous developments like the matchlock, and more recently the flintlock, would disappear once his gun came into common use. He'd worked equally hard at keeping it a secret until he could thoroughly test it and find appropriate buyers, buyers who would use it to keep the peace. In the wrong hands, it could destroy lives.

He fingered the parts still left to assemble on the weapon as he recalled the noisy squawking of that gaggle of geese. He had more important things to think about than some silly woman who couldn't cross the street! Still he couldn't quite shake her away.

Picking up a rag, he mindlessly polished the barrel of his new gun. He'd only been at it for a few minutes when a hard knock on his door shook him out of his reverie.

A man planted his feet and stood akimbo in the doorway, a man who presented an intimidating impression with his rugged good looks, his burnt mahogany hair and eyes. He announced in a firm voice with an English accent, "My name is Jonas McDever, and I am the captain of the *Scarlet Lion.* I have come to get the new weapon you are working on."

Reid looked up from his worktable as an uneasiness settled over him. He recognized the captain's name and his ship, the *Scarlet Lion,* as one reputed to attack and destroy any other ship unfortunate enough to get within spyglass range. This McDever was a pirate of the worst sort, and proud to be one.

"I dinna ken what ye're talking about. I have no new weapon to show ye."

McDever took a step forward and pressed his fists into his hips, using his height and stance to assert his power and control. "I'm not here to argue with you. I am looking for a gun that needs no spanner wrench to wind the wheel lock, only a trigger to cock it, and has a smaller flintlock. It also has a flash pan that only needs refilling every thirty shots. That is the weapon I am looking for."

"I dinna think such a weapon exists," said Reid as he walked around the table away from McDever.

"On that, my good man, I am certain you are wrong."

"I dinna ken where ye get yer information."

"Where do you think?"

McDever could have heard about his gun only one way. The Wardens of the Guild.

The Stirling Wardens of the Guild required every member to report original developments to them in order to monitor quality, to prevent the sale of below-standard work, and to maintain the prices a gunsmith earned. Earlier in the month, Reid had presented his new handgun to the Wardens, and knowing its impact on the world of weaponry, they had agreed to total secrecy until he finished it and it was ready for sale. Clearly word had leaked out. Most likely it came from a warden in his cups, bragging at some tavern, and now this pirate had shown up at Reid's door.

"Do you know anything about rifling the barrel?" asked McDever.

Reid took a deep breath through his nose. His most creative advancement came from rifling the barrel for improved accuracy. Other people had tried to rifle long guns, muskets, and such, but so far no one had been successful with a smaller piece, no one until Reid. Previously, carving each groove into the barrel one at a time was a tedious and lengthy process with questionable accuracy, but he'd designed and built a tool that carved all the rifling grooves in the barrel at once.

Hesitating for only a moment, Reid said, "I ken of the process. Many men have hopes to perfect it in large weapons sometime in the future, but I havena attempted it myself." Reid was glad the boring tool he had made to do the rifling was not out on the table.

With a haughty sniff, McDever said, "I am tired of this game. Reid Haliburton has made such a handheld weapon. Are you Reid Haliburton?"

"I am, but I have no weapons like ye describe to show ye. I have other work to do. Good day."

McDever, pushing his tricorne hat off his forehead, gazed out the open door of the shop. "Perhaps I can offer you this. I have seen your sons when you take them to school. Handsome lads. I captain my own ship, the *Scarlet Lion*, and a fine ship it is. I have need of another cabin boy. Would one or two of them like to become cabin boys on my ship?"

Reid whipped around. "Is that idle curiosity…or a threat?"

Turning his back on Reid, McDever said, "I will return on Thursday evening, and I will either leave with a weapon that pleases me, or I will have a new cabin boy. Good day, Reid Haliburton. I look forward to meeting your sons."

"Ye willna threaten me or my lads! Get out!"

In long strides, McDever left the shop and crossed the street to join two companions waiting for him in the alleyway that ran beside the inn. One of them, a tall bull of a man, wore a dingy linen sark that laced up the front and cinched at the waist with a silver belt buckle, while the other, a black-skinned Moor, dressed in baggy gray pants, an open vest, and tall leather boots.

McDever said, "Haliburton is a most uncooperative man. He's not the least interested in doing his duty."

The three men laughed.

"But if I feel generous," McDever went on, "I might let the gunsmith say a word or two before I slit his throat and walk away with the gun. I gave him until the end of the week."

The three men strode down the street and out the city gate.

Reid's gaze followed McDever and his men until they disappeared around the corner, and now he paced the length of the shop, breathing hard. How had his life's decisions led him to this debacle?

Having labored for years as a blacksmith with his father and finding the work boring and tedious, he finally convinced his father to let him apprentice to an established gunsmith. He worked his way up to journeyman, and after making a weapon that passed inspection by the guild, his "masterpiece" as it was called, he set off on his own, establishing his own shop and building a profitable business. He challenged himself to make the best weapons possible, and with this new handgun he was convinced that he had.

McDever could make himself a fortune by getting Reid's prototype to London and having it mass-produced by the hundreds of gunsmiths who worked there, induced to come years ago by King Henry VIII, who wanted to build England's arsenal. McDever could then sell it to whoever offered him the most. He'd have no scruples about who bought it, only that they paid well, very well. The results could be disastrous!

Reid had hoped to have some control over who acquired his gun. Enemies of Scotland and England were everywhere, but his intention had been to provide his homeland extra protection, ensuring a balance of power. How foolish he was!

Reid still believed that guns could, and should, serve to ultimately achieve peace. For centuries, men had served some form of military service in the protection of their families and villages. It was a common, accepted duty. Bearing arms, be it swords, bows and arrows, or now guns, was associated with being a Frank or a free man. A weapon meant freedom, something all men desired, the right to live their lives without the oppression of those who were stronger. Weapons of any kind were the great equalizer between the rich and the poor, the noble and the common. Even the clergy, monks, and priests who preached peace and kindness carried swords under their robes.

How Reid wished he could talk to someone, anyone, about the threat his gun now proved to his sons.

How could he protect them?

Reid pounded his fists in frustration on the worktable, making the pieces of the unfinished weapon bounce around. The ramrod rolled onto the floor. Picking it up, he sat back down to put finishing adjustments on each piece and to assemble it. Mayhap by the time he finished it, he could think of some way to escape what now seemed an inevitable calamity.

****

Just after sunrise the next morning, Reid pushed open the gate to the graveyard of the Church of the Holy Rood, and the gate gave its familiar creak, just as it had every morning for the last five years.

He found himself thinking about the woman he'd saved from the mud yesterday. She had asked how old he was. For certain, she was an odd one from the Highland country, but werena they all?

He noticed other things about her, too, like the smile that brightened her entire face, her round, nearly black eyes, and hair that fell down her back in waves of chestnut brown. Most noticeable were the pronounced, thick, even strands of gold that framed each side of her face, almost as if someone had painted them on. Even braided into several braids all held back with a clip, the golden tresses accented the shiny brown.

Extraordinary!

She'd been standing at the bench talking to his sons when he returned to the shop yesterday. In her arms she held two lengths of cloth, one green and one blue, and as he passed by, he had said, "The blue complements yer coloring better. Choose it."

Why had he said that? Why did he care what cloth she chose? She was a stranger in Stirling, so what difference did it make to him?

To his surprise, there she was again, that Highland woman, standing in the graveyard six rows back and eight graves to the left in front of the stone that read "Marjorie Haliburton, 'Maggie,' Cherished wife and mother, age 32 years, 3 months, 8 days."

"What are ye doing here?" he asked her gruffly as he approached the grave.

"Good morning. Is this yer wife?"

"Aye."

"And these two yer sons?"

Carved on the stone next to Marjorie's was "Thomas Haliburton, 'Tommie,' age 12 years, 6 months, 2 days." His firstborn. The other one belonged to his second son, "David Haliburton, 'Davie,' age 11 years, 1 day."

"They all died of putrid throat on the same day five years ago," he said. "I come every morning to spend time with them, and I've done that every day since they were buried in the ground. What are ye doing here?"

"I, too, spend time every morning in the graveyard at our home at Makgullane. 'Tis a hard habit to break."

He rested his hand on Marjorie's headstone as if to claim it and in some silent way let her know she was intruding on his private time.

"My husband, Johnnie, died eight years ago," she said. "Stepped on a rusty nail four days after we were married and died a week later."

"I'm sorry."

"Graveyards are no' for worshipping the dead, but for honoring the ones we loved, the ones we still love. I cherished every day I had with Johnnie, and I visit to remember him. It brings me some peace. I wanted to come here and get to know at least the names of people who have lived here in Stirling. I hope ye dinna mind that I lingered at yer wife's stone. And yer sons."

"The priest says they are waiting for me in heaven, but I need them here with me." His face went dark with inner pain. "I need to touch her cheek. I need to tousle my lads' hair." His words came quick and harsh. "I need to hear their voices! Hear their laughter!" He turned away from Leena.

"Johnnie and I loved each other for a year afore we wed," she said quietly. "He earned his living traveling around Scotland as a balladeer and teller of stories at fairs and festivals, and what a voice he had. The first time I heard him singing, I followed the sound until I found him."

She smiled, remembering. "He wasna what ye'd call a handsome man, with his long, fawn-colored hair. If the wind blew it over his face, it covered his gray eyes and his lopsided smile, but he drew everyone in with his outgoing nature. He made life an adventure.

"It took all my courage to leave him and come here to Stirling. My brothers, Taran and Dillon, had to practically drag me away from my last visit to his grave. This will be the longest I've ever been away." She laid her hand on her heart. "I was terrified that if I came here I'd lose him, forget him, but I find that he's still here with me." She patted her chest. "His life is in mine, no matter where I am, and it always will be."

Reid turned around to face her. "He sounds like quite a man."

Impulsively touching his arm, she said, "He wrote down some of his stories into chapbooks, a few pages, and sold them for a penny or two. Traveling chapmen sold other similar stories, but Johnnie's were the most popular. He wrote the one yer lads are reading."

"They're reading a chapbook?"

"Aye, 'tis a wonderful one filled with stories of a woman on a quest, a woman named…" She paused. "I can see ye disapprove of the book, just like the lads' teacher does, but ye should read it afore ye dismiss it. Lads like adventure, and this one is an exciting story. I love the idea that she is named after the stars."

He let out a slow breath before saying, "Could I have some time here alone?"

"Aye, of course, I didna intend to impose. Thank ye again for saving me from the mud."

She left the graveyard through the gate, but he kept an eye on her until she safely crossed the street at the corner. Such a clumsy woman needed watching. Then he turned his attention back to the Haliburton graves.

" 'Tis a bit chilly today," he said.

Some days the morning sun shone through the trees directly onto her grave, and he could almost hear Marjorie saying, "Good morn, my man!" On those days he smiled. But after nights full of troubled dreams of her calling to him, she stayed silent. Today, not a word.

His two oldest lads would be near grown now. What would they be like had they lived? Tommie would be tall and dark-haired, and he'd be working right beside his father, learning to be a gunsmith. Davie would have grown into a man more like his mother, one who loved to read and study. Davie would have made them so proud by going to university and becoming a scholar, but Reid would never know. No one would ever know.

His three youngest sons, Willie, Ramy, and

Hendrie, were his life now. Marjorie had wanted them called by their full names, William, Raymond, and Hendrick, and she often scolded him for not using their entire given names. He missed her scolding him.

Maggie'd be so proud of her sons. Each had a kind heart and brave soul, and their futures stood before them, but he needed to know what he should do to make certain they continued to grow up properly. He needed to know if he disciplined the lads too harshly, if her gentle guidance would be better for them. Together the two of them had made a balance, but alone his surety failed him.

He wanted to talk to her about the new handgun he'd designed and about the man who had come trying to claim it, but instead, after touching the gravestone of each of his lost beloved, he said, "I love ye, and ye are a part of me forever." Without looking back, he walked out of the graveyard.

Chapter Three

The next day, the sun shone bright with nary a cloud in the sky as Reid and his three sons stepped out the door of the gunsmith shop.

He'd had a long night working on the gun, and he had finally completed it. Still struggling with how to handle McDever and his demands, he reasoned that a finished weapon gave him more bargaining power and a better way to protect his sons.

"Fine day to test our weapon," said Reid, looking up and shielding his eyes from the glare.

"Is it truly that we dinna have to go to classes today, Da?" asked Ramy.

"Nay, no' today. Today we're spending the day together." Reid wanted to make this an adventure for the lads, not just a way to keep them within his sight and safe from McDever and his two friends. "Did ye get the bread and apples? How about the dried fish? Is the flask filled with beer? Enough for all of us?"

Willie held up a cloth bag filled with thick slices of bread, four apples, and leftover chips of the dried fish they'd had for their evening meal. "Here!" he said.

Dark-haired Ramy raised two flasks, calling out, "Beer!" while little Hendrie, a towhead with two front teeth missing, opened a square cloth filled with sweet oatcakes. "Mistress Ethel made these for us."

"Ye better no' eat them until we've had our share!"

said Ramy, giving his younger brother a poke in the arm so that he almost dropped the oatcakes.

"Hey, careful, or none of us will get any," said Willie.

"I have the gun in here," said Reid, patting a lumpy cloth bag slung over his shoulder, "and Willie has the tools. Looks like we're ready."

Just as Reid closed the door to the gunsmith shop, Leena Adair stepped out of the mercer's, fanning her face with a piece of linen. Spotting the gunsmith and his sons, she said, "Good morn to all the Haliburtons."

Hendrie ran up to her. "We dinna have to go to classes today!"

"Well, sometimes it helps to take a little break from the routine. Where are ye going on yer day off?"

"We're headed south of the city to an open area to test a gun," said Reid. "The lads help me with the targets and keep track of how well the balls fire. Then I can make adjustments."

"We canna have a gun that winna shoot straight," chimed in Ramy. "We do this with every gun Da makes."

"Anyone who buys a gun from Da kens he's getting the best," said Willie. "I'm going to be a gunsmith as good as Da someday."

" 'Tis a fine occupation," said Leena. To Reid she said, "Yer lads are proud of ye."

"And I am proud of them," said Reid. "What are ye doing out here? All done with yer shopping?" The gold streaks in her hair shone in the sun like a halo around her face.

"Nay, no' nearly. 'Tis very stuffy inside the shop, and the seamstresses are working on making linen patterns for me to take home so I can adjust the sizes for everyone. Ethel said everyone is starting to use patterns now. 'Tis the latest thing. French, I think. I've always had to piece each outfit on everyone one at a time and sometimes do it several times before getting it right. With these patterns, I can do one fitting per person, mark the cloth from the pattern, and be certain of the fit. There is naught for me to do right now, so I came outside for a breath of air. I might go to the bakery and find something to eat for midday."

"Ye could come with us!" piped up Hendrie. His tongue prodded through the gap in his teeth. "We have enough. Will it be all right, Da?"

Before Reid could answer, Leena said, "Thank ye for the invitation, but I'm certain yer da has work to do testing the gun."

"Ye winna be in the way," said Reid. "Ye might find it interesting, and we have plenty to eat."

"Come, please, come!" said Ramy and Hendrie in unison.

Willie, in a much more reserved mature voice, said, "Aye, 'twould be verra nice for ye to come with us."

"All right," said Leena. "Let me tell Ethel where I'm going, and then I'll be glad to join ye."

Hendrie grabbed Leena's hand and dragged her back into the shop. As soon as he spotted Ethel, he said, "Mistress Adair is coming with us. Dinna worry, we'll bring her back. Come on, mistress." The words were barely out of his mouth when he turned around and tugged Leena back toward the door. As he did, Leena looked over her shoulder toward Ethel. "I should be back in a few hours, if Hendrie lets me!" she said with a laugh.

Ethel crossed her arms and scowled.

The Haliburton lads ran ahead, leading the way out of town to Dumbarton Road and out to the open land south of the city wall. Once away from the crowded buildings of Stirling, the grassy, tree-lined meadow reminded Leena of home. Relishing the familiar feeling, she took in a deep breath of fresh air.

"The lads and I come here often," said Reid. "We enjoy being outside in the open space. I hope we're no' taking ye away from anything important. The lads didna consider that ye might be needed elsewhere."

"This is the perfect distraction," said Leena. "I think if I have to make one more decision about what kind of cloth or what color it should be or if the thread matches exactly, I'll lose my mind." She looked at him cross-eyed with her hands on her head and shook it back and forth.

He laughed. "The shooting can be loud."

"Again just what I need. One woman, Adelle, has the scratchiest voice I've ever heard, and high-pitched, too. My ears are still ringing." This time she covered her ears and quickly made a motion with her hands like her head exploded.

He laughed from deep in his belly, and the laughter filled his entire face.

By the time they caught up to the lads, they had already set up three targets. They nailed two to trees about ten feet apart, one forward of the other, and tacked a third target to a wooden post about twenty feet away off to the side.

"Look at how we put the targets in different places," said Willie. "That way Da can see how well the gun fires at different distances and angles. 'Tis important so the gun doesna misfire depending on where ye aim it. Ready, Da?"

Reid took the gun out of the bag on his shoulder. "Would ye like to handle it?" he asked Leena, holding it out to her. " 'Tis no' loaded yet."

"I would," she said, taking it from him. "My da and my brothers go hunting quite often. Sometimes for food, and sometimes to get rid of varmints that bother the crops or the livestock." She rubbed her fingers over the smooth barrel and handle. "Da believes in teaching women to shoot for protection, but Mum and I dinna get to practice much. Ammunition is too dear. This seems like a verra fine piece."

"If it shoots as well as I hope it will, mayhap ye can take a try at it."

"I'd like that."

The three lads gathered around their father as he loaded the gun and the flint, poured in the powder, tamped down the ball, cocked the trigger, took aim, and fired. He held the weapon steady despite the strong kickback. After loading the handgun three more times and firing at the same target, he said, "Willie, fetch the target so I can see exactly where the shots hit."

Once Willie returned and handed the paper target to him, Reid took out a caliper to measure precisely where each shot hit from the center.

"Is that where ye were aiming?" Leena asked with a wink and a smirk.

In all seriousness, Reid answered, "Nay, close, but no' exactly. I need to adjust the sight and the hammer." Giving Ramy the caliper, he took several other tools out from the backpack, sat down on the ground, and made his corrections. Reloading again, he fired at the second tree three times and again made his recalibrations. His next shots aimed at the target on the freestanding post to his right, and after he made those adjustments, the lads set up three new targets in different places.

Repeating the firing process, he gathered the targets and this time was satisfied with the accuracy.

"Would ye like to try yer hand with this weapon, Mistress Adair?"

"Please, call me Leena, and aye, I would."

He picked up the powder horn and tipped it toward the gun barrel to fill it. Putting her hand on his arm, she asked, "Would it be all right if I loaded it? I'll need yer help, but I'd like to learn."

She took the gun from him, and he carefully guided her hands along it. His touch sent a smooth sensation up her hand. It had been a long time since a man had touched her in such a familiar way.

" 'Tis no' loaded yet, but get the feel of it," he said. "Get used to the weight and the balance. Try pulling the trigger so ye can find how much strength ye need. Nay! Dinna point it at me!"

Leena winked again and pointed the gun away from Reid.

"Now we'll load it. I dinna have that much powder with me, so ye can only fire it a few times. Show me how ye'd do it."

She put the flint in the pan, poured in the right amount of powder, and tamped in the ball. She struggled to pull back the trigger wrench, but he patiently let her try without his interference. After she finally got it cocked, he said, "Fine job. Now take aim. Remember, 'twill have some kickback, so brace yerself."

She held the gun straight out toward the target, locking her elbow, and it wasn't long before her arm started to shake from the weight of the weapon. Reid stepped behind her to place his hand under her forearm. "A gun can be heavier than you think," he said as he redirected her aim.

He stood close enough for her to breathe in his smell of gunpowder and soap. Oh, how she missed the closeness of a man. It had been eight years since she'd been able to tip her head back and snuggle into a man's chest, and it took all her willpower not to do it now.

Taking aim at the first target, she pulled back the trigger. The kickback knocked her off her feet into Reid, and both of them fell, landing on the cold ground, tangled in each other while the slug flew well over the tops of the trees.

He started to giggle, softly at first, but it soon turned into raucous laughter, and after she caught her own breath, her giggles joined his. The lads had gasped as she first fell, but they soon laughed just as hard as their father and the woman. Before long all five of them had tears running down their cheeks.

"Ye seem to have a real knack for landing on yer backside, first on the street and now here," Reid said between guffaws. "Whoever taught ye how to stay on yer feet did a verra poor job."

After yet another giggle, she sputtered, "I remember my mum tying rags over my knees when I was little. Until now I didna ken why."

Gradually, everyone regained their composure, and once she and Reid were back on their own feet, she reloaded the gun by herself, only needing his help to get the amount of powder right, along with his quick touch to help her trigger the cocking wheel. She took aim. This time she put one foot behind the other to brace herself against the recoil, and she stayed on her feet, her shot hitting near the outer edge of one of the targets.

"One more time, please!" begged Leena. "I'll do much better this time."

Hendrie jumped up and down. "Let her do it again, Da."

Reid pursed his lips but eventually agreed. Handing her the gun, he said, "Ye will have to do it all on yer own. I'll cough if ye're doing it wrong."

Her tongue jutted out the corner of her mouth as she concentrated on each step, and he didn't cough even once. After she made the gun ready to fire, she took aim, braced her body, and shot, and then jumped for joy when the ball landed close to the center of the target tacked to the other tree.

Turning back, she caught his smile as he asked, "Is that where ye were aiming?"

"Of course!"

"Willie, ye can clean the gun while we get the food out to eat."

"Ye sit over there," said Hendrie, taking Leena's hand and pulling her toward a low stone wall along the side of the road. "Do ye want bread and an apple? I'll get it for ye." He dashed back to his father, took some of the food, and carried it to Leena. "Here, Da, sit here, next to Mistress Adair." Reid sat several feet away on the wall, but Hendrie shoved him closer. "Nay, here."

The three lads sat nearby on the ground to eat their midday meal.

"Hendrie's taken quite a liking to ye," said Reid.

"And I to him," said Leena.

"He was only a year old when he lost his mother, and he keeps looking for another. Ramy and Willie do, too, but they keep it to themselves."

Breaking off a piece of bread and taking a bite, Leena said, "Grief is hard on everyone." She paused to chew. "And everyone handles loss in a different way."

Reid didn't answer. He stared at something beyond the trees.

"We have to leave," he said. "Right now. Gather everyone up. Quickly!"

"What's wrong?"

"Willie, do ye know that man standing over there?" said Reid, indicating a tall man in a faded sark cinched with a silver belt buckle. "Have ye seen him before?"

"Aye," said Willie, "and that one over there, too." He pointed in the direction on the far side of the grove to a dark-skinned Moor in loose gray pants and high black boots.

"We have to leave," said Reid. "Did they speak to ye? What about ye, Ramy and Hendrie? Have either of them spoken to ye? Or mayhap came up close to ye?" The tension rose in his voice. "Tell me! Have they?"

"Nay, Da," said Willie with Ramy and Hendrie nodding in agreement. "We saw them on the street, but then they walked away."

"The Moor waved once," said Hendrie. "I waved to him, and he waved back."

"Is something wrong?" asked Leena as she handed her uneaten food to Willie, who rewrapped it and put it in the food bag.

"We have to leave," said Reid. His eyes flickered between the two men. "If ye see either of those men again, ye're to run home as fast as ye can. Hendrie, no more waving to either of them. Ye are to find me as quick as ye can. Dinna let either of them come close to ye. Do ye understand?"

Reid herded his sons in front of him, pushing them along until they had to run to stay ahead of him, and Leena kept up as best she could.

Turning his head back to her, Reid said, "Ye stay away from them as well."

"Why?"

"Do as I say."

"I'm a grown woman, Reid Haliburton. Tell me why I should stay away."

He didn't answer her but kept up his hurried pace until he saw the lads safely inside the gunsmith shop. He walked back to Leena, still catching her breath in front of the mercer's.

"I'm sorry," he began. "All I ask is that ye be careful."

"What is the problem? Is there anything I can do?"

"Naught. Please, Leena, 'tis something I have to take care of. I'm sorry to have ruined our outing. I'll visit ye tomorrow and try to explain. Will ye be at the mercer's?"

"Aye."

Ramy stepped out of the gunsmith shop door. "Da?"

"Get back inside!" Reid shouted as he strode back to his shop, leaving Leena dumbfounded on the street.

Chapter Four

Leena spent her third day in the mercer's shop learning about the latest styles in dresses and gowns, collecting sketches of those designs, and examining ells of material to make two dresses each for herself, her sister, and her mother. One outfit would be a fancier gown for attending dinners and celebrations with neighbors and friends near Makgullane, and these gowns required the best wools or satins with an assortment of trims and adornments. The second one would be plainer, but still attractive, to wear around the estate. These would be made of sammeron, imported Holland linen, or broadcloth.

After Leena decided on styles and patterns and calculated how much material she needed along with the appropriate notions, Ethel wrapped and tied everything for each gown in brown paper packages for Leena's sister and mother to unwrap and enjoy after she got home. Leena also decided to buy several ells of dornicks, a checkered table linen, for the estate's cook, Marta, and her staff, when they set the table for meals.

The day after the gun testing, Reid and his sons came into the mercer's shop just after the midday meal. Reid had a list of several tasks that he did in exchange for the mercer providing the cloth and for Ethel to do the stitching of clothing for his sons. Today they each wore the sarks and trews Ethel had made. With strict orders to sit near the window, the lads read while Reid worked. Leena noticed that each lad had one book. Willie's looked like one about guns and weapons with drawings and diagrams while Ramy's was the chapbook about Lyra. Every once in a while he whispered to Hendrie about the heroine's adventures, and soon the two brothers shared the book.

After Reid repaired a broken board in the workroom and then added additional supports for the upper shelves of cloth, he brought a stool near to Leena's worktable and sat down.

"Good afternoon, Mistress Adair," he said. "Go about what ye're doing. I'd like to see the choices ye have made."

She couldn't hold back her smile that he had come to the shop and now wanted to talk with her.

After Ethel and the seamstresses left to get more material, Reid said, "I want to apologize for the way I ended our outing yesterday."

"No need to explain," said Leena. "I only worried there might be trouble."

"I didna mean to alarm ye. I overreacted. I hope to make it up to ye with pleasant conversation while ye work today."

"I'd enjoy that."

Ethel returned to the table, muttering under her breath.

"Is everything all right?" Leena asked her.

Ethel replied very slowly, "Aye, mistress. Master Haliburton, are ye taking off work again today?"

"Aye, I am. Leena, tell me about yer family in the Highlands."

She didn't need much encouragement to talk about

the family she loved. "I have seven siblings, five older brothers, a younger sister, and a younger brother. My parents adopted the two oldest, Hugh and Fergus, but they're two of the brood just like all the others. My parents and the families of all my grown brothers, except Fergus, live on the estate. I saw them every day of my life until I came here. Well, except Hugh and Fergus. Hugh left home when I was wee and didn't come back for five years, but he's lived there ever since."

"What about Fergus?"

"He's a professor in Edinburgh. Has his head buried in a book too often for a family of his own, but Mum still has hope he'll look up long enough to find someone. What about ye?"

"I ne'er kenned my two older brothers or older sister. They all died afore I was born, so I ended up an only child. Because of that I wanted a lot of bairns for my own family. We would have had more…" He glanced over at his sons, sucking in a slow jagged breath. "A lot more, but some things…"

He straightened his shoulders before turning back to Leena, but Leena spoke up first. "I'm certain yer three sons fill yer heart."

"They do."

Ethel laid a bolt of cloth in front of Leena, saying, "What do ye think of this one?" Before Leena could examine it, Ethel added, "Master Haliburton, did yer lads like the oatcakes I made? It gives me pleasure to do something for them. They are fine lads, and I care about them so."

"The oatcakes were delicious, a real treat. Leena, I'll go and leave ye to yer choices."

"If ye have the time, I'd like a man's opinion."

"I'd be glad to offer it, for what 'tis worth."

"Ethel, do ye have this in a red or, perhaps, even a purple or violet? I think it would be a fine accent for this piece here," asked Leena as she reached across the table, indicating the cloth she had chosen for her mother's fancy dress.

"I will look, mistress," said Ethel.

Leena said to Reid, "Since we're getting to ken each other, tell me some of yer favorite foods."

It turned out that his favorite foods were beef stew and apples while hers were sausage and freshly baked bread. They exchanged more tidbits about their childhoods and their lives for nearly an hour until Ramy approached and put his hand on his father's leg. "Da, we've finished reading everything we brought with us, twice. Hendrie fell asleep. 'Tis almost time for the shops to close. Can we roll our hoops in the street now?"

"I didna realize how close it was to three o'clock. Leena, if yer packages are ready, the lads and I will help ye carry them across to the inn. Then, Ramy, we can play outside."

"I'd appreciate the help," said Leena. "Here, Ramy, ye can carry this one. We have to take them to our cart in the barn behind the inn. If we dinna, Taran and Dillon will fill the cart with tools and winna leave room for what I have."

As Reid took the packages from Leena, his first finger looped around two of hers, lingering as if he wanted to take her hand and hold it. He gave a small smile before pulling his hand back and taking the parcel from her.

The next afternoon Reid came again to the mercer, and he took his sons to the back room of the shop, assuring the owner they would play quietly and not disturb any customers. Following him back, Ethel knelt on the floor beside the boys, saying, "I have time to play with them for a while before I have to go back to work. I'll make certain they mind."

"They have carved wooden toy soldiers as well as their ball-and-cup toys for contests to see who gets the ball into the cup most often. I also promised them that if all went well, the four of us would go south of town to have mock battles with wooden swords and play blind man's bluff." Looking at Ethel from beneath hooded eyes, he said, "I winna tell ye what I promised them if all didna go well."

Once back out in the front part of the shop, Leena asked him, "So ye brought yer lads with ye again today?"

He hesitated. "Aye, there'll be no classes for the next two weeks."

Leena nodded. "My mum taught all of us, and now she does the same for the grandbairns. She is verra good at it and verra strict. We studied from the books in my grandfather's library. He brings one or two new ones back every time he goes to Edinburgh, where he represents the Highlands in Parliament."

"I'm self-taught like that, too. We couldna afford to pay school fees, but I read whatever I could get my hands on. The fees here in Stirling to send the lads to a proper grammar school are verra high, but Mistress Waltham offers lessons for a smaller fee. She is also verra strict like yer mum."

"Yer lads seem like quick learners."

"Aye, they are."

After a lull in their conversation, Leena asked, "Dinna ye have yer own work ye must do, rather than sit here with me?"

"I do my best work at night. Ye'll often find light in the shop after the streetlamps are lit."

"If ye're certain I am no' keeping ye from something."

"Ye are no'," he said. His eyes crinkled with his smile. "Tell me more about living with five older brothers. It must have been a challenge being the younger sister."

Chuckling, she said, "I learned before I could walk that to live with brothers, I had to be smarter and stronger in spirit, but to tell ye the truth, I didna always do it honestly. Sometimes, if they were mean to me, I told Da things that werena exactly true, and the lads took punishments they didna exactly deserve. I can be verra convincing."

"If I ever caught my lads doing that…"

"I'm no' as wicked as it sounds. I always told the truth eventually, and as I got older, my brothers came to respect me on my own and dinna treat me badly. Sometimes they can still be a bother, but we really do love each other verra much."

They continued to talk about things important and unimportant until the shop closed, and Reid carried her day's packages back to the barn behind the inn. As they crossed the road, he laid his hand on her back while gently steering her around ruts and holes, and the heat of his hand radiated through her.

On the fourth day, Hendrie burst through the shop door ahead of Reid and handed Leena a small, polished piece of mahogany wood in the shape of a teardrop. "Look what Da made for ye! I kenned ye would like it!"

The wooden teardrop had a wonderfully smooth and shiny feel in her fingers, and it made a unique trinket. "How lovely," she said.

Reid said, "I had this chip left over from the stock of a musket for the Earl of Arbor, and Hendrie thought ye might like it carved and polished so ye could make a necklace out of it. I can make ye a chain from some silver I have, if ye like it."

"I like it verra much, but ye dinna need to go to the trouble for me. I ken ye have much work of yer own to do."

His blue eyes twinkled, or perhaps only in her imagination. "I need to take a break once in a while. I can have the necklace ready by tomorrow, if ye'll still be in Stirling."

She nodded. "We leave in two days. Taran and Dillon will pick up the last of the tools tomorrow, and we'll be leaving on Friday. I would enjoy a necklace as a remembrance for my time here. Beautiful. Thank ye, Hendrie, for thinking of me."

"I found the piece of wood, but Da said it would make a necklace. Do ye really like it?"

"I truly do," she said, giving the boy a hug. She had the urge to hug Reid as well, but she kept her hands at her side.

"I'll start to work on it right now," Reid said, taking the wood from her hands. Her fingers touched his palm, lingering long enough for Leena to feel a tingle.

Before Reid left, he said, "Ethel, let me ken when

Mistress Adair is done here for the day, and I will help her carry her packages back to the inn again."

Ethel gave an obligatory smile. "Aye, sir."

As the door closed behind him, Ethel lowered her eyes and said to Leena, "He ne'er brought me or any other woman in town anything so fancy. Are ye certain ye should be taking favors from a man without yer brothers' permission?"

Leena snapped her head around in Ethel's direction. "I dinna need my brothers' permission to take a token given in friendship. Besides, he said 'tis just a leftover chip. I would hardly call that 'fancy.' "

Ethel, while folding the cloth on the table, said, "Have ye no idea how expensive mahogany wood is? Even a scrap costs Reid more coin than he can spare. Ye're taking advantage of a man who still mourns his wife after five years. 'Tis no' right!"

"Ethel!" snapped the shop owner, approaching the cutting table. "Ye canna speak like that to a customer. Ye are dismissed to clean up the shop tonight, without pay, while the others go home."

"Nay, please," said Leena quickly. "She only told me what she thought. Please, dinna penalize her."

The shop owner, a balding man with a bushy mustache, frowned, but said, "As ye request, Mistress Adair. Ethel, the others will stay and help ye, but ye will work in the back room for the rest of the day."

Ethel stared at the floor, curtsied, saying, "Aye, sir," before walking away.

"Please, forgive her," said the owner. "She has set her cap for Reid Haliburton ever since his wife died, but Reid still grieves heavily. Ethel willna accept that he might ne'er find another woman."

"I understand," said Leena, but a tiny part inside of her fell. She had hoped that in some small way the mahogany token might mean that he saw her as more than a friendly stranger, that he might miss her after she left Stirling, if only a little, just as she would miss him after she returned to Makgullane.

Each night Leena looked out her window in her room at the inn toward the lantern light shining out the windows in the gunsmith's shop. She promised herself to explain all about Reid to Johnnie. Reid had become her friend, and she his as well. Spending time with Reid didn't change the love in her heart for her husband. Johnnie would understand.

With a sigh, she closed her eyes and wished for morning to come quickly so she could spend time with the gunsmith again.

Reid didn't come to the mercer's shop the next day, her last day in Stirling.

Chapter Five

The mercer wrapped the last package of material with brown paper and tied it into a bundle, making it the twentieth bundle Leena had purchased from him.

"Yer business is greatly appreciated," said the rotund shop owner as he tied the knot on the last package. "It has been a pleasure working with ye."

"And I with ye," said Leena. "I dinna think I will ever be able to come back here, but I will have so much to take with me to remember my time."

"Have a safe journey."

Taran and Dillon met her at their cart in the stable behind the inn. While the twins were identical in appearance with thick blond hair, round blue eyes, and broad shoulders, Dillon often had to play peacemaker to Taran's quick temper.

"Where in the name of all the saints are we going to put these last four packages? No one needs this many clothes," said Taran.

"Then I winna make anything for ye!" said Leena. "Either of ye!"

Dillon spoke up. "Dinna include me in that. I could use a new sark."

"Then ye'll get two. Taran, if ye return one or two of these scythes, mayhap I could spare some material for ye. We have more tools than cloth."

Taran opened his mouth to retort, but Dillon lifted

his palm to him. "Enough. We have all the tools we need, and ye have all the cloth. The problem is no' how much, but how we can get it all in this cart."

"I have one more place to go," Leena told them. "I want to get new shoes for Da and Mum as a special treat. I'll find the way to the cobbler shop and buy what I can for them."

"We winna have room!" protested Taran.

"Boots dinna take up much room," said Leena, "but, if ye like, ye can be the one to tell our *mathair* and *athair* why they didna get new boots."

" 'Tis useless to argue," Taran said to Dillon. "If I live to be eighty-five and her eighty-two, she'd still be telling me what to do."

"Ye're right about that," answered Dillon. "Leena's been a force to be reckoned with from the day Mum birthed her."

Walking back to the mercer's shop, and pleased with herself for crossing the street without incident, Leena smiled at Ethel, who greeted her at the door. "Is there anything else ye want, mistress?"

"Can ye give me directions to a cobbler's shop?"

"Since we willna be seeing ye again, of course I can," she said.

Leena ignored the snap in her tone.

The cobbler was only two blocks away, and as it turned out, he had a great deal of inventory for Leena to choose from. Leena wanted new boots for her father and new turnshoes, sturdy shoes designed for women, for her mother. Also, knowing that getting shoe leather could be difficult in the Highlands, she purchased two large rolls to donate to the cobbler in Kirkcaldy near Makgullane. Gathering up her shoes along with the rolls of leather, she set off, making her way back the way she had come.

Eventually, she stood in front of the gunsmith shop, trying to decide if she dared attempt to cross the street with her arms so full. Just then the door opened behind her, and Reid stepped out. The sparkling sensation of him so close almost caused her to drop her parcels.

"Let me help ye with that," he said, taking the large rolls of leather from her. "I couldna come to the shop today. I had too much to do."

"I understand, but 'tis good to see ye one last time afore we leave in the morning. It has been quite an adventure here in Stirling. I've enjoyed it, especially getting to ken ye and yer lads." She looked up at him. His sapphire eyes glittered in the light, and she ne'er wanted to forget them.

"I…we enjoyed spending time with ye as well. I'll carry these across for ye," he said, taking the bundles from her.

As they started across the street, Leena slipped her arm in his. He looked down at her, and she said, "To steady myself."

Once across, they walked around to the back of the inn and packed both the shoes and the leather into a corner of the cart.

"I hoped I would get a chance to say goodbye to ye," he said.

"I as well."

They stood self-consciously beside each other until he put his arms around her and pulled her in for a gentle hug. "Goodbye, Leena Cullane Adair."

She wrapped her arms around his waist, but she

didn't answer. She couldn't. She wanted to stay in his arms a little longer, and it had been eight years since she had wanted to stay in a man's arms.

She murmured, "Hmmm."

With his finger, he tipped her chin up and gazed at her with a look so tender, the strong wall she kept around her heart for Johnnie alone cracked and crumbled. This man moved her. She loved Johnnie and always would, but he would never stand beside her again, never hold her close. She would always remember how he loved her, but she would never hear his voice, never feel his lips, never know his touch again.

She snuggled into Reid, trying to imprint everything about him in her mind—the strength in his embrace, how he breathed, and the feelings he created in her just by being near.

In the silence, Reid's eyes darkened. He leaned his head toward hers, and she stretched up until their lips met. Pulling her close, he kissed her.

She had loved a man before, and now she hungered for his lips. She needed his lips. The scratch of his beard stubble moved over her cheeks gently like the lick of a kitten's tongue. Their mouths moved and teased, refusing to leave the tenderness. Again, and again, they pulled each other closer, their lips, their arms, their faces. His heart beat against hers.

Today, he looked different, as if a halo of sunlight surrounded him. His was not a glow anyone else would notice, but one that shone just for her.

Did Johnnie have that kind of glow? Aye, he did, but it had faded over the years until all that remained was a memory. Reid's glow shone fresh and alive, and she wanted to experience more of it.

Was she ashamed to have these feelings for another man? Nay! Feelings didn't vanish in the wind. She would always love Johnnie, and Johnnie would understand.

After today, she would never see Reid again. Perhaps the saints might smile on her, and someday he might cross her path, but in reality she would live the rest of her life alone, having loved two men, in two very different ways. Those memories would have to be enough to sustain her.

She and Reid stood face to face, their lips joining and their breath mingling, and he held her safe and strong. A quick breeze blew her hair across his arms, but she didn't feel the chill.

She had no idea how long they kissed, but after he lifted his head, she still wanted him. She reached for him again, but he stepped back. Losing his closeness, she now shivered with the breeze.

Reid opened his mouth to speak, but no words came out. Touching the side of her face with his palm, he again started to say something, but again stayed silent.

"Reid," she whispered.

A moment later he spoke, but his voice sounded hoarse and raw. "Think of me sometimes. I ken I will think of ye."

He released her, and his long strides took him away. She didn't take her eyes off him until he reached the gunsmith shop, went inside, and closed the door behind him.

She stood there in a daze as a window on the second floor at the back of the inn clattered open.

"What are ye doing?" shouted Taran, leaning out. "Who is the man? I'll teach him no' to accost my sister! Who is he?"

****

Across the street, Reid pressed his hands against the worktable, closed his eyes, and prayed to turn back time.

In the last four days, Leena had been on his mind almost constantly from the moment he swept her up in his arms to keep her from falling in the street. At first, his preoccupation with Leena disconcerted him, as did the physical reaction of his body to the sight of her. He hadn't been aroused like this since the days before Marjorie took sick, and he had thought that with her death sexual expression might be over for him, but Leena's presence brought it back. A sense of contentment filled him by just catching a glimpse of her. Their conversation came easily, and a lump formed in his throat every time he had to leave her.

She had never given him any encouragement, not like other women in Stirling. She never sidled up next to him, never brushed smudges off his jacket, and she never tossed her head back and laughed at everything he said, no matter how ordinary. He accepted, however reluctantly, that Leena regarded him as a friend, someone she wouldn't think about after she went back home.

Yet today, he had overstepped the bounds of propriety by kissing her. He had taken advantage of her, and even as desperately as he had wanted to kiss her, he should have shown restraint. Although she returned his kiss in kind, pleasing him greatly in that moment, he had no excuse for his behavior.

Suddenly one word popped into his head. Marjorie! He had betrayed the mother of his children, the woman he loved in his youth, the woman he promised never to forget.

At the sound of someone at the shop door, his head whipped around.

A man in a faded sark with a silver belt buckle yanked open the gunsmith shop door, and an African Moor followed him inside.

Chapter Six

Magnus and Shipopi, two of the *Scarlet Lion* crew, had kept a close watch on the gunsmith and his shop all week. Magnus, a huge man with beefy fists and a pockmarked face, who treasured his stolen silver belt buckle, had been with McDever since his captain first commandeered a ship. Shipopi had only been on the *Scarlet Lion* for a few months.

On the ship's last trip along the Mediterranean coast, Shipopi, a tall muscular man with skin the color of coal, round brown eyes, and tightly curled black hair, had walked aboard at a port in northern Egypt and, not knowing a word of English, made it clear that he wanted to join the crew. McDever took a chance on him, and Shipopi proved his worth. While the presence of Moors had become more common in England and Scotland, his shouting in his native language intimidated even the bravest soul.

The two men had reported back to McDever a series of encounters between Reid Haliburton and a woman with sun-streaked hair. This woman did quite a lot of business at the wardrobe mercer's store, and every time she came to the shop, Haliburton found a reason to be there, too, and then carry her packages back to the inn.

Whatever this woman might mean to Haliburton, he couldn't be bothered to look into it. Haliburton's business with a woman, any woman, did not concern McDever. He had a bigger prize on his mind.

The pirates also recounted the target practice time south of town that included that same woman, and also that Haliburton had spotted and recognized them.

"Good," McDever said. "Keep your presence known to the man. Maybe he'll work a little faster."

On the evening of the Thursday deadline, McDever leaned against the wall in the narrow alley between the inn and the tavern across the street from the gunsmith shop, growing impatient for Magnus and Shipopi to return with the gun. They'd been in there for some time, but so far hadn't returned. McDever, used to giving commands and having them answered within seconds, didn't relish dealing with a man like Haliburton. Any other man would have pissed himself and delivered the gun immediately, not deny its existence as this gunsmith had. Even the threat to snatch his sons hadn't been enough to cow Haliburton, and instead of working on the weapon day and night, this man had sat in a dress shop wasting time.

McDever's expression hardened with each irritated tap of his foot. *What was taking so long?* He'd give them five more minutes.

Two young women walked by the alley arm in arm, and one of them caught a glimpse of McDever leaning against the wall. He nodded and gave a casual wave of his hand. The women walked on by, but the taller one turned her head back and winked at him. As a handsome man, he enjoyed such reactions from women, so he smiled and ranged his eyes up and down her body. Too bad he didn't have time to pursue her and find out what else she might offer him beyond her wink.

Magnus, leaning out of the doorway of the gunsmith shop, signaled him. McDever shifted his eyes, scanning the block in both directions along the virtually deserted street. Walking quickly, he crossed the road with his long stride, avoiding the ruts and puddles, until he stepped into the shop.

The inside shocked him.

The workshop, previously cluttered with all varieties of shapes and sizes of wood pieces for handles and chunks of metal, stood empty, completely empty. The cupboards holding guns in need of repair, the mainstay of any gunsmith's livelihood, were bare, and Haliburton's tools were nowhere in sight. Gone were the screwdrivers, wrenches, pliers, and hammers along with the chisels, saws, and clamps needed to work on a weapon. All had disappeared along with his calipers and his rifling tools. The only things left in the shop were his worktable and his stool.

"Found it this way, Captain," said Magnus.

McDever looked around the barren shop, and then fixed his stare on Reid leaning against the wall, clutching his stomach. Shipopi, a man nearly equal in size to Magnus, had obviously already greeted Reid with his fists, and now he pressed the gunsmith against the wall with his hand on Reid's chest.

"Where's the gun you owe me?" said McDever as calmly as if he had requested the time of day.

" 'Tis no' here," coughed out Reid.

McDever's voice tightened. "I can see that, ye yaldson! So where is it?"

Reid said nothing, merely coughed again.

"Are you trying to be clever, Haliburton? Do you

think if we found naught in your shop, we'd give up looking for the gun?" He leveled his dark eyes at Reid and bared his teeth. "Wrong! I intend to get your gun, make certain it gets to London, and have hundreds made, but first I need the original. Hand it over. There are many ways to get what I want, and I always get what I want."

Reid's eyes flickered between the three pirate men. "I ken ye have ways, but ye willna get the gun from me. 'Tis in pieces and scattered to the four winds, and with naught in the shop, ye canna make me recreate it."

"You are a clever man, Reid Haliburton, but still only a man. Magnus, Shipopi, persuade him to change his mind." He turned his back while Shipopi clenched his fist and sent an exploding punch into Reid's stomach and another to his face. Reid doubled over as blood spurted out of his nose.

Wiping his bloodied face with the back of his hand, Reid said, "Ye canna have the gun, and ye ne'er will. I will do whate'er I must to keep it away from the likes of ye." That remark cost him two more vicious blows to his body and face.

McDever paced the width of the narrow shop as Magnus and Shipopi took turns beating Reid, who fought back as best he could. A quick jab from Reid bloodied Magnus's nose and cracked one of his teeth. The big man stepped back to nurse his wounds, and Reid landed several powerful blows to Shipopi, but they were not enough to win the battle. After Magnus entered the fray again, the two men soon overpowered Reid and forced him to the floor.

McDever, pulling himself up to his full height, strode close enough to Reid to smell the blood.

"Perhaps we can end this difference of opinion if I tell you that I ne'er had a son of my own. I always thought he would bring joy to my life, just as I am certain your sons bring joy to you."

"Leave my sons out of this," said Reid as he struggled back to his feet.

"I cannot do that. No matter where you think you have hidden them, I will find them. If you care to save me the trouble, I would greatly appreciate it, but it will not change anything, except how kindly I treat the boys."

Reid growled.

"If I decide to treat them unkindly…"

Reid lunged at McDever, but the pirate stepped aside and let Shipopi slam the gunsmith into the wall again.

McDever saw the boy at the back door of the shop first.

"Ah, this is your eldest, Willie, I believe," he said.

"Run, Willie, run!" shouted Reid. "I told ye to stay away! Run!"

But instead of doing as his father said, he came into the shop. "Here is the gun. Leave my da alone." He held out the gun in his hand.

Reid's shoulders slumped. "Nay, Willie, nay. I told ye to stay where ye were."

"We couldna leave ye," said Willie. "I put the gun back together, and they can have it if they leave ye alone. Do I have yer word?" he asked McDever.

"Take the gun from him," said McDever to Magnus, but Willie jumped out of the way and scooted under the table before Magnus could reach him.

"Let my da go," said Willie. "Ye want the gun

more than ye want him. As soon as Da is out on the street, I'll put the gun on the table, and ye can do whate'er ye want with it. Do I have yer word?"

Ramy and Hendrie emerged out of the shadows at the back of the shop.

"Ye are all verra brave," Reid said to his sons, "and I am proud of yer courage, but ye're no match for these men. This ends now. Willie, put the gun on the table, and run afore they catch ye. Take yer brothers with ye."

Willie hesitated.

Reid spat out the words. "I said, 'Put the gun on the table!' "

Slowly, Willie slipped out from under the table and laid the weapon on the edge. None of the men in the room made a move, although their heavy breathing rasped through the empty space in the shop.

In a voice dripping with exasperation, McDever said, "Take it." As Magnus reached for the weapon, Reid charged at him with both fists raised, landing a blow on the pirate's back and sending him sprawling. Shipopi grabbed Reid by the arm, swung him back around, and at the same time McDever moved to grab the gun. Willie proved quicker.

Snatching up the weapon, Willie tossed it behind him to Ramy who, with Hendrie, dashed out the back door into the open area behind the shops. McDever started after them, but Willie jumped onto McDever's back and latched onto his belt, hanging there, slowing the tall man down, until Willie hooked one leg between McDever's and sent him flat on his face. On the way down, McDever knocked his head on the corner of the table and lost his senses, giving Willie enough time to step across the pirate's back and run out the door after his brothers.

Magnus and Shipopi helped their captain to his feet, and after McDever refocused his eyes, he shouted, "Now make this fool regret defying me."

Magnus and Shipopi started pounding on Reid again, but the gunsmith found the strength to hold his own until his three sons had made their escape. Eventually, Reid gave up the fight, taking the beating as the two pirate brutes overwhelmed him.

McDever's head whipped around as the shop door opened and a voice called out, "Reid? It's Angus. Are you all right? I heard the ruckus through the wall from next door. Hey, what's going on? Get your hands off him!"

The three men gave Angus only a glance before they ran out of the shop through the back door, each turning in a different direction.

Stepping cautiously over the broken table, Angus made his way toward the back of the room. In the shadows lay his friend and neighbor in a crumpled heap.

Chapter Seven

As Leena finished packing for their trip home, she tried not to think about the man who had worked his way into her heart so quickly. Perhaps she would write Reid a letter once she got home, thanking him for all his kindnesses and for helping her across the street. Perhaps he would write her back.

The journey home to Makgullane would take several days longer than the trip coming to Stirling. The cart, loaded with heavy tools, now needed two mules to pull it, and they would have to stop more often to trade for fresh horses and mules. If none were available, the going would be even slower so as not to wear out the animals.

They wanted to get to the Beatson's farm by midday on Saturday, where they could rest for another day before going on. It would be four more days, possibly more, of hard travel and sleeping outdoors, before they reached the abbey for a proper meal and a proper bed. Then, depending on how long they rested at the abbey, it would be one or two more days before they reached the Freebairns' inn, and at least one more full day to Makgullane. Of course, rain and the possibility of an early snow would delay them even more.

The small stone cottage that called itself an inn housed the Beatson family downstairs and could sleep three persons in the loft and another four in the barn. Anna Beatson, known for serving the best meals found on the road, also kept the straw mattresses free from bed bugs, a blessing to all travelers.

Taran and Dillon led the two horses and two mules into the barn while Leena fetched their bags from the cart. Throwing back the tarp, she jumped away as three pairs of eyes glinted back at her. She shouted, "Taran, Dillon, badgers in the cart! They better no' have eaten away at the cloth!"

"We havena eaten anything. We promise," came an unexpected voice from inside the cart.

Cautiously leaning over the side, she peered in. Three lads crouched between and under the packages of fabric and the tools, all shivering from the chilly night air.

"Well, what do we have here?" she asked as Taran and Dillon came running up behind her.

"What is it?" Taran asked. "Squirrels? Badgers?"

"Nay," said Leena. "It looks like we have stowaways. Come out, lads. Let us have a look at ye."

The oldest stowaway lifted the two younger lads over the side to the ground one at a time. Then he climbed out and stood in front of them as the other two cowered behind him.

Putting his hands on his hips, Taran straightened up to his full height. "So who are ye, and why are ye in our cart?"

The oldest lad matched Taran's gestures with his hands on his hips while stretching up as tall as he could, although he only came to the middle of Taran's chest. "My name is Willie, and these are my brothers, Ramy…" He patted the next smaller one on the shoulder. "And the wee one is Hendrie."

"I ken these lads," said Leena. "They're the Haliburtons."

Dillon took a step closer to the lads, who all stepped back in unison. "And what are ye doing in our cart?"

"We're on our way to the Highlands," said Willie with all the bravado he could muster with men the size of Taran and Dillon staring down at him.

All three adults scoffed. "The Highlands? What do ye expect to do there?"

Sticking his chin out, Willie said, "We can make our fortunes in the Highlands. We are hard workers." The other two lads nodded in agreement.

Dillon said, "Well, we dinna carry passengers for free, wherever they're headed."

"We can pay," said Willie as he pushed aside the lumpy cloth bag tied across his chest. Pulling a small leather pouch off his waistband, he jiggled it as it made the sound of clinking coins.

"Da gave us those," said Hendrie, the wee, light-haired boy, "so we could pay our way."

"Hush!" said Willie. "Name yer price."

"Let's look in here," said Taran, taking the pouch out of Willie's hands. He opened it and dumped the contents into his palm. "'Tis a tidy sum ye have here, and what is this?" He held up a silver chain with a polished wooden teardrop dangling from it.

"Oh, my," said Leena. "That's the necklace Reid made for me. Give it to me. Willie, did ye ken ye had this?"

"Nay, mistress. Da gave us the pouch and said to use the coin wisely."

She looped the chain over her neck and gently rubbed the smooth mahogany teardrop with her forefinger until Taran reached up and tugged on the necklace. "The skellum who assaulted ye behind the inn made ye a necklace? Why? To remember him by? And ye're accepting it? Are ye mad?"

Smacking his hand away, she said, "I told ye afore. He did naught against my will. And I am a grown woman who kens her own mind, and I willna be scolded by my brother." Taran gave her a withering look but stayed silent.

With a glint in her eyes, she said to the lads, "If we take yer coin for yer ride, what will ye use to eat until ye get to the Highlands?"

Willie shrugged, Ramy shook his head, and the smallest lad began to wail. "We havena eaten at all today. Please, dinna take our coin!" cried Hendrie.

Immediately, Leena stepped up and wrapped her arms around him. He sobbed into her skirts.

"We ne'er let our passengers go hungry. Yer coin may be yer fare for the ride, but ye will eat with us tonight…and tomorrow morning. Give him back his pouch."

"What?" exclaimed Taran. "We're feeding this band of fugitives? Then what are we going to do with them?"

" 'Twill be decided in the morning," said Leena. "Now, lads, go with Dillon to the pump and wash yer hands and faces afore we eat. Taran, ye do the same."

Taran grumbled while walking toward the water pump. "She's always telling us what to do. I'm older by three years, mind ye. I should be doing the telling."

Ramy looked up at him. "Willie is always telling

us what to do, too. He thinks because he's older he kens everything."

"I ken what ye mean," said Taran, "but I'm the older one, and she still does the telling."

"Hush up," said Dillon while pumping the water into the trough. "Put yer hands under the water, lads. Taran, ye listen to yer wife, Winnie, often enough. Ye just try calling her 'bossy,' and find out where it gets ye."

"According to her, she's no' bossy. She's determined, but I trust her judgment. She's always done right by me, but I canna say the same about Leena. 'Tis foolish to take in these three. Ye ne'er ken what kind of trouble these runaways are in."

None of the Haliburton lads said a word.

"Again, hush," said Dillon. " 'Tis only washing yer hands. Naught worth fussing over."

Once inside the house and seated around the wooden plank table by the fire, the young lads ate heartily of the lamb stew set before them. Between bites, they each in turn said, "Thank ye, mistress." Leena insisted they have only the weakest mead with their meals, none of the strong ale her brothers drank.

After everyone had finished eating, Leena moved the empty bowls to the end of the table for the innkeeper's wife to wash, and said, "Now that ye're fed, 'tis time to tell us where ye're going and why."

"We didna ken 'twas yer cart," said Willie. "We saw 'twas loaded and ready to go, so we climbed in. We're old enough to head out on our own. Da said we should go. He didna want us anymore."

Leena raised an eyebrow in a questioning slant. "I dinna think ye're telling me the truth. Hendrie, is Willie telling me the truth?"

Tears burst into the wee lad's eyes, but he didn't speak, only hung his head.

"If ye're hiding from the law, ye could get all of us in trouble," barked Taran.

"Nay!" said Ramy. " 'Tis worse!"

"Hush!" said Willie, giving his brother a strong fist in the chest.

"There'll be none of that," said Leena. "Willie, tell me the truth. Why did ye run away?" Willie hesitated, so she added with sternness, "Or perhaps Taran or Dillon can get it out of ye."

Taran and Dillon both scowled at the lads, and the eyes of all three young ones popped open wide. These big men who looked just alike with their yellow hair and blue eyes might have some unpleasant ways of getting at the truth.

"Aye, mistress," said Willie, swallowing hard. "I'll tell ye the truth. It has to do with this." He looped off the string on the sack across his chest and laid the bag on the table. Slowly, he untied it and pulled out a handgnome, a handheld pistol, one with a polished wooden handle, two shiny metal triggers, an unusually shaped flintlock, and a metal ring around the muzzle. A fine weapon indeed. Leena recognized it right away.

"Where did ye get this?" asked Taran.

"Our da made it."

"Why do ye have it?"

The silence dragged on until Taran stood up and, in a voice that could make a bear back down, said, "Why do ye have it?"

Willie answered quickly, "A man came to get it, but Da said 'Nay,' and the man started to beat him."

"All the men beat him," said Ramy. " 'Twas no' right. Three against one!"

"Da put us in yer cart afore the man came," said Hendrie, "but we didna stay. We couldna leave our da alone." He laid his trembling hands on the table.

Immediately, Leena reached across and grasped them. "Ye're safe with us, but one of ye has to tell us everything. Willie, will it be ye?"

Willie bit his lip. "Aye, mistress. Da told us that a bad man wanted this gun. 'Tis a special one. Da made it, and 'tis the only one like it in the whole world. The man wanted it, so Da took the gun apart and hid the pieces in different places. He hid everything in his shop so they couldna force him to make another."

"It looks to be in one piece now," said Dillon. "How did that happen?"

Willie's lip twitched as he furrowed his brow.

"Ye have to tell them," said Ramy. "Ye canna get in any worse trouble. We all agreed. Tell them."

Taking a deep breath, Willie began. "After Da put us in the cart, we got out and found the pieces of the gun. I helped him build it, so I kenned how to put it together."

"Then what?" said Taran.

"Then we went to the shop and saw what they were doing to Da. They were hurting him…so I said I would give them the gun, but I didna. I threw it to Ramy and Hendrie, and we all ran. And now we're here with ye. Da said we would be safe with ye."

"I dinna like how all this sounds," said Taran. "Do ye ken the man's name who wanted the gun? The man who beat yer da?"

" 'Twas Dawson."

Ramy piped up, "Nay, 'twas McDill, I think."

"Was it McDever?" asked Dillon.

"Aye!" said the three lads in unison.

Dillon's grim face told everyone that the name McDever meant serious trouble. "I heard that pirate was in town. 'Twas the talk in the tavern."

Before Dillon could explain more, Leena stood up and ushered the lads away from the table. "I think 'tis time for ye to get some rest tonight. We'll talk and make our decisions in the morning. Willie and Ramy can sleep with Dillon and Taran in the barn. Hendrie, ye will bed with me in the loft. Dillon, ye mind the weapon."

Dillon reached for the gun, but Willie put his hand on it. "I can keep the gun with me," he said.

"Nay," said Leena. " 'Twill be safer with a grown man. Give it to him."

Very slowly, Willie slid his hand off the gun. "All right," he breathed.

"Thank ye, Willie." Waving to the innkeeper's wife, Leena said, "More blankets, please, and tell my brothers what the extra charge for these three little ones will be. This way, lads."

Chapter Eight

Jonas McDever had never been so livid in his life! Outsmarted by a simpleton gunsmith and a boy. He wouldn't have it. They would suffer!

Captain McDever ordered his crew to leave the *Scarlet Lion* and come to the campsite outside the city wall. Only the three-man skeleton crew left on board would escape his fury. The unlucky ones got a lash across the face, the lucky ones ducked in time, but they would all face worse if they didn't find that boy who stole the gun.

"Scour this town! Look in every nook and hiding place," McDever bellowed. "Every house, every shop, every corner of this pitiful town. A reward to the one who brings me the boy. If he does not have the gun on him, bring him alive. If he's carrying the gun, slit his throat and leave him for the buzzards! 'Tis the gun I want!"

"What does the lad look like?" shouted out one man. McDever grabbed him by the throat, dragged him to the fire, and threw him on the flames. The man's screams continued long after he crawled away.

McDever drew his sword from its sheath, waving it in his men's direction. "Any more questions?"

There were none.

"Do not return empty-handed, or you'll taste your own blood!"

The thirty-two men of the crew of the *Scarlet Lion* scattered into the night in search of a young boy and his gun. By morning, McDever still hadn't found Willie. He spent the night watching the gunsmith shop on the chance the boy might return.

Obviously, the gunsmith still lived because other people came in and out of the shop, always carrying things like food or blankets but leaving empty-handed. First, came the grocer from next door, followed by his wife, then the physician, and now the wardrobe mercer's shop girl.

Not finishing off Haliburton had been the pirate's biggest mistake, the worst of many in this fiasco. First, he'd underestimated Reid Haliburton. McDever had never met a man who defied him the way Haliburton had, and he did it in a most ingenious way. Hiding and destroying everything he owned was ridiculously clever and maddeningly effective, but the only thing Haliburton hadn't planned on was for his son to put the gun back together and try to rescue him. With the gun now in one piece, all McDever needed to do was find the brat.

The only person who had not come to visit the gunsmith at his shop was the constable. A town the size of Stirling could always find someone to take the post, despite the paltry salary, because the title came with substantial authority and influence. Usually, the constable sent an underling out for low-level crimes like vagrancy or public drunkenness, but a constable could make a name for himself by bringing the criminals to justice after beating a respected citizen.

So that made the question, "Why hasn't Haliburton notified the authorities?"

The only explanation could be that he had something to hide. Could it be he didn't want anyone looking for his sons or for his weapon? If so, why not? With no sign of the gun or the sons in Stirling, could someone have taken them away? Who did Haliburton know who might leave with both?

****

The next morning Leena came down from the loft at the inn to find the three Haliburtons and Taran crowding around Dillon seated on the bench beside the table.

"What's going on?" asked Leena.

"This is a most remarkable weapon," said Dillon. "Willie's started to tell us all about it. 'Tis the only one like it in the country. Go ahead, Willie. Tell Leena what ye told us so far."

Willie proudly held up the gun. "Look right here," he said, pointing to a round metal piece just above the trigger. "That's the wheel lock. Ye used to have to get out a spanner wrench to wind it up so that it would pull down the flint and set off the charge in the pan. Then those sparks would set off the larger load of gunpowder and the ball in the barrel."

"I've fired that gun," said Leena. " 'Tis quite a special weapon."

Taran and Dillon looked doubtfully at their sister, but Willie went on before they could say anything.

"But Da put a new kind of spring behind the wheel lock so that it winds itself just by pulling back this trigger here." He pointed to a smaller trigger behind a larger one. "Ye dinna have to wind it yerself. All ye have to do is pour a little powder in the pan, and ye dinna have to do that every time. Ye close the pan and ye're ready. If ye want to fire it, ye pour more powder in the barrel with the ball and tamp it down with the ramrod. Cock the wheel lock trigger and fire. 'Tis so much faster that way." Willie's enthusiasm caught on.

Dillon held out the gun and took aim.

Leena gasped.

" 'Tis no' loaded," he said, "but if ye had this weapon, think how many shots ye could get off afore yer enemy could reload and fire his."

"I dinna want to think about killing people," said Leena.

" 'Tis no' so much about killing people as 'tis about defending yerself," said Dillon.

"But a gun's only real purpose is to shoot and kill. Give one to a weak person, and they feel stronger than they really are and try to prove it to others."

"Ye're right." He shook his head. "Sometimes evil takes over."

Taran interrupted. "Arguments like this have been around ever since the invention of gunpowder. We need to hope that people in the future will figure it all out. As for this gun, ye say this pirate, McDever, wanted it."

"Aye, and he didna want to pay for it," said an indignant Ramy. "Da said 'Nay,' but no' because he wouldna pay. McDever wanted to use it to attack ships and steal their cargo. He wouldna use it to protect other people, just to make himself rich, and that's a wicked purpose. I'm worried about Da."

"And I'm certain yer da is worried about ye," said Leena.

Taking Leena's hand, Dillon led her away from the table. Speaking quietly, he said, "McDever is the worst kind of pirate. There are tales of him overrunning cargo ships and murdering everyone on board or selling them as slaves on the Barbary Coast. He empties the ship of all its cargo and scuttles it. No survivors. Whoever has this gun is in danger."

Leena's face paled.

"McDever willna stop until he finds this weapon and the ones who took it. We canna send these lads home."

A most terrible thought came to her. "Do ye think they killed Reid?"

"I dinna ken. If McDever thinks that Willie has the gun and can put it together, Willie is the one he'll be after. Taran and I've been talking. We think ye and me should take the lads to Makgullane like Haliburton wanted us to. Taran'll ride back to Stirling and find out what's become of Haliburton and, if he's alive, bring him to Makgullane as fast as he can. Taran agrees 'tis safest to get the lads as far away from Stirling as possible."

"Are ye certain sending Taran to get Reid is the right thing? Taran thinks the man violated me. Ye ken how protective Taran is, and he might murder Reid afore he brings him here."

"He promises to get Haliburton here in one piece." He winked. "But I canna promise what kind of shape the man will be in."

"Dillon!"

" 'Twill be all right. Taran may be hot-headed, but he kens that getting the lads back with their father is the important thing. He may grumble the whole way, but he'll bring Haliburton to us."

Leena forced a smile, and they went back to the table where Taran held up a coiled wire.

" 'Tis the wheel lock wire," he said. "It willna fire without it. We also took off the flintlock. 'Tis a lot smaller than a standard one, but it could be replaced by something similar." He laid the wire on the table beside the flintlock, saying, "Are there other pieces we can take off this thing so no one can use it?"

No one noticed Willie taking the wheel lock wire off the table. He turned away and after a few minutes turned back.

"Where's the wire?" exclaimed Dillon as he patted the table looking for it.

"If ye can find it," said Willie, "ye can have it."

Taran stood up. "Tell of yer own free will, lad, afore I make ye regret playing games with us."

Willie's breath quickened before he pushed the end of the thin coiled wire out of a small hole near the hem of his vest and threaded it about halfway out. "See," he said, "it moves with the curve of the hem, and 'tis strong enough and thin enough that nobody looking for it could find it. 'Tis safe with me."

"Clever," said Taran.

"But dangerous," said Leena.

"I'll take the flintlock," said Ramy. Sitting on the floor, he took off his left boot, pried down the heel, and then twisted it. It opened, revealing a small compartment, just the right size for the new, smaller flintlock. "The cobbler made them special for Willie a couple of years ago, and they're still plenty big enough for me to wear." He held up his boot. "These nails here are shorter, so I pull the heel and it turns on the larger nail at the back." He slipped the flintlock inside the heel, put the boot back on, and stomped on it. "See, 'tis no' loose or anything."

Dillon smiled. "What have ye been hiding from yer da in there?"

Hendrie spoke up before his brothers could stop him. "Sometimes the ladies give us bits of candy, ye ken, nuts soaked in sugar, and sometimes dried fruit, ye ken, 'suckets.'"

"We ken all of that," said Dillon. "Our mum makes them for us sometimes, but why do ye hide them?"

"The ladies want us to tell Da how nice they are, but Da doesna want them to think he likes them, so we hide the candy in the boot and eat it later," said Willie. "We always say 'Thank ye, mistress.' There's one more part I have to tell ye about. 'Tis a part ye canna take off the gun."

He turned the gun and put the barrel close to his eye. "This is what makes the gun best of all. Look."

"Aye, rifling," said Taran before he even put it to his eye.

"What is that?" asked Leena.

"Ye make grooves inside the barrel and the bullet spins, and ye can be more accurate at yer target. 'Tis like what archers do to the feathers on their arrows so they'll fly straighter."

Willie explained. "Da studied how some men rifled or barreled their weapons in Germany, but they had to put in the grooves one at a time, and it took way too long, but Da made a tool to spin and cut a lot of grooves at once."

"Where is that tool now?"

"Da smashed it when he took everything out of the shop."

"Nay, he didna!" said Hendrie.

"Quiet!" said Willie.

Leena laid her hand on Willie's shoulder. "Ye must tell us everything. We can only help yer da if we ken it all." Willie looked up at her with his rich blue eyes from under long eyelashes, so much like his father's.

" 'Tis verra important, Willie."

Willie licked his lips before saying, "Look in yer cart."

At first glance, nothing in the cart appeared amiss, but removing one of the ploughshares and several of Leena's packages revealed a stash of unfamiliar tools.

Willie pulled out one with a blade on a rotating bar. "This is da's rifling tool. 'Tis the only one ever made."

Dillon and Taran examined it carefully before putting it back in the cart under the ploughshare and the packages.

"Then we have to keep it out of McDever's hands," said Taran.

Chapter Nine

Ethel set the bowl of soup on the small table beside the bed in the upstairs room of the gunsmith shop. "Can ye sit up for me to spoon it to ye?" she asked.

Reid lay on the bed with bandages around his chest and knuckles, but they couldn't hide the swollen-shut left eye or the gashes on his jaw and cheekbones. Although his internal injuries couldn't be seen, they pained Reid the most. He needed around-the-clock care, and Ethel eagerly stepped up to give it.

"I am no' hungry," said Reid. "Take these poultices off my stomach. They're no' helping, and the salve itches."

"The physician said ye need to keep them on so the bruises and yer ribs can heal."

"I dinna care what that ignorant physician says," said Reid, struggling to sit up. "If he kenned anything, Marjorie would be here instead of ye!"

Ethel's face fell.

"I'm sorry," said Reid. "I'm in pain."

" 'Tis all right," said Ethel. "I ken ye're hurting. Let me take away the poultices, and mayhap then ye'll want to take some soup. Ye need to keep yer strength up, even I ken that."

As she carefully pulled up the patches of poultice and gently wiped off the salve from his stomach, she asked, "Do ye want to talk about how this happened to ye?"

"Nay, dinna ask me again."

Ethel ducked her head and tossed the last of the poultices onto a rag on the floor. "I'm sorry. I only wanted to help."

He flopped back on the bed and closed his eyes.

His wounds would take more than a couple of days to heal, and he needed to make certain his sons were safe, provided they'd hidden in the Cullane cart as he told them.

"Ethel, may I ask ye a favor?"

"Of course, Reid, anything."

"Will ye go to the inn across the street and ask if the Cullanes have left Stirling?"

"The Cullanes?"

"Aye, but ye canna tell anyone that ye're asking for me. 'Tis important."

She wrinkled her nose. "Leena Cullane Adair? Why do ye want to ken if she's gone?"

" 'Tis of no matter to ye. I'd be most grateful if ye would find out."

Ethel hurried down the stairs and across the street. The innkeeper, quite generous with his information, said, "All of them left yesterday morning. Got two mules, a couple of horses from the blacksmith, and took their cart. They took verra good care of their rooms, no' like some that leave a terrible mess for me to clean up afore I can rent it again."

Ethel asked, "Were any of the lads with them?"

The innkeeper shook his head. "I saw three lads sneaking around the barn, but I chased them away afore the Cullanes left."

"Thank ye, sir," said Ethel before she turned and

strode out the door. Sitting down on the bench outside the gunsmith shop, she mulled over her choices now that the woman was gone, along with Reid's sons. Aye, his sons were with her, and after Reid was well again, he'd leave and marry her. *I canna let him go!*

Back upstairs in Reid's room, she told him, "The innkeeper said she and her brothers left this morning. Oh, and I saw Willie behind the inn."

Reid forced himself up on his elbows. "Are ye certain ye saw Willie? What about Ramy and Hendrie?"

"I only saw Willie. He said they were waiting for ye to get better. He said to tell ye he and his brothers were staying with their teacher, Mistress Waltham, until ye are well."

Reid squeezed his eyes against the pain as he sat up. "Are ye certain that's what he said? Mistress Waltham's?"

"Aye. I can go to Mistress Waltham's and check on them for ye. I'll go afore I bring ye supper, but ye must lie back down and rest." She pushed gently on his shoulders, and he lay back down on the pillows.

"Ye can go back to the shop. I am certain Master Owen misses ye."

"But I would rather be here taking care of ye. I am no' a verra good shop girl. I'd make a better wife and mother. I like taking care of others. Can ye no' see that?"

She smiled at him adoringly until she saw he had closed his eyes and snored softly.

She pulled a face. *At least he isna out looking for his lads. The longer I can keep him here, the farther away she will be.*

She picked up the soup bowl and walked down the

stairs, muttering to herself. "I'll have plenty more chances to soften Reid's heart. He will no' be on his feet any time soon. What will I make him for supper tonight?"

****

Reid waited until he heard the door to his shop close behind Ethel before opening his eyes. *She's lying.* Three days ago Mistress Waltham had written him that she would be visiting her sick sister on the coast for at least the next two weeks.

Why would Ethel tell him this tale about seeing Willie and the lads staying with Mistress Waltham? Was it to ease his mind or did she have another motive? It occurred to him that she might want to keep him in bed so she could keep waiting on him hand and foot. He had never encouraged the feelings she had for him, and he'd always treated her like a younger sister and never like a woman he might want to court. Had he really been that callous to her feelings? Had he become so selfish and careless about the lass that she would do anything, even lie about his sons, to win his affection?

Ethel's lie convinced him his sons had hidden in the Cullane cart and were no longer in Stirling. They were clever lads, and they did what they had to do. They were with Leena.

Leena. He closed his eyes again, and his mind filled with visions of his hands encircling her waist and then wandering down over her hips and over her firm, round bottom. He could hear her softly hum as he unlaced her kirtle and slipped his hand inside to stroke and tease her breasts to taut peaks. Sliding her dress off her shoulders revealed luscious milky skin, and she stood before him waiting.

He envisioned her hands going under his sark, untying his belt, and pushing his trews off his hips and then his legs. Together, naked, they would use their eyes and then their hands to give each other pleasure. He touched her in places forbidden to all but those who are bound to each other by trust, commitment, and love. She moaned, saying, "More," and he gave her whatever pleased her, and that pleased him. He would then lay her down on soft silky sheets, spread her legs, and join with her in sweet lovemaking.

Sucking in a noisy gasp, he opened his eyes, and instead of finding the beautiful woman who kindled long-buried feelings, he saw the bare walls of his room and winced with the lingering pain of the beating he'd taken. She was the keeper of all his dreams now, and she was on her way back home with his sons, never to return.

All because of the gun. Until the first day McDever showed up, he'd been so proud of making it. *Please, Lord, save my sons from my pride!*

That evening Ethel brought him a stew for his supper and told him she'd been to see the lads, and Ramy had the sniffles, but she would tend to him. After she left, Reid swung his legs over the side of the bed and took his first steps unaided across the small room to the wall and back. He would fight to regain his strength.

****

Jonas McDever entered the wardrobe mercer's shop and walked straight over to a shop girl with ginger hair pinned into a bun at the back of her neck, the woman he had seen going into Reid Haliburton's gunsmith shop.

"Mistress," he said to her. "Are you able to help

me find something for my mother?"

"I am just about to leave to attend a sick friend, but I am certain I can get someone else to help ye. Adelle, will ye come here, please?"

"I am so sorry, but this will not take long. Is there no way you can help me yourself? Will your friend not wait a few minutes for you?" He touched the crook of her arm and gave her a pleading look.

She returned a demure smile to this tall handsome stranger. *Aye, Reid can wait a few minutes.* "Aye, sir, how may I help ye?"

With a sigh of relief, the man said, "If I may introduce myself. I am Wellington Falconer. I know 'tis a mouthful, but my parents wanted it to be memorable. Forgive me, I digress. I brought my mother to Stirling to get her mind off the recent death of my father."

"I am so sorry," Ethel interrupted. "Ye both must grieve."

"Aye, mistress, we do, but my chore today is to purchase something pretty and fancy to cheer her up. Have you a lovely handkerchief or perhaps a pair of gloves she might like?"

"Of course, we do. This way and I can show ye our selection of both."

Wellington Falconer occupied Ethel's time for nearly an hour as he struggled to make a decision. His mother liked very specific colors and styles, and so did he, but despite narrowing it down to two choices, he still couldn't make up his mind.

"These are both verra nice," said Ethel, her impatience showing on her face. "Mayhap she would like both. Would that please her?"

"Why, I believe it would. You're a clever lass and

quite an excellent seller. Will you wrap them both up for me?"

"If 'tis all right with ye, I will have Adelle wrap them for ye. My sick friend is waiting for his morning meal, and I am afraid I have kept him waiting too long as it is." She handed the gloves with embroidery on the cuffs and the equally fancy embroidered silk handkerchief to Adelle, but before she could leave, Master Falconer took her arm and gently turned her toward him.

"Forgive me again for keeping you so long, but I must tell you the truth." He put his hand to his mouth and cleared his throat. "I saw you in the window yesterday, and since then I have not been able to take my eyes off you. You are so lovely, and I had to find out if you were as charming as I imagined. You have proven yourself to be more than I could possibly hope for. If I may be so bold as to ask if you would walk with me, and perhaps help me become more familiar with this town of Stirling. If I could get to know you better, I would greatly appreciate it."

Ethel blushed from her neck to her toes. No man had shown her favor in a long time, especially no one so handsome, charming, and obviously well-heeled. She could not, and would not, pass up this chance for a possible future with a man, one she had only dreamed of.

"I...I...I will be honored to show ye Stirling."

"Thank you so much," said Falconer with a deep bow.

To the shop owner, Ethel said, "I will be taking the rest of the day off." Before the owner, Owen, could answer, Ethel put her hand into the bent arm of

Wellington Falconer and left the shop. Less than a minute later, she stuck her head back through the door. "Adelle, take the bread and milk to the gunsmith. 'Tis on the table in the back." The door slammed shut behind her.

Ethel did not return to work the next day, as she and Wellington spent their time strolling around Stirling, eating their meals from local street vendors and in the evening dining at a high-class tavern with a fine selection on their menu. A delicious kiss followed that meal before Wellington dropped her off at the rooming house where she rented a room from a married couple.

Conversation came easily with Wellington, who wanted to know as much as he could about her. He listened intently and encouraged her to share all about her life, never believing it to be dull or ordinary. His stories about his own life as a wealthy landowner of a large estate south of the border in England enthralled her as did his fine manners and gentle touch. On the second day, he turned the conversation to the "sick friend" in the shop next to the mercer.

"If I may be so bold," Wellington asked, "is your friend…more than a friend?"

"What do ye mean?"

"I…well…I mean, if I may be so bold, that I am becoming quite attached to you…as perhaps more than a friend, and if I overstep my bounds because another has your heart, I…will with great reluctance step aside. Is this friend more than a friend?"

Wellington Falconer had shown her devoted attention, while Reid Haliburton took advantage of her every kindness with barely a word of thanks, and obviously Ethel had wasted her time for five years. On the other hand, in two short days Wellington had already said he wanted her in his life. She made up her mind.

Wellington frowned. "Your hesitation tells me that I have indeed overstepped, so—"

"Nay, it doesna," Ethel said quickly. "My sick friend is just that, a sick friend. I have kenned him for several years, and it will ne'er be anything more, but I wish to ken ye better, for ye to be…more than a friend…if that is what ye wish." She bowed her head at her brashness.

Wellington lifted her chin and lightly brushed his lips across hers. "I wish to be much more than friends. I wish to introduce you to my family, who will find you as delightful as I do." He kissed her again and convinced her that she'd found the man of her dreams.

After a long walk through the park in the center of Stirling, and after long, sweet kisses behind an oak tree, Wellington asked, "This friend, has he a name I might have heard? My mother knows many people in Stirling."

"Reid Haliburton," said Ethel, her face flushed with swirling feelings for Wellington. "I doubt yer mother would ken him. He's a gunsmith, a widower with three sons."

"Did he send the boys away when he became ill?"

"He ne'er said, but he had to. They are nowhere in sight."

"He must want a mother for his sons. Has he tried to find someone since his wife died? Has he shown interest in anyone besides you?"

Rubbing the back of his hand with her finger, Ethel

said, "He has no' shown any interest in me, but he has been attentive to a woman who did business with the shop. She only stayed here for a few days. I think she has gone back to where she came from. Her name was Adair, but she left with her brothers, the Cullanes, a few days ago."

"That is curious. Did ye ken where Mistress Adair came from? Or where these Cullanes were going?"

"Let me think. She mentioned that her mother and sister lived in a place in the Highlands called…Let me think…"

"Think, Ethel, think!" said Wellington with unexpected irritation. "Where did this woman come from?" He grabbed her arm and shook it. "Think!"

Ethel gave a start of surprise. "Why do ye speak so sharply to me?"

Immediately, he released her arm. "My sweet one, I am so sorry. I didn't realize how harshly my words came out. Forgive me, please. To frighten you is the last thing I want." He kissed her forehead. " 'Tis only idle curiosity as to where this woman is from, nothing more. Do you forgive me?"

"Of course, I do. I think she mentioned a place called Kirkcaldy. It must be a verra small place to bring her to Stirling for so much cloth."

McDever gave her an approving smile. "My dearest lady, I would like to escort you to your room so you can rest before the magnificent evening I have planned for us."

"Really? What is it?"

" 'Tis a great surprise, and I do not want to spoil it by giving you even a hint. But 'twill be a night you will not forget." He gave a slight bow and offered her his arm. "This way, milady."

Ethel practically floated all the way back to the room she rented from Master and Mistress Kyle. After giving Ethel a deep lingering kiss at the doorway of the boarding house, Wellington Falconer strode out of Stirling to the campsite of the men of the *Scarlet Lion* outside the wall.

"Four of you get ready to ride," he said to the men waiting there. "The rest will go back to the ship and start sailing north up the coast. We'll catch up after we get the gun. The five of us are going toward the Highlands where someone will know about an estate owned by the Cullanes or a town called Kirkcaldy. Along the way we will find a cart, three boys…and a gun."

Chapter Ten

Taran headed south back toward Stirling with a pack full of bread, slices of lamb, and oatcakes made by the innkeeper's wife, but not before grousing that he only did it under duress.

"And I thank ye heartily," said Leena as she kissed him on the cheek. "I ken how protective ye are of me, and I do love ye for it, but Reid Haliburton doesna deserve yer scorn. He is a good man, and ye will learn that if ye get to ken him."

"I only do this because ye're my sister, no' because Haliburton deserves anything."

"We thank ye for going after our da," said Willie who stepped up to shake Taran's hand, quickly followed by Ramy and Hendrie.

Taran, taken aback by this gesture of gratitude from the lads, gave a quick nod before mounting his horse and riding away, leaving behind one horse and two mules.

With the cart loaded and the mules hitched, Dillon, Leena, and the Haliburton lads prepared to head north. It would be at least three long days or more before they reached the abbey and could find shelter for the night.

"I can drive a team," said Willie. "I have done it afore when Da delivered guns to men who lived outside of Stirling. Ye can trust me."

"Aye, ye can," said Ramy and Hendrie almost in

unison.

"All right, we will," said Dillon. "Hendrie will ride with me for this first part while Leena and Ramy will take turns walking and riding in the cart. Then we'll switch." With that he lifted Willie onto the seat in the cart and handed him the reins while Leena and Ramy decided to walk together first. Dillon climbed into the saddle on his horse and lifted Hendrie to sit in front of him. A quick snap of the reins, and all were on their way.

Hendrie sat straight against Dillon's chest for a time until his back ached. Slumping down, he turned his head to look up at Dillon. "Do ye think I will grow to be as big as ye?"

Leena, listening to their conversation, felt encouraged by how wee Hendrie warmed up so easily to everyone in the family, and they to him.

"Is yer da as tall as me?" asked Dillon.

Hendrie twisted around even farther to get a better look. "Aye, I think mayhap bigger."

"Then I think ye will grow up to be quite a man."

"But I am little now."

"Everyone is little to begin with. 'Tis in the growing that yer size is made."

Hendrie pondered this for a minute before righting himself on the saddle, leaning his head back on Dillon, and falling asleep.

As she walked and then rode on Dillon's horse throughout the morning, Leena's anxiety gradually eased as the landscape changed from the level, forested ground into the craggy, sometimes barren terrain of the Highlands. While others might view the empty Highland glens as lonely, Leena never had. These were places where someone could breathe in clean air and admire the expanse of blue sky. How lucky she was to have been born and raised here!

Yet despite the increasing comfort of coming home, a troubled sensation settled around her heart. She hadn't been honest with Reid Haliburton. She had enjoyed their conversations, even if it were about something as trivial as choosing the right color thread, and she had relished the warmth of his hand against hers. By accepting his invitations to spend time together, she had encouraged him.

She saw it in his eyes, in his smile, and in the taste of his kiss, how he, too, liked their time together. She had encouraged him, but she had no right. She closed her eyes and prayed he might never find out the truth. Otherwise, he'd regret saving her from that fall in the mud.

Johnnie had known the truth about her, and it hadn't mattered to him. The way he loved her flourished, constant and deep, but other men couldn't love her like that, not if they found out she could never give them a child. Barren. What a terrible word!

A woman had a duty to give the man a piece of himself to live on as his heritage, and she couldn't do that. Wiping a tear from her eye, she sucked in her breath and exhaled the pain, knowing that she could never be a complete woman, or wife, to any man, especially not to a man like Reid Haliburton who deserved only the best a woman could give him.

At age fourteen, she'd fallen out of the hay loft and landed on a pitchfork. Her grandfather, Bretane, had saved her life, but he could not save her ability to have a child. The pity she saw in his eyes when he told her the news created greater pain than any she'd endured, but she fought against that pity, fought hard so no one would pity her again. She couldn't bear to see her shame in Reid's eyes.

Leena, the lads, and Dillon spent the first night in tents in a small clearing about fifty feet off the main road, if anyone could call it a road without laughing. The next day the rocks and ruts slowed their pace considerably, and all of them were near exhaustion when Dillon called for them to stop at dusk.

A group of traveling merchants heading in the opposite direction camped nearby after a summer in the Highlands selling everything from pots and pans to medicines and carpets to buttons, starches, and dyes. Bandits and thieves were commonplace on the road, and it was only by luck they had not encountered any so far on their trip. Although not all travelers were trustworthy, there was safety in numbers, and he hoped being near these people might help him have a peaceful sleep tonight, instead of jerking awake at every sound.

Dillon strode into the circle of three wagons to ask if he and his family could camp nearby. He needed to find out the honesty, or lack thereof, within this group.

He came back to Leena and the lads beside the road a few minutes later, saying, "They are chapmen traveling with their families. I saw several women and two children, so I think we'll be safe here for the night."

"I can help ye lay out the bedding in the tents," said Ramy. "I do it for Da if we are away overnight."

"That would be verra kind of ye," said Leena.

Ramy took her hand in his. "Thank ye for taking us with ye. Willie said we could make it on our own in the

Highlands, but I dinna ken how. Da said we would be safe with ye."

"Ye and yer brothers are fine lads, and I would ne'er turn ye away. Even if I didna ken yer da, I wouldna leave ye alone."

Ramy dropped her hand and went about laying out the bedding for the five of them to spend the night in the tent.

After eating a meal cooked over the fire, Leena and the two younger Haliburtons curled up together on the blankets while she read aloud from another of Johnnie's chapbooks that she always carried in her pack.

Dillon asked Willie to walk with him over to a group of men to find out about the conditions ahead.

"If it doesna rain and the roads stay dry, mayhap ye can make it to the abbey by nightfall tomorrow. At the latest by midday the next day," said a blacksmith who worked his trade at crofts and estates too small to have their own blacksmith. "How are yer horses and mules fixed for shoes?"

"I checked them, and all look fine," said Dillon. "I wish there were a station between here and the abbey to get fresh animals, but we'll have to make do until we get there."

At sunup, Willie, Ramy, and Hendrie bid a reluctant goodbye to their new friends in the children of the merchants. By midday, they had come nearly eight miles and were ready to stop at midday to rest and eat. Dillon unhitched the mules so they could graze alongside the horse. Even though the grass and underbrush were scarce between the rocks and rough terrain, the animals were quick to find a snack.

After eating, Dillon told the lads to clean up the

site while he resaddled the horse. The mules were next, and he had the harness over one of them when all at once the animal started braying frantically, kicking, and running in circles. This set off the other mule and the horse who, still not knowing where the danger came from, desperately tried to save themselves, leaving Dillon trapped in the middle of a frenzy of hooves and terrified animals.

The mule tossed Dillon from side to side, lifting him off his feet until the mule slammed him into the side of the cart. At the same time, the other mule kicked back on the other side. The cart, not used to such rough treatment, promptly splintered and collapsed on top of Dillon, sending the wheel and then the heavy tools tumbling out to bury him. He lay still and silent as the wild screaming of the animals continued while Leena and the lads stood helpless until all three animals ran in different directions out of sight.

"Dillon! Dillon!" screamed Leena as she lifted a pile of smaller tools off her brother. "What happened?" she cried. "They all just went mad!"

Willie, Ramy, and Hendrie followed her lead, tossing packages of cloth, bundles of leather, and buckets of nails, screws, and files onto the ground away from Dillon. One of the iron-rimmed wheels and two heavy ploughshares remained across his chest and legs.

"Help me," said Leena as she and the lads grabbed onto the plough on his chest and started to drag it off. "Stop! The sharp edge is cutting him! We have to find a way to lift it off."

"I ken what happened!" said Hendrie. "I saw that mule run off. He had snakes, a lot of them, hanging onto his leg."

"Adders," said Ramy. "He must have stepped into a nest hidden under a rock and got bit. Now all the animals are gone. Are you all right, Dillon?"

Dillon gasped, "We can look for the animals later. Just get all this off me."

"I have an idea," said Willie. "Mistress Waltham taught us about Archimedes and the lever. Ramy, get that rock over there to use as a fulcrum. One of these boards from the cart could be the lever."

Ramy quickly brought back a large rock while Leena and Hendrie tore a loose board from the side of the cart. Arranging the rock and the board under part of the plough, Leena balanced the plough while the lads put all their weight and strength to the board.

" 'Tis moving," said Leena just as the board snapped in half and the plough fell back onto Dillon. He grunted.

"Try two boards," gasped Dillon.

Finding two undamaged boards proved difficult, but eventually they put one board on top of the other, situated it over the rock, and again the lads put all their weight against the boards while Leena balanced the plough and slid it off her brother. They did the same with the plough on his legs. Only the cumbersome iron-rimmed wheel remained.

"I dinna think the boards are strong enough to move the wheel," said Willie. " 'Tis too heavy."

"What if we pull out the wooden spokes first?" asked Hendrie. "That would make it lighter."

"Wise lad." Dillon panted. "Hurry. 'Tis on my chest, and I'm having trouble breathing."

Working together, Leena and the lads pulled away the broken spokes and sawed off the others. Very carefully they cut the wooden part of the wheel held together by the iron rim into pieces and took them out one at a time. Only the iron rim remained, so they stuffed a blanket under the rim until they could pull the blanket and slide the rim to the ground. It took all they had, and they fell repeatedly, but eventually they freed Dillon.

Leena checked him for injuries, which were unexpectedly few, only consisting of several broad bruises across his chest and a few small cuts. The only one of any consequence proved to be a twisted and clearly broken lower right leg.

"We're in a bit of a mess," said Dillon, gritting his teeth against the pain. "I canna walk, and the cart is useless."

"First things, first," said Leena. "We take care of this leg. I've seen Da and Mum fix broken legs afore, and I'll do the best I can. Ramy, bring two shorter boards, and Willie, use yer knife to tear strips off that blanket."

While Leena and the older lads made the preparations, Hendrie knelt at Dillon's head and lifted it onto his lap. Stroking the man's brow, Hendrie started to sing a sweet song.

Go to sleep, my baby,
Close your pretty eyes.
Angels up above you,
Peeping at you dearly from the skies.
Great big moon is shining,
Stars begin to peek. Time to go to sleep.
Close your pretty eyes and sleep.

Dillon's shoulders relaxed, and he closed his eyes.

"Where did ye learn that?" asked Leena.

"Willie sang it to me when I was just a wee one. It helped me go to sleep after my mother left us."

Willie handed Leena two boards long enough to reach from Dillon's midthigh past his foot. "Our mother sang it to us every night after she put us in bed, but Hendrie was only a babe when she died. Da wanted to sing it, but he has a terrible voice, and Hendrie would cry, so I sang it to him."

Leena's heart melted for these motherless lads who took such good care of each other, and for their father who so obviously loved them. Hendrie's song also brought back a memory for her. As a grown man, Hendrie's voice would sound remarkably like Johnnie's.

"First, let's get him off the cold ground," said Leena. They made a bed of quilts and blankets and helped him scoot over on top of them. Next, they set up the tent around him to keep the now-sprinkling rain off his head.

"I'll work on straightening this leg well enough until we can get proper care at the abbey." Gently feeling Dillon's shin, she found where the bone had split. "It doesna seem too bad, no' much separation between the ends of the bones. Can ye feel yer toes?" She pinched one.

"Aye!" said Dillon. "Tie the boards, spacing the strips along my leg from my thigh down to beyond my ankle. Now carefully twist the boards until ye pull the leg down, and the bones should slide together."

After tying the boards in place, she grasped Dillon's foot and ankle and slowly turned and pulled until the lump on the side of his leg moved inward. She repeated the procedure twice more, each time feeling the bone with her fingers until the ends of the bones were as close together as she could get them. Finally, she tightened all the strips along the boards to hold his leg as still as possible.

Dillon, in a cold sweat from the pain and exertion, appreciated the warm quilt Willie and Ramy tucked over him.

Now they needed a plan to get help for Dillon and to get them to a safe place off the road.

"One rider can make it to the abbey to get help," said Leena. "But 'twill be at least tomorrow eve afore I could get back. I canna leave ye alone that long."

Willie threw back his shoulders, trying to seem older than twelve. "Ye will have to ride the horse, if we can ever find it again, but we can take care of Dillon. Ye can trust us."

In unison, Ramy and Hendrie said, "Aye, ye can!"

" 'Tis the only way," said Willie.

"The lad's right," said Dillon, shifting his weight on the blankets. "Ye have to ride to the abbey and come back with a friar and a wagon to carry me. Without the heavy load of the cart, ye can make good time. Lads, go find the horse and the mules while I talk to my sister."

The lads took off running in search of the runaway animals while Leena sat down on the ground next to Dillon.

"I dinna want to leave ye alone," she said.

"We have no choice. Ye have been on this road afore, so ye ken the way to the abbey. Ride as fast as ye can, resting the horse only when ye must. We dinna have much coin left, but take what's in my pouch. A donation will help persuade the friars to come and help us."

"What about ye and the lads?"

"I can tell the lads what needs to be done, and they can do it. Their da trained them well to take care of themselves, so they can take care of me. I want ye to take the gun."

"We have no iron balls, and Willie has the cocking wire in his vest. The gun is useless."

"That may be, but if ye're threatened on the road, they dinna ken that. Scare anyone with it and then ride away as fast as ye can. 'Tis the only way. 'Tis late in the season for travelers, so the risk is low that someone will come upon us here, and we have our knives. Leena, ye have to do this."

The horse whinnied as Willie led it toward the tent beside the broken cart while Ramy tugged on one of the mules. Luckily, neither animal was injured.

"We couldna find the other mule that got snake bit," said Ramy.

"We can make do with these," said Dillon. "Help Leena get ready to go."

Leena organized the remaining foodstuffs and got a fire started. A campfire might bring thieves, but as they got farther into the Highlands, the colder came the nights, and they couldn't go without a fire for warmth. The three Haliburtons had shown themselves to be brave and willing helpers and guardians, giving added confidence to Leena that she could leave them and go to the abbey by herself.

She changed into a pair of Dillon's trews and sark, wrapping his belt around her to keep them on, tucked her hair under a knitted cap, and put a small loaf of bread and a flask of water on her saddle. The unworkable gun went into her waistband.

"*Beannachd leat*," she said as she kissed Dillon on the cheek.

"What does that mean?" asked Hendrie as he wrapped his arms around her waist and waited for his kiss.

" 'Tis Gaelic for 'good luck.' If ye're going to live in the Highlands, ye'll have to learn Gaelic. Mum will insist on it."

"I want to learn," said Hendrie.

"So do I," said Ramy.

Willie hesitated. "I will if Da will learn it, too."

She saved her hug for this lad so near to manhood who understood better than his younger brothers the possible consequences of everything that had happened. "Taran will bring yer da. I promise."

"Be off," Dillon said. "We want to see ye back here afore tomorrow evening."

The eight-hour ride to the abbey was fortunately uneventful for Leena. After she explained her situation to the friars, they packed a wagon with supplies, and even though the sun had already set, they started on their way back to the campsite with Leena.

" 'Tis dark," said a young monk by the name of Brother Thaddeus. He had a thick head of hair and an easy grin "But even if we did no' ken the road, which we do, we have lanterns to light our way. We have to get back to yer brother and the lads as soon as possible."

By noon on the next day, the wagon arrived where Leena had left her injured brother and the three Haliburton lads, only to find uninvited visitors waiting for them there.

Chapter Eleven

Taran, in no great hurry to get back to Stirling to find the man he disliked, took his time on the road, making it nearly two days before he got there. After finally reaching the gunsmith shop across from the inn and taking his horse to the blacksmith for the night, he walked back to the shop and peered through the window. No light anywhere. He knocked on the door. No answer.

As he turned to leave, Angus McGregor, the grocer, came out to toss a pile of spoiled vegetables into the garbage trough in the center of the road. "If ye're looking for the gunsmith, he's sick abed upstairs. He's been injured and willna be doing any gun work for some time."

"I only want to talk to him," said Taran. "On a personal matter."

"In that case, I can take ye up."

The two men climbed the stairs with McGregor calling out, "Reid, Reid, 'tis Angus, and I have a visitor for ye."

"Come ahead," Reid called back, "but ye'll have to light a lamp."

As soon as Angus lit the lamp and Reid saw his visitor, he pulled himself up to a sitting position. "Who are ye?"

Putting up his hands in a sign of surrender, Taran

said, "I'm Leena's brother, Taran, and I come in peace. I'll give ye my message and be on my way, if 'tis what ye want."

Reid eyed him cautiously before saying, "Is Leena all right?"

"Aye, but I didna come about her."

"Angus, ye can leave us. Thank ye for bringing him up."

"Are ye certain?" asked Angus.

"Aye."

After the two men heard the door close behind McGregor, Taran said, "We have yer sons."

Reid threw back the quilts and swung his legs over the side of the bed. "Are they all right?"

Again, Taran put up his hands. "Do ye think us evil monsters that we would hurt bairns? They're safe. We found them in our cart."

Reid's shoulders slumped. "I beg ye to take them somewhere safe."

"Willie already told us all about the gun and McDever and why ye put them in our cart. Right now they're on their way to Makgullane with Dillon and Leena. I am to bring ye to them."

Reid's head shot up. "Ye came to get me?"

" 'Twas no' my idea. I didna ever want to lay eyes on ye again, no' after I saw ye kissing my sister, but Leena kens the lads need their da, even if 'tis ye. Ye look in bad shape. The lads told us that ye took a beating. Do ye think ye can ride?"

"It looks worse than 'tis. I have been abed for five days, and I had to get my own meals for the last two, so I am much better. I can ride. I didna think I'd ever see my sons again. I thank ye."

"We'll leave in the morning, but first we'll talk. Has McDever been here since he did this to ye?"

"Nay, but I havena been out of this room."

Taran walked to the front window and looked out onto the street. "By the time we can catch up to them, Leena and Dillon should be at Makgullane with the lads. Once they get there, they'll be safe even if McDever follows them." Taran turned back to look at Reid. "I passed several riders about one day out of Stirling. I dinna ken who they were, but they didna look like typical Scots. One was a black Moor."

"McDever and his pirates. The Moor is Shipopi."

"One of them stayed back to ask me if I ever heard of a place called Kirkcaldy. That made me suspicious. No one goes to Kirkcaldy who doesna live there, but if they've heard of it, they mayhap ken of Makgullane. I dinna ken."

"We have to leave tonight," said Reid, his breath quickening. "They'll be nearly three days ahead if we dinna."

"Nay," said Taran. "We have to get ye ready to travel and get fresh horses. Besides, I ken the way, and they dinna. We can travel faster than they can, so we'll catch up soon enough. Ye can trust that Dillon will protect them all, and I tell ye true, Leena is verra good at taking care of herself. She made me come back here, and that was no small feat."

Reid's chuckle matched Taran's.

By sunup, the men had reached an uneasy truce and were prepared for a week or more on the road. Both agreed they should leave from behind the shops and stay to the side streets and alleys until they were outside the city wall. The fewer people who knew they were gone, the better, especially if McDever's men wanted to follow them.

As they rode away, neither of them noticed Ethel sweeping out the back step of the mercer's shop, her eyes red and swollen from crying. Wellington Falconer had never arrived that night, and she admitted he'd made promises he had no intention of keeping, and now Reid Haliburton was riding out of town. Her dashed hopes to wed and have a home of her own would painfully churn inside her for a long time.

****

Reid kept up with Taran's steady pace despite the increasing pain with every bounce in the saddle, but he couldn't show Taran any weakness, not to that arrogant man who had begrudgingly come for him. Late in the afternoon, Reid begged a stop so he could relieve himself, and Taran agreed he needed to do the same.

Easing himself off his mount, Reid grasped the saddle and steadied his legs for several minutes before taking a step toward the trees. Despite his best efforts to walk straight, he limped badly from having stayed in a riding position for so long. To his surprise, Taran took him by the elbow and supported him until they were both behind separate trees to do their business.

"We're stopping for an hour," said Taran as both men walked back toward their horses. "Get something to eat. We can sit over there on that mound."

"We need to make time. 'Twill be dark soon," said Reid.

"And if ye fall off yer horse from exhaustion and pain, and I have to carry ye, we'll make no time at all. Use yer head, *a'dhuine!*"

"What did ye call me?" snapped Reid.

"Take it easy. 'Twas Gaelic. It means 'man.' Ye are a man, are ye no'?"

"As much a man as ye are!"

Reid took the cheese and bread from his pack and hobbled to the grassy mound under a lone tree. He'd only taken a few bites of his food before he fell asleep, and Taran let him sleep until almost dusk.

Once back on their horses, the men were thankful for a full moon that let them get in nearly eight more miles before stopping for the night. They slept on the ground, wrapped in blankets. At first light, they were on the road again.

"We should be at the abbey by the evening meal," said Taran. "We'll get news of Leena, Dillon, and the lads since they will have reached there two days ago. 'Tis only two more days beyond the abbey to Makgullane, so we can be certain they're at home by now."

Reid slumped in the saddle, both from exhaustion and from relief that his sons would be protected. Whatever happened now, Willie, Ramy, and Hendrie were safe, and the gun stayed out of the hands of McDever.

****

"Something's wrong," said Leena as the wagon from the abbey came over the rise in the road at midday. "Stop." The wagon kept moving until she cried out to the driver, "Stop! Something is wrong!" Thaddeus reined in the horses.

Surrounding the broken cart were five additional men whom Leena didn't recognize. One had his hands on Willie's shoulders, shaking the boy.

"Leave the lad be!" she shouted as she jumped

down from the wagon. She kept her distance, hoping the mere presence of other people might scare the intruders away. "Dinna touch him."

"Stay away," called Dillon to her from the ground. "Go back!"

A man standing next to him promptly pounded Dillon's chest with his boot. Dillon grunted and lay still.

The man with his hands on Willie stood up, pushing the boy to the ground. Leena didn't recognize the tall, muscular man with ebony black hair and eyes, a handsome man except for the grimace across his face. "Those chapmen on the road told us you were coming in this direction. Otherwise, we'd have gone farther north and missed you altogether. Your bad luck, but my good fortune."

Leena could make a good guess who had been following them, but she stood silent until the man spoke again. "I have been waiting for you and the monks to come from the abbey. You might be more willing to give me what I want than these fellows here."

The young friar leaned down from the wagon seat and put his hand on Leena's shoulder. "Let me handle this," he said. To the men, he said, "We are only here to take the injured man and the lads back to the abbey. We are men of God and willna harm ye. Let us pass."

The dark-haired man threw back his head and laughed. "Ha! You think I tremble at the feet of men of God?" The other strangers joined him with their own laughter. "Here's my proposition. I will not harm you if you turn that wagon around and go back where you came from."

"We canna do that," said Brother Thaddeus, "no'

when a man is hurt. We only ask that ye let us tend to his injuries. 'Tis a godly request."

The man grabbed Willie around his neck and pulled him off his feet while asking, "Do you know who I am?"

Willie grasped McDever's arm and dangled with his feet off the ground.

No one answered.

"I am Jonas McDever, a man with no soul who looks forward to the Hell your God promises so I can make your devil do my bidding. Now if you do not want me to break this boy's neck, you will go back where you came from, but leave the woman."

Brother Thaddeus stood up in the wagon. "That willna be happening. I ask ye to listen to reason. I have coin here, so ye willna leave empty-handed. All we ask in return is to take the injured man and the lads back to the abbey."

A look of pure venom slid across McDever's face. "That will not be happening." With a jerk of his head, the other four pirates, Shipopi and Magnus among them, drew their swords and charged at the wagon. The pirates quickly defeated the monks, who carried only small dirks hidden in their robes. All the holy men soon lay wounded and bleeding in the wagon with Leena screaming beside it.

Shipopi leaped up into the seat of the wagon, slapped the reins, and, turning the wagon around, drove it back in the direction it had come. The sound of the rattling wheels on the road gradually faded into the wind.

Leena started toward the broken cart. "Take what ye want and leave us be."

"Nay," called Dillon. "Dinna come closer, Leena."

McDever's eyes perked up as he tossed Willie back on the ground. The boy landed hard, but didn't cry out. Instead, he crawled over beside Dillon and tugged his brothers close to him.

"So you're the woman Leena. I'm glad to finally meet you. I have heard about you from Ethel. You have something I want."

"And what might that be?" hissed Leena.

"These lads are very tight-lipped. I know they had what I want at one time, but they don't have it now. That only leaves one other person. You have it."

"We didna tell him," said Hendrie.

"Hush!" said Willie, giving Hendrie a slap on the arm.

Leena sucked in a deep breath and threw back her shoulders. "I still dinna ken what ye're talking about."

McDever stared at her silently for a long moment before saying, "Ye want to play with me like that fool of a gunsmith did?" In one stride he moved beside Hendrie, lifted the boy by the collar, and held the tip of his knife to his cheek. "Give me what I want, or this boy will wear my scar for the rest of his life." The brutal detachment in McDever's voice sent shivers down Leena's spine.

"I have it. Put the lad down."

McDever dropped his knife to his side, but he didn't release Hendrie. "Show it."

Leena slid the gun out from her belt under her jacket and held it out. "Let the lad go, and I'll toss it to ye."

She heard Shipopi's footsteps approaching as he loped back to the campsite alone. "Over edge," said

Shipopi in his broken English. "No see again." He laughed. "Nobody see, mayhap their God!"

Ignoring Shipopi, Leena repeated to McDever, "Let the lad go, and I'll toss ye the gun." The wind swirled around her as she waited for him to release Hendrie. Instead, McDever winked just as Shipopi reached over her shoulder, snatched the gun out of her hand, pushed her onto her face on the road, and walked over to his captain with his prize.

McDever stroked the weapon almost gleefully. "In case you're wondering, I already have the flintlock. The one without boots gave it to me if I'd go away." He pointed at Ramy and laughed. "He is so trusting." Aiming into the distance, he cocked the wheel lock trigger, but without the tension of the wire, the trigger released and snapped back to its original position. "There's no wheel lock wire. Where is it?"

Leena came up on her elbows on the ground. "I dinna ken anything about the gun." Standing up, she brushed off her trews. "Take it and leave. We dinna ken anything about how it works. Ye'll have to go back to Stirling and ask Reid Haliburton."

"Mount up, men," McDever said, and the five pirates jumped onto their horses. "That is not entirely true. One of you does know." With that he leaned over, snatched up Willie, and threw him across his saddle facedown. "I won't have to go to Stirling. Haliburton will come to me."

The pirate men rode off to the northeast.

Ramy and Hendrie ran after them, calling to their brother, until the horses were out of sight. After they trudged back to the remains of the cart, Leena took them in her arms and tried to comfort them, but her own tears gave away her hopelessness.

"This is all my fault," said Leena to Dillon. "If I'd told McDever about the wire, he wouldna have taken Willie. He would have his gun, and he would have left us alone."

" 'Tis no' yer fault," said Dillon.

" 'Tis! I kenned what he wanted. If I'd just given over the gun, the friars from the abbey would be alive today. I killed them!"

"Nay! Nay!" cried Dillon, reaching out for her. "McDever would have killed us all. 'Tis the pirate's fault. Aye, if I had been more careful with the horse and mules, I wouldna be lying here with a broken leg, and we'd all be safe at the abbey, but 'twas McDever who stole Willie. He is the guilty one! Hendrie, Ramy, please forgive me."

The lads knelt on either side of Dillon.

"The three of us talked about this last night," said Ramy, "and we ken 'tis no' yer fault. We blame the snakes, creatures with no brain at all."

Hendrie spoke up. "Willie is verra brave. That bad man winna hurt him."

Leena clutched her stomach. *McDever could do worse than hurt him. He could kill him, and I couldna live with myself.*

She vomited into the grass.

"Do ye have any ideas?" Ramy asked. "Willie always has ideas. We have to get some."

Leena straightened up, wiping her mouth. "Ye're absolutely right. We need ideas."

For the next hour, the four of them nibbled on bread, cheese, and dried meat while they made suggestions, dismissing them, and making better ones.

At the end of the hour, they had a plan.

The tools in the cart proved helpful as they nailed and lashed together pieces of boards, dragged the second wheel over, and tied it together with the first wheel rim. Now they had a platform big enough to carry Dillon. Using the remaining boards, they filled in the iron circles, and stuffed the spaces with blankets. The hitch hadn't been damaged, so by tying it to the first iron rim, they harnessed Dillon's carrying cot to the mule. The mule brayed and kicked, not entirely happy with this arrangement, but Hendrie proved to be an excellent mule driver. He agreed to ride on the mule's back and guide him, and the mule seemed satisfied with this part of the plan.

Once Dillon situated himself on the makeshift bed, with the few tools they might need stuffed around him, including Reid's rifling tool, Ramy and Leena took turns riding the horse and walking beside the bed to steer it around rocks and ruts in the rough road. Heading in the direction of the abbey, their pace was slow but steady.

Chapter Twelve

"If we can keep up this pace," said Taran, "we'll make the abbey by nightfall. How are ye managing?"

"I'll make it," said Reid. "The sooner I get to my sons, the better."

Reid had paid the price for his injuries over the last two days' ride from Stirling, but his determination to see his sons and Leena again made the pain worth it. Willie, Ramy, and Hendrie would be as excited and relieved to see him as he would be to see them, but he worried that Leena's reaction might be different.

The last time they were together, he had let his emotions erupt to the surface in their kiss behind the inn. How could he have done something so inappropriate at the least, and abusive at worst, something unacceptable for a man who had not proclaimed his intentions to court her? He held out only the smallest hope that she might forgive him, that he might see her smile at him again and mayhap allow him to touch her cheek.

But did he have the right to expect anything from her? His heart ached for Leena, but his commitment to Marjorie continued even with her death. He tried to blame Leena for his tumult of emotions, but he couldn't fault her because he had been thunderstruck by her smile, captured by her deep love for her family, and amazed by her strength and independence of character.

Or that the simple lilt in her voice or the sound of her laugh charmed him. Or that she made him feel genuinely happy for the first time in five years. Or that until the moment she fell into his arms on the street, he had forgotten how gladness could ease the constant lump in his chest.

Marjorie would want him and her three sons to lead good lives that amounted to something, but would she want him to find happiness with another woman? Until death do ye part had been his vow. Aye, she had parted from him in death, but death had not taken him. Would it be breaking his vow if he loved another?

Love? He tried to tell himself that he hadn't known her long enough to call it love, but if his heart beat faster at the mere sight of her, it could be nothing but love. He acknowledged it to himself, but could he tell her?

A cold, hard breeze ruffled his hair and chilled his ears, and he tugged the hood on his cloak tighter around his neck.

"What's that pile of rubbish by the road up ahead?" Reid asked. "Who would leave ploughs?"

"I think I ken," said Taran as he whipped his horse into a run. Reid followed.

Arriving at the broken cart, Taran jumped off his horse and quickly poked through the pile of abandoned tools and pieces of broken wood. "This is our cart! These are the tools we bought in Stirling." He held up a caliper, a handful of screwdrivers, and a brass hammer. "These are yers. And look at all this cloth!"

Reid scattered the wood from the cart out of his way until he reached the bottom of the pile. "Where are Ramy or Hendrie?" Scanning the countryside, he shouted, "Willie! Willie! Where are ye?"

"Stop yer shouting, *a'dhuine*! See what ye can learn from the tracks. There are too many prints to be only our horses and mules. Somebody else stopped here."

Reid gave the ground a slow, deliberate search. *Taran is right. The lads are no' here, but calm, meticulous thinking is the only way to follow the clues and find out what happened.*

"There are some horse prints moving north," he said. "I'd guess four or five horses went that way, but the tracks to the west are harder to figure." He knelt to get a closer look. "Something heavy made a wide rut in the mud." He followed that rut up the road for about a furlong before coming back to Taran, who still circled the broken cart trying to decipher the tracks.

"There are footprints, too. They're small, maybe Ramy's."

"Could they be Leena's?"

Standing side by side, Taran and Reid looked down the road in the direction of the abbey. "Whatever happened here, our best bet is to follow the tracks that way. Dillon would make certain all of them got to the abbey, no matter what."

"I agree," said Reid as he leapt back onto his horse and started down the road. Taran hurried to catch up.

For the next mile, Reid called out the names of his sons over and over. He kept a nearly breakneck pace until Taran caught up, grabbed his reins, and tugged him and his mount to a stop.

If Reid's glare had been his fist, Taran would be flat on his back in the dirt.

Talking quickly, Taran said, "We could miss them

at this pace, ride right past them. Slow down and look around before ye go calling out their names. Use yer head, *a'dhuine*!"

With a long sigh, Reid said, "They're my sons, the only ones I have left."

This time Taran glared. "Are ye thinking I dinna care for my sister and twin brother as much as ye do for yer sons?"

"I...I didna mean ye didna care. I ken ye do. Did ye say twin brother?"

"Aye. He's the nice one, but if ye can tell us apart, I'll give ye this dirk." He pulled a jewel-studded knife out of its leather case. "My grandfather gave this to me on my fifteenth birthday, thus announcing I was a man. Ye name me and Dillon and 'tis yers."

"A fine piece 'tis. And what if I canna tell ye apart?"

"I get to call ye '*a'dhuine*,' no' yer name, for as long as I ken ye."

Reid studied Taran for a few moments before saying, " 'Tis a bargain. I can feel that dirk hanging from my belt already."

Putting the dirk back in its sheath, Taran said, "If ye win the bet, *a'dhuine*, ye'd be the first one ever. Leena is the only one who doesna have to study us afore deciding. Let's keep moving, but slower this time."

Another mile passed with excruciating slowness for Reid until something in the distance caught his eyes. He pointed. "Do ye see that up ahead?"

Squinting, Taran said, "I do. 'Tis worth taking a look."

They headed off the road toward movement to the

northwest. As they came closer, the wind carried a low murmur of voices to them.

Reid dug his heels into his horse's flanks. "Willie! Ramy! Hendrie!"

Ramy and Hendrie's heads turned in his direction, and as soon as they saw him they started running toward him. "Da! Da! We kenned ye'd find us!"

Reid pulled his horse to a stop, jumped off, and hauled both lads into his arms. "Are ye all right? Ye're no' hurt?"

"We're no' hurt. Leena took good care of us, and we took good care of Dillon," said Ramy.

Reid noticed the blond man lying on a makeshift cot hitched to a mule. "I'm guessing that's Dillon," he said to Taran, already kneeling at his brother's side. "Pay up."

"Nay, *a'dhuine*," said Taran, throwing his arms around Dillon. "We have to be standing side by side afore I pay ye."

Before this conversation escalated into a brawl between his hot-headed brother and the still frantic Reid, Dillon interrupted. "We came into a bit of a mess when a nest of snakes bit one of the mules. In the fracas, I got my leg broke. Leena's over there." He pointed to the edge of a cliff several dozen feet away.

Reid saw a slim figure kneeling at the rim of the ridge overlooking a deep glen as Hendrie started pulling him in that direction. "Hurry, Da! We need yer help. Leena! Leena! Da is here!"

The figure stood. Leena! Reaching out her arms, she called, "Hurry! He's badly hurt!"

As Reid came closer, she put her hands on her hips and asked, "Yer face is bruised and cut. What happened to ye?" Before he could answer, she said, "Ye'll tell me later. We have to help him now." Taking him by the hand, she tugged him closer to the edge.

Peering over the rim, Reid saw a deep picturesque glen of lush hills and stony ridges surrounding a shimmering cobalt blue lake.

"Lovely," he said, but without warning she jerked on his arm, nearly dragging him over the side. Looking down, he saw a man in brown monk's robes lying prone on a small ledge about twenty feet below. A puddle of dark blood surrounded his chest. "What happened? How did he get there?"

In a strained voice, Leena said, "McDever came here. His man forced the wagon and two other men over the cliff, but Thaddeus landed on the ledge. We can't get him up." Dried tears streaked her face. "Help him. Please, help him."

"McDever was here?" Reid asked.

"Aye. I'll explain everything as soon as we get Thaddeus up here. Please, Reid. He needs yer help."

Reid's scorching look didn't change, but he said, "Have ye got a rope?"

"Aye." She took off running back toward Dillon, passing Taran on his way to the edge.

"Bring a blanket, a big one," shouted Reid. To the injured man on the ledge, he said, "Can ye move at all?"

In a raspy whisper, the man said, "Aye, a little, but no' enough to pull myself up. Praise God for sending ye."

"Wait until we get ye up here afore ye praise God."

To Taran, he said, "Yer going to have to lower me down with the rope around my waist. I'll wrap him in the blanket and tie him around my chest. Then ye'll have to haul both of us up. I'll hold on as best I can, but 'twill be up to ye to get us to the top."

"I can help," said Hendrie.

"So can I," said Ramy.

" 'Twill be dead weight so 'twill take all of ye. Where's Willie?" said Reid.

A sickening look came over all their faces.

"Is he dead?"

"Nay, nay!" said Leena, handing Reid the rope and the blanket. "We'll tell it all after ye're back up top with Thaddeus. Please, Reid, he's a brave man. Please, afore he dies."

Reid's gut churned. McDever's presence explained everything, the broken cart, Dillon's broken leg, the abandonment of the tools by the side of the road, and Willie's absence. He wanted to roar in frustration, but instead he swallowed his dread at whatever evil McDever had done and focused on rescuing the monk before he died alone on that ledge.

With the rope securely around his waist, Reid lay on his stomach and swung his legs over the rim. Taran, Ramy, Hendrie, and Leena held tightly to the other end of the rope, bracing their feet in the dirt as they lowered him down.

"I'm here," called up Reid when he reached the shelf.

"Hendrie," said Taran. "Hitch up the mule and bring him so he can help pull the two of them up." Hendrie ran back to the cart made from the iron rims.

"Thaddeus, we're going to get ye out of here," said Reid. "I canna promise it winna hurt. It will, but I'll do all I can to keep ye safe until we reach the top. I am going to roll ye into this blanket, and I'll tie ye across my chest, but ye'll have to put yer arms around my neck because I'll need my hands on the rope. Are ye ready?"

Thaddeus moaned as Reid lifted him onto the blanket and wrapped it around him, leaving his arms free, the sticky blood on his robe now soaking into the blanket. "Can ye put yer arms around my neck and hold on?"

"My right arm is useless, but I'll hold on to ye as tight as I do to the cross."

Reid stood, shifting Thaddeus's weight until he had balanced the man evenly across his chest and shoulder. He tied the rope around both of them before he called out, "Ready!"

"Here we go!" shouted Taran. "Pull with all ye got! Hendrie, start the mule to moving. Dinna let the rope slip off his harness."

Hendrie, sitting on the mule's back, kicked his feet, and the mule started to walk forward.

Bracing his feet against the rock, Reid held tight. The palms of his hands bled against the rubbing of the rope as he moved upward, but he never loosened his grip. Sweat broke out on his forehead from the effort, as he determined not to let his own injuries stop him.

"Dinna look down, Reid," called Taran.

"I already have. How'd ye think I got down here? Pull harder...*a'dhuine!*"

Gradually, Reid's head appeared over the edge of the ridge, followed by his chest. Then Thaddeus and finally Reid's feet were safe on top. Taran and Leena untied the monk from around Reid and laid him gently on the ground. Once free of his burden, Reid pressed his hands under his arms and took deep breaths as his body relaxed from the exertion.

Quickly, Taran and Leena unwrapped the blanket and examined the monk's wounds. The bones in his shoulder had crumbled into broken pebbles, so she would have to immobilize it. He winced as Leena gently pressed her fingers along his chest.

"Broken ribs," she said. "Get my saddle bag, Ramy. I'll stitch this gash on his chest. Hendrie, bring the canteens so I can wash the wound first."

As Leena went about her work, Taran said to Reid, "Help me check that Dillon's broken leg is in the proper place. Leena did the best she could, but she's ne'er done it afore. Then we can brace it with wood and wrap it. If we dinna, he'll ne'er walk straight again."

As the men came back toward Dillon's makeshift carrying rig, Taran asked, "Are ye going to be all right?"

Reid nodded.

"Have ye ever set a leg afore?"

"Why do ye think me a fool all the time? I've done it on bigger men than yer brother. No wonder Leena says ye're a mumblecrust."

"She doesna say that," protested Taran.

"She ought to."

By the time Reid and Taran finished resetting Dillon's leg, both the Cullane brothers had gained new respect for the gunsmith, despite his having brought all this trouble to them.

After the men laid Thaddeus on the wheelrim cot with Dillon, Leena reached out for Reid's hands. "Let me look at them."

He held out two hands with dried blood covering

the fingers and palms from gripping the rope.

"I can tend to those."

"I'd appreciate it."

With the gentleness of a great healer, Leena washed away the blood, applied salve, and wrapped both hands with strips of cloth torn from the checkered material she'd bought for the tablecloths for Marta, the cook.

He held up his red-and-white-covered hands. "I'm sorry you had to waste the cloth on me."

"Marta will understand. Do they pain ye much?"

"Nay," he lied.

"Ye were verra brave when we lowered ye down the cliff."

He narrowed his eyes. "Only a lunatic without his senses wouldna be afeared of going over the edge and that far down. If ye dinna think me afeared, ye must no' think me much of a man."

"Ye didna show it."

"Fear is an odd thing. When the men were beating me in the shop, I wasna afeared. I was angry, but I kenned I could take it. I just hoped they didna kill me, but then my lads showed up, and fear nearly swallowed me." He clenched his fists as best he could through the bandages. "And the whole time I lay in bed until yer brother came, the fear tore at my gut that they hadna hidden in yer cart. Now that Hendrie and Ramy are safe with ye, all I've got is fear in my verra soul for Willie."

" 'Tis because ye love them. Love and fear tangle up in each other."

He looked away for a moment, and then turned back. He had to tell her that he experienced the same fear for her. If he did, she might forgive him. "And I feared…I feared I'd ne'er see ye again. That I might ne'er…" He leaned into her, putting his hands on her shoulders, and their eyes held each other. He bent his head toward hers.

"*A'dhuine, a'dhuine!*" called out Taran. "Help me build a fire. Yer lads are hungry, and my sister can wait."

Leena turned and scowled at her brother. "He's right," she said to Reid in a low, husky voice. "I can wait."

By nightfall, they had set a tent around both injured men, who now lay side by side on the bed made from the cart rims. A low fire burned nearby, and by combining what leftover foodstuffs they had, everyone ate until they were full. Ramy and Hendrie laid out their bedrolls next to each other and were asleep almost as soon as Leena kissed their foreheads.

Thaddeus chanted a prayer for their safety. Soon both he and Dillon were asleep and snoring while Taran, Reid, and Leena spread out blankets around the fire and tried to get some sleep of their own.

The stars twinkled overhead while each person slowly closed their eyes, but sleep didn't come easily. Reid soon found himself pacing behind a tall outcropping of rocks a short way from the campfire. Opening and closing his fists, he tried without success to calm his racing mind about what would come tomorrow. He would go after McDever and Willie, and leave the others. A woman, two small lads, and two injured men with only one man to take care of them proved a desperate situation, but if he stayed until they got to safety, it put his son at even greater risk. A dilemma with no solution!

He turned his back to the rock and slid down to sit on the ground against it. Then he saw her.

Stepping out of a copse of scrub bushes, she brushed down her skirt, and looking up, she saw him. "Couldna sleep either?"

He nodded.

"I used needing to relieve myself as my excuse." Crossing her legs, she sat down beside him. "We've gotten ourselves into quite a twisted bundle, haven't we? Which way to go? Who needs us the most, and who needs us first? I canna put my mind around it." She scooted closer to his side and rested her head back on the rock. "Any thoughts ye care to share? Good or bad?"

"Nay."

"No' even any thoughts about the beautiful, clear sky tonight?"

He turned to look at her, scowling. "Nay."

Gazing upward, she said, "I always wanted to know, if ye could get up there, what a star would be like. Is it fire? They look too white for that. Fires are more yellow and red. Would it be really hot or would ye be able to sit and stare down at us, right where we are? People write poems and songs about the stars even though they've ne'er been up there. What do ye think?"

"I've got too many other things on my mind to care about it now."

She scooted closer and rested her head on his shoulder. "Are ye thinking about Willie?"

"Aye, and yer brothers, and that monk, and Ramy, and Hendrie, and ye. I canna leave ye to look for Willie, and I canna look for Willie unless I do. Do ye see an answer in yer stars?"

Reaching her hand across his chest, she touched his opposite cheek with her fingertips and turned his face to hers. "I canna find it in the stars, but I do see it in yer face that ye will find the right answer."

"Are ye certain of what ye see?" he asked. "Are ye certain 'tis me, no' some imagining of a man ye barely ken?"

She pushed away from him as her eyes shot daggers. "Do ye think me a glaikit, a stupid, foolish woman who doesna ken anything? I ken my mind, and I ken a great deal about ye, mayhap more than ye do. Ye're a man with strength and character. I dinna imagine it. 'Tis true. Mayhap ye carry a sadness, but 'tis one ye dinna deserve."

Her faith in him filled him up with the sense that he might someday become a whole man without the reservations that held him back. "Do ye understand how dangerous McDever is? If by some wild chance I can find Willie, do ye think he will have kept him alive for me?"

"McDever is a treacherous man without morals, but there's nothing to gain if he harms Willie. 'Tis a working gun he wants, and he kens he winna get it unless ye give the say so."

He wished he could see her face better in the shadows, especially as he now confessed the worst of his sins. "But dinna ye understand, I put my sons and ye at risk by creating that weapon? I am a master gunsmith, and I've always been proud of the work I did, proud of my skill in producing a quality weapon. But this time what I made will no' protect the ones I love. It will murder them. I will murder them!" He put his bandaged hand over his eyes.

"Nay, nay," she said. " 'Tis no' what ye made. 'Tis the man with evil intentions. No' the gun, 'tis the man. Ye have to believe that." She came to her knees in front of him and put her hands on his cheeks. He had not shaved in several days, and the bristles of his beard prickled her fingers. "Look me in the eye. Tell me ye believe 'tis no' yer fault."

He pulled her hands down and held them in his own. "Ye are too good a woman for me."

"I am just a woman."

Guilt ate at his being. In addition to what he'd just told her, she deserved better than a man tied to a wife buried in a grave. His heart wanted to make a commitment to Leena, and his body wanted to show her how much, but would it be right? Did he have the right to take only a moment with her? He belonged to another, and in reality, so did she. Still, could one more kiss of her sweet lips be so bad? He wouldn't be breaking his marriage vow with only one kiss, would he? He needed her kiss. He needed her comfort. He desired her.

Slipping his arm around her back, he tugged her to him. She did not resist. She couldn't. She could only stare at his full, rich lips, wanting to taste them. The air around them grew thick and silent.

Leaning in, he brushed his lips against hers for a small taste of her sweetness. Again, she did not resist. He pressed closer, realizing she could fill the empty cavern inside his heart. Even if for only a moment, he needed her. He wanted her, and his body responded.

As their kiss grew stronger, a rush of her acceptance swept over him. She hummed deep in her throat as his tongue slipped into her mouth, and she used her own tongue to invite his kiss to linger. Leaning over her, his breath grew ragged. His hand slid from her round, firm breast to her waist and the unbandaged tips of his fingers kneaded her soft body. At the same time her hands moved to caress the back of his neck. If only he could have her completely, if only. He pulled away and pressed his forehead against hers, and together they took in deep jagged breaths.

Unable to stop the deepening physical attraction, she leaned back against the ground, and he followed her down until he lay on top of her, holding his weight up with his elbows.

"Reid," she murmured. "Reid."

He whispered, "I ne'er imagined what it might mean to me when I pulled ye out of the mud in the road." Running his thumb over her lips, he wiped off their intermingled saliva. As he pressed his lips onto hers again, she lifted her hips into him and moved against him. She melted into him, and he ached for her. Sliding his hand down her thigh, she bent her knee so he could reach farther down her leg.

"Leena," he moaned quietly as he kissed her neck and shoulder.

Could he take her now, behind these rocks? He wanted a memory of her to last for the rest of his life before he left her behind. Did he have the right?

Suddenly he lifted his head and looked down into her flushed face. "Leena?" he asked, but not knowing the right words. "Can we…? Is it…?"

Locking her fingers in his hair, she said in throaty softness, "Aye. Aye. I have always trusted my heart, and I do it now…with ye."

Stroking her cheek, he said, "Ye are…" His hand

slid under her kirtle.

"Ahem!" said someone clearing their throat.

Chapter Thirteen

Both Reid and Leena lifted their heads and quickly sat up.

"Ahem, ye two couldna sleep either?" said Taran, standing at the corner of the rocks with his arms akimbo. "Leena, Thaddeus has torn apart his stitches with his tossing and turning. Have ye naught in yer bag to make him sleep?"

Leena flicked the clinging strands of hair off her face and, giving Reid a conspiratorial smile, pulled herself out from under him and to her feet. "I have some lavender and mayhap a little valerian. I'll look."

With her cheeks flushed and her breathing rapid, she said to Taran as she strode past him back to the campsite, " 'Tis my life. I told ye that when I met Johnnie, and I'm telling ye that now. My life."

Reid, too, came to his feet, tugging his sark over his obvious physical need for her, and started to follow, but Taran put his hand on Reid's chest to stop him. "My sister deserves better than a man who expects us to risk our lives to help him. McDever is yer trouble, no' ours, and the sooner ye get that trouble away from us, the better."

"I regret that ye're involved in this, and I'll do whatever I can to keep ye safe."

"And another thing, Leena may think she cares for ye, but 'tis yer sons she really cares about. She canna have bairns of her own, so she is drawn to the bairns of others. Dinna think ye can pull her to ye with yer sons. I winna let ye."

Reid cocked his head in concern. "She canna have bairns?"

"Do ye think 'tis something she's proud of?" snapped Taran. "Something she'd brag about to a stranger she met on the street? 'Tis a sorrow that haunts her. She fell out of the loft onto a pitchfork when she was fourteen, and she would have died if my grandfather, Bretane, hadna seen similar wounds in battle. He treated her, and she lived, but she will ne'er be able to have bairns." He swallowed hard. "Now do ye ken why I willna let her…" He didn't finish his sentence.

Putting his hand on Taran's shoulder, Reid said, "I wouldna care about that."

Shaking off Reid's hand, he barked, "But I would!" He gasped in a heated breath. "I pushed her out of the loft. I am the reason she's barren, and I'll protect her until the day I die!" Taran's shoulders shook as he fought to calm himself.

Reid waited silently until Taran's breathing became steady again.

"She married afore. What about her husband?" asked Reid.

"All Johnnie wanted to do was sing and write stories. He lived in his head. He loved Leena, and he treated her verra well, but his music and stories filled his life. He died after they'd only been wed a week, so she ne'er had to face the looks and the talk about no' giving him bairns. I willna let her be a matter of gossip."

"I wouldna either."

Taran's whole body stiffened. "I dinna care what ye would or wouldna do. Stay away from her. She will ne'er be yers, and I willna let her be hurt or mayhap killed by that pirate who is after ye. Ye're dangerous to her, and I willna let ye have her."

Storming away, Taran left Reid behind the rock more troubled than ever. He brushed his hands through his hair and sucked in a deep breath. Did the feelings he had for Leena justify the danger he had brought to her and her family? The lingering truth was still that even if they all escaped McDever with their lives, he had his vow to Marjorie. Leena would never be his.

****

Leena brought her saddlebag over to the fire, poured some water into a pot, and set it on the logs to heat up a tea of valerian for Thaddeus. He had indeed torn his stitches, but the wound had not opened completely, so she only needed to tighten the bandages to close it again. His risk of developing a fever and infection worried her, but so far, his forehead stayed cool. After steeping the valerian leaves in the hot water, she let it cool enough to give him sips. In time he relaxed. Although not asleep, he rested easier.

"Thank ye," Thaddeus said.

"Dinna talk," she whispered. "Ye need yer strength."

As she ministered to Thaddeus, she strained to hear what Taran and Reid said to each other, but she could only pick out tones of anger, not the words, although she could guess what Taran told him.

Taran had been overly protective of her ever since the accident in the loft. She didn't remember much of it except the pain, and then the despairing look on her grandfather's face when he told her she would never carry a child. She couldn't bear the way everyone treated her after that, as if she were a china doll and easily broken. She hated people seeing her as frail or helpless. With determination and sheer strength of will, she soon convinced the others in the family that her life could be meaningful without children, and they abandoned their pity. All except Taran.

He continued to defend her fiercely because of his guilt, but she had forgiven him long ago. She loved him deeply, and she prayed he would eventually forgive himself.

She had other worries for Reid. He tried to hide it, but he had feelings for her even though he wanted to deny them. She saw it in the easy way they talked to each other about the simplest things, and how he conveyed his true feelings each time he kissed her. His kisses were fervent, passionate, and filled with urgency, the perfect expression of the emotions that a man and a woman shared. He did care for her, but she had seen how hard he tried to hold himself back. For some reason he could not, or would not, give himself to her, not entirely. Could it be the shame over making the gun that brought McDever and his danger to them? Or could it be the same reasons that had been hers for the past eight years? Could it be his dead wife?

She didn't want to keep living in this half-life between her dreams of loving Reid Haliburton and the reality that he might never be hers. The torment left her confused and uneasy.

Taran stomped past her to the horses to check their lines.

Had Taran convinced Reid to stay away from her? Would she ever see Reid again after he left tomorrow to find Willie? For the first time in eight years, she had opened her heart to another man. Could it be only to have it broken?

Chapter Fourteen

At morning's light, everyone gathered around the campfire to make plans. Their first concern had to be getting Dillon and Thaddeus to a safe place for proper medical treatment.

Taran, slapping the front rim of the injured men's makeshift cot, said, "The abbey's no' far, but we have to make it there by the end of day afore this pieced-together rig falls apart."

"I winna be going with ye," said Reid, staring at the ground. "I have to find Willie, and the longer I wait, the farther away he is." He lifted his head and scanned the group. "I'm sorry to leave ye in this time of need, but 'tis what I'm going to do."

"Da, will ye leave us?" whined Hendrie.

Reid held out his arms and drew both his sons in. "Ye'll be safe with Leena, Dillon, and Taran until I can come back with Willie to fetch ye."

Ramy tried his best to hold in his tears, but wee Hendrie wailed and sobbed. "Dinna go!"

Leena said, "Do ye ken the story of the shepherd and the lost sheep from the Bible?"

The lads didn't look at her.

"Every night the shepherd counted his one hundred sheep until one night he only counted ninety-nine. So, he left that ninety-nine and went to look for the one lost sheep, and he searched and searched until he found it.

He brought it back to the fold because he couldna bear to lose even one. Every night yer da counts his sons, one, two, three sons, but if one is missing, he will go find him and bring him home." The lads looked up at her now. "He couldna bear to lose one of ye. That's how much he loves ye, each of ye."

Ramy and Hendrie threw their arms around their father's neck. "Bring Willie home," said Ramy. "We'll stay with Leena until ye come back."

"We'll be good lads, so ye'll be proud when ye come home with Willie," said Hendrie, sniffing loudly.

Reid hugged his sons as he nodded his thanks to Leena.

"That leaves me and Leena to get Dillon and Thaddeus to the abbey," said Taran. "The other problem is the cart now carries two men, and 'tis too heavy for the mule."

Dillon lifted himself up to his elbows. "Now that my leg is in a splint, I think I can ride on one of the horses. Will ye walk beside me, Taran?"

"Ye ken I will. 'Twill slow us down, but we have no choice. Leena, ye and the lads can take turns walking and riding on the other horse. Let's put out the fire, pack up, and be on our way. We need to reach the abbey afore nightfall."

"We dinna have much food left," said Leena, "but we can divide up what we have."

"Dinna give me any," said Reid. "I can take care of myself."

Leena started to protest, but Reid put up his hand to stop her. "I said, 'Dinna give me any of yer food.' I winna take it. I brought this trouble to ye, and I winna make it any worse by taking yer food."

"But Reid…" began Leena.

Taran interrupted. " 'Tis his choice, Leena. The wee lads and the sick ones need it more."

"Ye can give my share to Dillon," said Ramy.

"And mine to Brother Thaddeus," said Hendrie. "I'm no' hungry."

Reid pointed at each of his sons in turn. "Ye're brave and generous lads, but Leena and Taran will give what is needed to everyone. I will be verra upset if I come back with Willie and ye two are scrawny and thin. Eat whatever Leena gives ye. Do I have yer word?"

"Aye, Da," said the lads in unison.

Leena and the lads cleared the campsite, and she changed into trews and a sark for easier traveling while Reid hitched the mule and saddled the horses. He went to each person in camp to say his goodbyes. Putting his hand on Dillon's shoulder, he said, "Take care of yer leg, and 'twill heal properly. Next time I see ye, I expect ye to be running."

Dillon answered with a smile. "Aye, next time."

Reid did the same to Thaddeus, who struggled to keep his eyes open. "God's blessing on ye," he said in a near whisper. Making the sign of the cross, he added, "The Lord be with ye and yer son."

To Taran, Reid spoke hesitantly as an uneasy tension still existed between them. "I want to thank ye for everything ye did for me and my sons. If ye hadna come to get me in Stirling, I ne'er would have kenned what happened to them."

"Leena made me do it."

"She is a woman who kens her own mind and doesna hesitate to tell others."

Taran went back to adjusting the harness on the mule, not looking at Reid. "We'll take good care of yer lads...for the rest of their lives if need be."

The thought that Reid might never see his sons again knocked the breath out of him. He closed his eyes, and after he opened them again, he said, "Ramy and Hendrie will be in good hands with ye, and I will be grateful." He turned and walked over to his horse, pressing his forehead against the saddle.

He didn't know how long he stood there contemplating the worst until someone laid a hand on his back. He twisted his head and saw Leena standing behind him.

"I'm going to be leaving soon," he said, tightening the cinch.

"Ye have to go."

He couldn't look at her. "I'll miss the lads," he said to the woman who had entered his life and now owned his heart and all his dreams. Still not looking at her, he said slowly, "And I will miss ye."

She laid her head against his back and wrapped her arms around his waist. "I'll do naught but worry until ye come back. Nights will be the hardest, the no' kenning if ye found Willie or if McDever..." She couldn't finish. "I wish I could go with ye."

Whirling around to face her, he said, "Nay! Dinna do that. I must do this alone. Willie is my son. Ye have duties here with yer brothers and my lads. I beg ye, dinna come after me. I will rest easier if I ken ye're here and safe. My sons need ye."

She ducked her head for a moment before bringing it up, saying, "There is one thing I want to tell ye afore ye go. When ye carried me out of the mud that day on the street, I learned something. Yer eyes, they were the bluest I'd ever seen, and while I may no' have fallen into the street, I did fall into those eyes, and I suddenly understood things differently. I thank ye for that."

Gently holding her hair at the back of her neck to keep it from blowing across her face, he began, "Leena…" But he couldn't finish. The mere sight of her made him whole again, and that made saying goodbye so much harder. "I…I…"

"Ye dinna have to say anything," said Leena. "I just want to thank ye for…for being ye. Ramy and Hendrie remind me of ye, and I will be grateful to have them with me. Stay safe and bring Willie back to us."

She started to pull away, but he stopped her, stammering out his words. "That flock of noisy, runaway…geese brought…ye into my life, and I count it a blessing, no' only for me, but also for my sons. I…I…"

"Please, Reid, tell me I'm not a fool for caring so much."

He did not answer. He couldn't. He had already suffered the loss of Marjorie, Davie, and Tommy. He could lose Willie to a vile pirate, and the last of his sons would leave with her. He'd be alone, and the only thing he had left was to know she cared.

Taran's shout interrupted them both. "Leena! We're ready to leave. Ramy and Hendrie will ride first, so ye'll walk for a while. Hurry!"

She reached up and laid her hand on Reid's cheek. Neither of them had anything else to say, and the way he blinked away the moisture forming in his blue eyes told her all she needed to know.

"Leena!"

Just then the low rumble of wagon wheels floated over the rise in the road. Everyone's head turned in that direction of a rickety wagon drawn by two swayback horses and driven by two monks in coarse brown robes. One of them stood up in the seat and shouted, "We're looking for our friends, a monk called Thaddeus and two other brothers with him. We sent them out to fetch some injured travelers. Have ye seen any monks?"

Taran ran over to the wagon and latched onto the side. "We're so glad to see ye!"

Brother Thaddeus pulled himself up on his good elbow as best he could. "I'm here!" he called in his weak voice.

" 'Tis Thaddeus!" said the monk in the wagon as he leaped down and ran over to him. "What happened to ye? Where are Thomas and Amos? And the woman?"

"Here I am," said Leena, running toward them. "We were attacked by a pirate named McDever. He wanted something we had, and when yer three friars tried to defend us, his henchmen attacked them and drove the wagon over the cliff. Only Thaddeus survived, but he is verra injured. We must get him back to the abbey where ye can give him proper care."

"Of course, of course," said the man. "My name is Father John, and this is Brother Mark. Mark, help me get Thaddeus into the wagon. As pitiful as our wagon is, 'tis better than whatever he is lying on now."

Mark, a broad-shouldered man in his thirties, lifted Thaddeus and carried him to the wagon while Taran and Ramy pulled some of the blankets off the wagon rims and spread them out on the floor of the wagon before Mark laid Thaddeus on top.

"Carefully," said Father John. Now satisfied that Thaddeus was as comfortable as possible, he asked, "What did this pirate want from ye?"

"A gun, a new kind of weapon," said Leena. "That man over there invented it, but he refused to sell it to a man like McDever." She pointed to the outcropping of rocks, but Reid had disappeared. In the distance, she saw him riding away to the east. Her heart sank. She wanted one last kiss before he rode out of her life, and she prayed silently, *Please, bring him back.*

"McDever kidnapped Reid's son, and Reid is determined to find him," she said to Father John. "These two are his other sons, and they're entrusted to our care until he comes back."

"My brother broke his leg. Can he ride in yer wagon?" asked Taran. "And the lads, too. My sister and I will ride our horses back to the abbey with ye. We can tie the mule behind."

"Of course, of course," said Father John. "We'll get ye to the abbey and come back for the bodies of Thomas and Amos."

"I'm afraid 'twill be impossible," said Taran as he helped Dillon hop on his good leg over to the wagon. "Thaddeus landed on a ledge, but the wagon, horses, and the other men went over the edge and into the loch. We're so sorry."

Father John crossed himself. "Show me where they went over into the loch. I need to say a prayer for the dead before we leave. I can come back and give the last rites later to ease their passage into heaven. Even without the bodies, the rites must be performed."

Taran, Leena, Ramy, and Hendrie walked to the ridge with the priest and the monk, and all knelt, bowed their heads, and listened to Father John's prayer in Latin.

On the way back to the wagon, Leena took Taran's arm. "Ye can take Dillon, Thaddeus, and the lads to the abbey. When Dillon is ready to travel, ye must take Ramy and Hendrie to Makgullane. That's what Reid wanted when he put them in our cart."

" 'Tis my plan as well. If we can borrow a cart to carry Dillon, we should be back home in a few days. After that we can come back here and look for any of the tools and yer cloth that might still be by the side of the road. 'Tis the best we can do. Reid Haliburton caused us all this trouble. From the verra start, I kenned he'd be bad luck."

Leena jerked his arm back. " 'Tis no' Reid's fault. Dinna ye blame him. 'Tis McDever's."

"We can argue about whose fault it is after we're back at Makgullane. Mount up."

Straightening up to her full height, which came to just over Taran's shoulder, she said firmly, "I willna be going with ye today."

"And where will ye be going? And if ye say to follow Haliburton, I'll stop ye."

She gave him a smoldering look. "Ye willna stop me. I'm going with him. Tell Da I will look out for myself, and I will come home…with Reid and Willie."

"I can tie ye up and carry ye with me."

"And I would hate ye for the rest of my days."

Those were the worst words she could have said to Taran. One thing he couldn't abide would be if she hated him. After her fall from the loft, he'd done everything he could to earn back her love, which in reality, he never lost, but his guilt drove him to defend her for as long as he lived.

"I'll take that chance."

"Will ye? Will ye truly risk it?" she asked.

A heavy silence passed between them before Taran, letting his breath out slowly, said, "Ye do what ye have to. I'll explain it to Da and Mum." He paused. "Ye're a woman like no other. I dinna ken how Johnnie put up with ye."

She glared at him. "Ye leave Johnnie in his grave."

After another long moment of silence, Taran said, "I love ye, Leena, and I'll pray for ye every day."

"I love ye, Taran. Tell Dillon and the lads I love them, too." Stretching up on her toes, she kissed her brother on the cheek.

She strode to her horse, climbed into the saddle, and rode away in the same direction as Reid Haliburton.

Chapter Fifteen

Reid had lost his chance with Leena. How could he profess his love if nothing would ever come of it?

He tried to form an image of Marjorie in his mind. He saw her lying on her sickbed, but her face remained cloudy. He saw her gravestone. He tried to remember what her voice sounded like, but in his head he heard only Leena's voice.

For the first time he questioned if he could stay devoted to his marriage to Marjorie to the rejection of everything else. Could he, should he, keep using Marjorie as the chain that held him back from living his best life? Could he keep his sons tied to her memory when their future lay in front of them? Did he even have a future himself knowing that his oldest son could die, that he could die, because of the weapon he invented? Could he live the rest of his life without his sons?

Leena had also made vows to Johnnie which were as binding as his were to Marjorie, and if the two of them stayed tied to the past, could there be any hope for a future?

She couldn't give him children, and while that didn't matter to him, for a woman, it brought disgrace in the eyes of the world. If she carried shame about being barren, any marriage would disintegrate over the years. After he found Willie, could he take Ramy and

Hendrie away from her and start his own life somewhere else? Could he leave her behind again?

He couldn't, but first he had to find Willie. He'd been on the road for several hours before he rode up to three crofts bunched close together at a crossroad. "Hello! Good afternoon!" he called out.

A plump woman with a kerchief over her gray hair came out of one of the huts and answered him in Gaelic, followed quickly by English. "Guid efternuin to ye! Good afternoon! We dinna get many travelers on this road. Would ye come in for a bite to eat?"

" 'Tis most kind of ye, but I dinna have time to stop. Mayhap some water and some oats or barley for my horse would be much appreciated."

"Follow me to the stable." She led him to a small outbuilding behind the croft and directed him to the trough for water and the manger to feed the horse. She left and came back with a small cloth sack. Handing it to him, she said, "I can tell a hungry man from a long way off. Take this with my blessing. 'Tis no' much, only some dried meat, an apple, and warm bread."

"I do welcome it. Have there been other travelers recently? Mayhap four or five men with a lad about twelve years?"

She scratched at the whiskers on her chin. "Aye, a few days ago, but the men took water and food for their beasts without even asking me. I didna give them anything to eat. I only slipped a piece of cheese to the lad."

"How did the lad look?"

"He had a bruise on his cheek, and he slumped in the saddle. No' a happy lad. Rode in front of the Moor."

Reid gritted his teeth thinking about what his son

had to endure with those pirates. "Which way did they go?"

"I didna watch, but one of them said something about going to Perth, so they would go to the south from here." She pointed to the road that took off to the right. "Why are ye looking for them?"

"The lad is my son. I'll be following them as soon as my horse has rested a bit."

"Do ye want me to look at yer hands, mayhap change yer bandages? I ne'er saw red-and-white ones afore."

"Nay, they're healing quickly, but I do want to ask ye another favor. Later today or mayhap tomorrow, a woman might be coming this way. Her name is Leena Adair, and her hair is a chestnut color with wide sun-bleached stripes around her face." He handed the woman a coin from his pouch. "Could ye give her food and a place to sleep? And if ye could talk her into going back to the abbey, I'd much appreciate it. I doubt she'll go, but if ye could try, it would be a boon to me."

"A woman is following ye? A woman alone? Why dinna ye wait for her here?"

"I dinna want her to follow me. I told her so, but she's a stubborn woman, and she does what she wants. I'd throttle her if she'd let me."

"Let ye? When does a woman have to let a man do anything?"

"She's one of a kind, and ye'll find out what I mean if she comes this way. I hope she stayed behind with her brothers, and I'll be much relieved if she did. Please, take the coin as thanks for the food for me and my horse."

"*Gu'n deanadh Dia maille riut*," said the woman,

slipping the coin into a small cloth bag tied at her waist. Reid nodded his thanks, hoping the Gaelic words were a blessing.

Reid's next rest stop came at dusk in the small village of Castleton. Stopping at a traveler's inn on the outskirts of town, he left his horse in the stable behind the inn and settled down to sleep in a narrow bed in a tiny room at the back of the building.

After several hours of dreamless sleep, he wanted to ignore the pounding on his door, but finally, he dragged his feet across the room and opened it.

The owner of the inn, a scarecrow of a man, said in a low voice, as if his pounding hadn't already woken up everyone in the place, "The woman ye left the money for is in her room. I didna let on that ye paid the rent or what room ye were in."

Reid's lips curled into a smile. "I dinna think ye'll have to. Winna ye come in?"

After the innkeeper stepped across the threshold, Reid put his hand on the man's chest and pushed him back. "No' ye. Her." He pointed to Leena Cullane Adair standing in the hallway behind the innkeeper with a smirk on her face.

Startled to see her, the innkeeper said, "Oh!" and scampered back to his own room.

Leena entered, sat down on the stool in the corner, and started to pull off her boots. "Ye paid for a room for me. How did ye ken I'd come?"

"We may only have met a fortnight ago, but I ken a lot about ye, and following my orders isna one of your skills."

"Yer orders?"

He raked his fingers through his hair in frustration.

"Leena, 'twill be verra dangerous if I find Willie and McDever. I dinna want to have to look out for ye as well."

She stood up, putting her hands on her hips. "I came to help ye get Willie back, no' get in yer way. If I fall behind, ye can leave me."

"I could leave ye here with the innkeeper."

"I got Taran to let me go without much of a fight. Do ye think that scrawny wisp of a man could stop me? But since I canna be certain ye winna sneak out without me, I will be sleeping right here." Dragging the narrow, lightweight cot across the room until it sat crossways at the door, she flopped down, tossed her boots under the bed, and shoved her feet under the thick layer of quilts.

"I could go out the window."

"I doubt it. Directly underneath that window is the inn's midden. Dinna people in this part of Scotland ken how to dispose of garbage properly? Instead of just piling it up somewhere? 'Tis why this room is so cheap. If ye try it, I'll follow the smell until I find ye. Good night." She closed her eyes.

"Where am I supposed to sleep?" he asked.

"I dinna care."

Scratching his head, he tried to swallow his grin at seeing her again, but couldn't bring himself to frown at the risk she took by following him.

Jerking back the quilts, he crawled into the bed and pushed his back right up next to her, shoving her against the door. Wiggling his hips to get himself comfortable, and so enjoying the sensations it gave him, he took delight each time her bottom bumped into the door. "Good night. Sleep well."

The words were barely out of his mouth when a

good hard kick from Leena landed him on the floor, followed by a quilt landing on his face. With a sigh, he wrapped himself in the quilt and closed his eyes to spend the night where he lay.

The next morning just as the sun came up, the innkeeper pounded on the door again, shouting, "She ne'er slept in her room! I dinna ken where she is. She's gone!"

Reid dragged the bed into the center of the room with Leena still on it and opened the door. "She's here."

As soon as the innkeeper saw Leena in the bed, his eyes widened. "She stayed here with ye?" Pulling himself up to his full meager height, he said, "We run an upright establishment. We dinna allow for whores or the men who use them."

Sitting up, Leena said, "Dinna worry, fine sir, we're married. There is good reason why my husband rented two rooms." She pushed Reid out of the way to look for her boots under the bed. Popping her head up, she said, "I caught him with another woman, and I threw him out of the house."

"Oh?" The man's eyebrows shot up.

"Aye, but I decided to forgive him, so I followed him here."

"Oh." He gave her a long slow look.

"He is a regretful man, and I am a forgiving woman, which explains why the bed is now by the door." She added with a wink, "We spent the night engaging in vigorous matrimonial relations."

"Oh!" The innkeeper blinked furiously before hurrying away.

"He'll ne'er let me stay here again," said Reid as he, too, pulled on his boots.

"Were ye planning on coming back?" Leena asked as she tucked Taran's sark into her trews and slipped her arms into her coat.

"Well, nay, but ye besmirched my reputation."

"So ye think ye'll be embarrassed by all the people who will ne'er set eyes on ye again, or who might frown at ye on the streets where ye'll ne'er walk again?"

He shrugged.

"Ye should thank me for stopping him from throwing us out before we had a chance to get dressed properly."

Rubbing her fingers over her cheeks, then pinching them, she tried to make herself presentable. Giving up, she tugged her knitted cap over her hair. "Ye can pay the stable boy for taking care of our horses while I get us each a slice of bread with butter, and mayhap some jam, and water for our flasks." She held out her hand.

"What's that for?" he asked.

"Coin for the bread. I dinna think the cook will give free bread to a scoundrel like yerself." She winked.

"Ye're quite the liar," he said, handing her three silver coins.

Pocketing the coins, she said, "No' a lie, just a slightly different version of the truth. I only changed one word from the truth. Did ye want to have relations with me?"

He gave a sly grin. "Aye, I did."

"So 'twas only the change of one word. From 'want' to 'had.' I said we had relations while the truth is we wanted to have relations. Only one word different. Barely a lie. As for us being married, I didna say we were married to each other. Besides, who wouldna believe this face?"

He smiled again. He'd believe just about anything that beguiling face told him.

Reaching up, she kissed him on the cheek.

Leena met up with Reid at the stable after getting food from the kitchen, just as the stable boy led their saddled horses out of the barn and into the yard. Reid handed him two coins and checked the cinches on both mounts.

"Been a lot of strangers around here lately," said the young man as a strand of straw dangled from his black hair. "The last ones didna pay. Two of the mounts had loose shoes, and I fixed them, but they rode off with nary a 'by yer leave.' And Master Blackstone took it out of my pay! How did he think I could have stopped all five of them? Big men they were."

"Five riders, ye say. What did they look like?"

"They were no' from around here. One had a big shiny belt buckle, and one was a black Moor. I ne'er seen a Moor afore. I heard about them, but I ne'er seen one. They had a lad with them, younger than me."

Reid glanced back at Leena. "Where did they say they were headed?"

"The one who did all the talking told me to tell anybody who asked that they were going to the sea and to hurry up. Then they rode off without paying a penny."

Reid opened his pouch and handed the stable boy four more coins. "To cover what they didna pay."

"Did they say anything else?" asked Leena as she mounted.

"The lad came over like he wanted to tell me something, but the Moor snatched him up."

"Did the lad look all right? No' injured?"

"He looked right thin but no' hurt. Thank ye for the coin!"

Reid and Leena headed toward the sea.

Chapter Sixteen

They rode in silence, heading southeast toward the seaport of Perth, through stretches of land for grazing or farming, followed by open rocky spaces with no life except for the birds. They'd been on the road for several hours when Leena tapped him on the arm. "Will ye let me practice shooting a gun again? All this trouble is over a gun, and I want to be good at it afore we find Willie."

Reining his horse to a stop, he jumped off and opened his pack, pulling out a handgnome. "This one is no' quite like the one ye practiced with afore but close enough. Let's go closer to that grove where we can use some of the trees as targets."

Leena dismounted and followed him.

He handed her the gun, saying, "This weapon is a little heavier than the other one, so get the heft of it first. Also 'tis loaded."

She held it straight out in front of her, prepared for the weight this time, and she kept it steady.

"I dinna have verra much powder or flint or bullets with me, so ye can only fire it a few times. Mayhap a town closer to Perth will have some ammunition we can buy. Aim for one of those trees over there."

Taking careful aim, she squeezed the trigger. The nearly deafening sound of the shot made her ears ring. "I didna expect it to be so loud."

" 'Tis louder than the other one. Now load it all by yerself. One difference is that ye have to wind this one with a spanner wrench." He lifted a metal wrench on a leather strap tied to his trews. "I'll show ye how to do it."

Carefully, she put the flint in the pan, followed Reid's directions on how to wind the wrench, and bit off the cap from the powder horn. Scrunching up her face, she said, "This tastes terrible!" After pouring in the powder, she pressed the cap back on the powder horn. "I ken this is no' verra ladylike, but…" She spit on the ground. "How do ye stand to do that every time? Really does taste awful."

"Ye get used to it," he answered with a grin. He handed her an iron ball from his bag.

Tamping it in, she wound the wrench and took aim toward the grove again.

"I did it!" she cried. "I did it! I hit the tree right where I aimed it. Can I try it again?"

Putting his arm around her shoulder, he gave her a quick hug. "Proud of yerself, are ye? Well, ye should be. I'll bet I could make a crack shot of ye. I wish I could spare more ammunition to let you practice, but at least I have enough for ye to take one more shot."

Again her tongue jutted out the corner of her mouth as she concentrated on each step of loading the gun. After getting it ready to fire, she winked at him, took aim, braced her body, and pulled the trigger. The ball landed in the heart of an oak tree at the edge of the grove.

Turning back, she caught his smile.

"Well, ye're still standing! Is that the tree ye were aiming for?" he asked with raised eyebrows.

"Of course!"

Once mounted and on their way again, the silence between them returned.

****

He looked over at her as she sat confident and sure on the horse, which responded to every slight movement of her knees in directing the animal. But Reid couldn't focus on the gun or her practice or even her horsemanship, but instead on her, on her courage, on her cleverness, on how much he had grown to care about her, and on how much he would regret it after he sent her back home alone. He needed to make good use of every minute he had with her until then.

"Tell me about Johnnie," he said.

She pulled a face. "Why do ye want to hear about Johnnie?"

"I dinna want to bring back sad memories. I only want to ken about the man because he means a lot to ye."

Looking at him oddly, she said, "All right. He always carried his flute and mandolin."

"Ye said he was a balladeer."

She chuckled. "He did much more than sing. He traveled around to fairs and festivals, singing and telling tales, but he also wrote down some of his stories, wonderfully magical tales they were, drew pictures to go with them, and sold them. He became quite well-known in the Highlands as a storyteller and an artist."

"Can ye make a living doing that?"

"Johnnie did. He always had coin in his pocket. He'd ne'er be rich, but that didna matter to him. He said he had riches in everything except money. He woke up every morning with a smile on his face, and he could hardly wait to see what the day would bring." Her gaze wandered off in the distance. "He always carried his flute with him, hanging from his belt. Whenever he worked alongside the other men—he wasna afraid of hard work—he'd sing or mayhap stop and play a tune. The men liked it. We all did."

"How did ye meet him?"

"With a song."

This time Reid looked at her askance.

"It sounds strange, but I visited the fair in Kirkcaldy with my family, and I followed the most beautiful voice I'd ever heard, and there he stood on the front step of the burgess's house, singing 'The Hunting of Cheviot.' Have ye ever heard it?"

He shook his head.

" 'Twas written a hundred years ago, but the words and tune changed. Johnnie's was the best." She started to sing.

"The Percy out of Northumberland
A vow to God made he
That he would hunt in the mountains
Of Cheviot within days three.

"There are fifty-nine verses, and after I'd heard them all, I kenned I would be his.

"I was twenty-three at the time, an old woman by most everyone's thinking, but I wouldna settle for anything less than the love my mum and da have. Other men asked for my hand, a few of them because they saw Makgullane as something they might inherit someday. Others came calling because they cared about me, but as soon as they..." She hesitated before adding, "But I kenned I didna care for them. I didna ken what love could be until I met Johnnie. 'Twas so amazing to me."

Leaning forward, she patted her horse's neck to give herself time to breathe before going on. "I followed him from fair to fair for nearly a year, my da begging me to come home, but I understood my own mind long afore I was twenty-three, and there'd be no changing it. I wouldna give him up unless Johnnie himself told me to go, but he didna.

"Still Johnnie wouldna marry me without my da's blessing, so he paid for me to stay with a traveling perfume merchant's family to protect my reputation, but that didna stop us from being together, truly together."

She paused to look at him. "Do ye think me a disgraced woman? Women have yearnings and desires as strong as men do, but women are expected to be ashamed of giving in to such feelings. I am not. I cared for Johnnie like the Highlands love the spring, and he loved me the same way."

She waited for his reaction. *Reid will either accept me for who I am and who I have been, or he will not. Better to find out now.*

Noticing her watching him, Reid said, "If ye're expecting me to say something crude or mayhap condemn ye, I willna. Ye and Johnnie loved each other and were faithful." He turned his face away from hers and looked out at the horizon.

She relaxed. "I ne'er afore wanted anyone as much as I wanted him, and he me. I cherish every moment we had together. After a year, Da accepted that I wouldna leave Johnnie, and we married in the yard at Makgullane. We were only wed for four days when he stepped on a nail. He died a week later."

They rode in silence until Reid said, "I'm sorry ye lost him."

"I learned something on this trip to Stirling. Johnnie is no' the bones in the ground. He is in my heart, and because of that he'll always be with me. No matter where I go, he will always be a part of me. I canna lose him no matter what…or who comes into my life."

"But once a man and a woman take vows, they can ne'er truly be separated."

"Aye, 'tis true. They canna leave each other's hearts even after they have left their bodies, but the one left alive still has to live that life and no' fall into the grave with the one who is gone."

He didn't answer.

"Tell me about Marjorie," she said.

"We kenned each other since we were children. We grew up together, and she didna choose another, so getting married seemed the right thing to do."

"Did ye love her?"

He paused. "I couldn't have asked for a better wife and mother, and we spent hours talking. I miss her every day, but 'tis funny, I ne'er asked her to marry me. We just went to the church and 'twas done. Now we're bound together for all time, like ye and Johnnie."

The sound of rushing wind and the clomping of the horses' hooves on the rough ground bit through the air.

" 'Tis getting dark. We need to look for a sheltered place to bed down." He pointed. "There."

Just off the road stood the battered, crumbling walls of a small, deserted castle. The towers had fallen, leaving only low walls and a splintered door that opened into the center courtyard. It had a strange but beautiful look about it. Someone must have lovingly cared for it years ago, but no more. The land had reclaimed much of it, and eventually any evidence it had ever existed would disappear completely along with the memory of the people who lived there.

As Reid and Leena dismounted just outside the walls, she gathered her courage to ask the question that had bothered her ever since she met him. "Do ye think ye could love another? Now that Marjorie is gone forever, I mean, will there ever be room for another in yer heart?"

His shoulders sagged, and his voice grew low as he pushed open the door in the wall. "It doesna look like the animals have taken over yet. Bring the horses inside. I think we can bed down in that alcove over there."

Once the horses were inside the walls and unsaddled, she asked again, "Do ye have room in yer heart for another?"

Dragging the saddles into the alcove, he said, "Leena, try to understand. I want to love again, but then I remember that Marjorie died as my wife, and she will always be my wife. My vows said, 'Until death do us part,' death for both of us."

He pulled the blanket out from under his saddle and spread it on the ground for a makeshift bed. He did the same with Leena's blanket in the corner about four feet away. He straightened but didn't face her, and with his back still turned, he said, "Leena, I want ye to understand. Ye're an amazing woman, and I have kissed ye twice, kissed ye because…ye fill me with feelings and dreams and hope." Slowly turning and now looking her in the eye, he went on. "If I were a stronger man, I ne'er would have kissed ye because ye might think... Forgive me for making ye think I might...I might..."

He bit his lip. She opened her mouth to speak, but he shook his head. "I have made a ruin of my life, and I brought ye and yer brothers into it. My son suffers, and all because I believed I could make a better weapon."

"Reid, I do understand."

"Nay, ye dinna!" He turned away again, but quickly whirled back to face her. "Leena, I do want ye. Ye canna ken how much, but I canna have ye. I am no' worthy of ye, and we are both bound to others. I am sorry, so sorry."

She took in a deep breath, gritted her teeth, and stomped her foot. "That's enough!" she cried. "That's enough!"

He stared at her with a startled look on his face.

"I'm right here! She's gone!" She pointed at him and then pointed to her chest. "Ye canna touch her or hold her in yer arms, but I am right here! All ye feel is sorry for yerself. Enough!"

Stomping her foot again, she shouted at him, "And I will decide who I give my love to. No one owns me, and as long as I am a free woman, I will decide what is best for me! No one else!"

He swallowed hard. "But what about yer Johnnie? Have ye given up on him?"

"Ne'er! He's forever a part of me just as Marjorie is forever a part of ye as long as we both live." She walked up and smacked him on the chest. "She's in yer sons, and she is in yer heart, but she is gone from this world. And I am right here in front of ye. Canna ye see me?"

Her breathing slowed. She reached out and ran her fingers down the back of his hand and placed his fingers on her shoulder. "Right here," she said softly. "Right here. If ye dinna want me for who I am, I understand and will no' bring it up again, but to no' want me because I am no' yer dead wife? I canna, and I willna, accept that."

He stepped closer. The gap between them lessened, but the tension did not.

She said, "I canna have ye be the keeper of my dreams at night and filling up my thoughts during the day. I must ken if ye are what I believe ye to be. If ye are real, if ye think me real. If ye think we can be real together. If ye think there is life still left for both of us."

He didn't speak, but his hands reached for her ever so tenderly, barely touching her, but still sending excitement through her entire body.

"I have no' kissed a man since Johnnie died until ye, and for eight years I thought I ne'er would, but now I must ken if my future is with ye, if I should go after it or if I should go back to the way things were, back to living my life alone. I must ken if the time we spent in Stirling, however short, if it made ye stronger the way it did me."

She leaned into him, and he put his arms around her and held her. His body heat banished the chill in the evening air.

"Johnnie will let me go, but will Marjorie let ye go? Will ye let Marjorie go? My heart made me follow ye here, and I will follow ye until we find Willie, but right here, right now, in this moment, I have to ken if I will go home alone afterward. I will live with whatever ye say, but I have to ken which. Ye draw me in, and I can only see the right of it. Can ye?"

She felt his body respond to hers, but a man's body and his heart and emotions didn't always act in unison. She wouldn't settle for one without the other.

His breath hitched before he said, "I canna think of much else but ye since I met ye. I used my grief over Marjorie as my excuse to no' get involved with other women, but after meeting ye, ye opened a wanting in me. I wanted more. I wanted ye, and I hadna wanted anything for a verra long time. I didna understand what happened to me, how I changed, but I couldna stay away from ye. With ye, I had to finally tell myself the truth."

He tipped up her chin with his finger to look into her eyes. "Ye spoke the truth to me just now, and 'tis a hard truth for me to accept. No' because it isna true, but because it changes my life."

"Oh, Reid," she whispered.

"Let me say it all, say it while I have the words. The truth is that for the rest of my life, 'twill be only ye. I tried to fight it, to tell myself that I had betrayed the life I'd lived for five years by loving you. I tried to close my heart. I couldna, and now I have to accept that for the rest of my life 'twill be only ye. Ye are the only woman I will ever want beside me. I canna fight anymore. Ye overwhelm me, Leena Cullane Adair, and I welcome it."

He leaned in until his warm breath whispered against her neck. His first kiss tested, but then deepened and grew. She stretched up higher. He tugged her closer, and together they melted into each other.

Lifting his head, he murmured, "I will ne'er forget Marjorie, ne'er forget she gave me five blessed sons, and ne'er let the three sons I have left forget how she loved them, but ye give me hope, something I lost five years ago, and I dinna want to ever lose hope again."

This time he kissed her with all the joy of a man jumping off the scaffold into freedom. Together they blended into an overwhelming desire for more…and more…and more of each other.

He lifted his head, his mouth open and his lips swollen, but still wanting more. And she wanted more, wanted it all.

She rammed her hands into his chest and gave him a hard shove, forcing him back into the alcove. Before he could recover, she stepped up and shoved him again until his back pressed against the wall. Her next steps brought her arms around his neck, and her breasts flattened against him. Their lips never parted as their fervor burned brighter. His hand reached for the tie strings on her sark. She hooked her fingers under his belt and slid open the ties.

His hands roamed from her breasts to her hips, and she used her hands to encourage him and keep him close. His lips caressed her neck, cheeks, and then back to her lips. She groaned every time his mouth left hers and hummed every time he found it again.

"I've been asking myself," he whispered in her ear, breathing hard, "why I feel so strongly about ye, but all I ken 'tis because ye are ye, and I need ye in my life. It came so fast, and I tried to stop it, but I couldna. Ye wouldna let me." Gazing into her face, he said, "I have been a fool. I hurt ye, and I promise, with everything I am, ne'er to do it again. Forgive me?"

"Naught to forgive. The spark began the minute I saw the blue in yer eyes, and it hasn't stopped yet."

His smile created captivating crinkles around those eyes.

"That spark began a fire deep in me, one I didna think would ever burn again. But it did, and I canna put it out. Together we can keep that flame alive, and no' have it be just a smoking pile of ash for the rest of our lives."

He pulled her tight, but suddenly stopped. Fingering the wooden teardrop on the chain around her neck, he said, "I first made up my mind right before I slipped yer necklace into the bag I gave to the lads. I hoped ye would ken I cared even if I couldn't say the words." His head dropped to his chest. "But this is no' the place I want to declare my commitment to ye. I'd wish it to be in a palace with shiny lights all around, and music playing softly on a harp."

"This place is a palace to me."

"Ye're a woman like no other, Leena Adair. Ye fill the empty places in me, places I didna even ken could be filled."

"Until I met ye—"

He put his finger to her lips. "I am the one who pushed ye away, and I will be the one making it up to ye for as long as I live. I give ye my heart, Leena, my body, and my soul. Now I tell ye, I will always be grateful to those geese who brought ye to me. For the first time since Marjorie died, I have dreams, dreams of a life and a future."

She rested her head on his chest.

"My words are coming out like a waterfall, but I must say them all. I canna control the hungers ye awaken in me, no' when ye are this close, no' when I touch yer hair or yer cheek or feel yer soft skin, no' when we are alone like this. And if this makes me weak, then weak I am, but if I hear yer voice or catch a glimpse of yer face, my soul is no longer my own."

She smoothed her hand over his cheek. "Ye are no' weak, Reid Haliburton. Ne'er think that."

"Are ye certain ye want this?"

Locking on his incredible blue eyes, she said, "Yer eyes captured me the first time I saw them, but then I discovered yer voice, yer laugh, and yer kindness. I want ye completely, and I'll settle for nothing less. Do ye want me in the same way, completely?"

"I want ye like I crave the air I breathe. For as long as I live, I will crave ye. Even if I ne'er told ye, even if I ne'er held ye in my arms, I would crave ye like a hunger in my belly."

"I am no' a young woman, and I ken what loving is between a man and a woman, and 'tis from ye I want it again, every part of it, every word, every touch." Putting her hands behind his head, she tugged him to her lips again. "But only if ye can put Marjorie in the corner of yer heart, ne'er to forget her, but to hold me with the rest of ye."

"I can," he breathed. "The words…my first words hurt ye, and now I ken they werena true words." He kissed her.

"But first I have to tell ye something," said Leena once the kiss ended. "And I have to ken before…I have to tell ye…something that may change everything." Her eyes locked on the ground, but she couldn't lose his touch. "I canna…I canna ever…"

"Give me a bairn. I ken. Taran told me about the accident in the loft, but it doesna matter. It doesna change how I feel about ye, and 'twill ne'er change how or why I want ye. It willna ever change what we have together, what we will always have together."

Her eyes flashed. "Taran had no right to say anything."

"He did it because he loves ye, and he didna want ye hurt again. He kenned of other men who turned ye away when they found out."

She raised her eyes as he said, "I swear if I ever hurt ye again, ye may cut out my heart. I will have no use of it. Of this I am certain."

She laid her head on his shoulder, tears glistening in her eyes.

Speaking in a low, soft voice, he said, "I see how ye love my sons."

"I do love them."

"And that makes them yer sons now." Lifting her chin with his finger, he said, "Ramy, Hendrie, and Willie are yer sons. They already love ye, and no' instead of Marjorie, but with Marjorie's blessing. With my blessing."

"My sons," she murmured.

He lifted her chin even higher. "If ye love me, I promise we will have each other from now on."

"From now on," she answered as his head dropped to hers, and their lips melded in the truest kiss.

Pushing aside her sark, he pressed his hand against her breast, first one than the other, until he found her nipples, and one at a time they rose against his callused fingertips. At the same time, she slid her hands under his sark and ran her fingers over his chest from his shoulders to down below his waist.

"Reid, Reid," she whispered.

A raw heat sped through her body as he lowered

her onto one of the saddle blankets, pushing down her trews, caressing the flesh of her legs and bottom until he found the warm spot between her thighs. Following his cue, she tugged down his trews and set free his strong, firm manhood. His hands and mouth roamed across her body from her neck to her knees as old, familiar sensations washed over her. It had been a long time since she'd experienced arousal like this, over eight years. She had so missed having a man close to her, to make love to her, and allowing her to love him in return.

He lay on his back and pulled her on top of him, and her soft places slid over his strong chest and stomach. Her exploration of his body began. His body, so different from Johnnie's, was more muscular, with rougher skin and more dark, curly hair covering his chest, but he moved in much the same lovemaking way. He whispered her name over and over, and as she responded in kind, he moaned slowly, "Aye, aye."

He tenderly pushed her over onto her back and brought her nearly to climax with his fingers and his mouth before he knelt to take her. Both gasped as he filled her completely. Together they moved in a sensual rhythm, deeper, clutching, falling into the joy of a new love, and relishing the feeling of a familiar act of lovemaking.

He exploded within her at the same time she peaked, and together they relaxed into each other's arms with his body pressed against hers.

They slept and then loved each other again.

Chapter Seventeen

Leena opened her eyes to a thin stream of sunlight coming through a crack in the crumbling roof over the alcove. Reid slept, his breathing slow and soft, and his eyes moving under his lids. What might he be dreaming about? She didn't want to know. His dreams were his own, and hers had all come true.

For the past eight years she'd stumbled through life, holding her breath, waiting, but she'd wait no more. No matter what happened in the future, whether they were able to find Willie and make it back alive, or wherever she existed after that, her life belonged to her again. No more waiting!

Reid's eyes blinked open. He shifted against her and came up on his elbow to look at her, and lifting the blanket, he scanned her body from head to toe. "This is how I want to wake up every morning, next to ye with the sunlight on yer face." Dropping the blanket back to cover her, he leaned his head to meet hers and kissed her deeply. "But I want ye to go back to Makgullane."

"That is no' what I expected to hear after the night we just spent together. I had hoped for something more like 'I love ye, Leena. Let's make love again.' "

Reid ignored her invitation. "I'll come to Makgullane after I find Willie, but 'tis too dangerous for ye to go with me. Now that I've found ye, I dinna want to lose ye. 'Twill be easier for me if I ken ye are safe."

"I understand yer need to protect me, and I thank ye for it, but I have the same need to protect ye. If ye're in danger and out of my sight, my heart will near pound out of my chest. Now that we have each other, I willna let ye go again. Besides, if ye are thinking ye can chase me away, ye canna. Ye left me once, and I followed ye. I will follow ye again."

Pulling her over on top of him, he said, "I think ye're more stubborn than an ox and a mule put together. I'm begging ye to go home and let me go on alone."

She slid off his chest and sat beside him. "I hear what ye say, and I ken ye think 'tis for the best, but I winna go home until we have Willie with us."

He scowled and started to speak, but she interrupted him. "I ken the danger. I truly do, but I have made my choice, and 'tis to be with ye, where'er that may be."

He sighed.

"Do ye remember how I told ye that I followed Johnnie for nearly a year afore we wed? My da tried everything to get me to come home, but I kenned what I wanted, and I didna regret a minute of that year, and the same is true with ye. I canna, I willna, miss a minute with ye. No matter where it takes us."

He reached up to stroke her breast. "Together we're stronger." He tucked a strand of her hair behind her ear. "For a long time, I didna think I needed someone in my life, except my lads, but ye...ye, Leena Cullane Adair...and Haliburton, if 'tis what ye want, I need ye because I love ye."

" 'Tis what I want, but only if ye love me like ye did last night."

His mouth found her breast, and their loving came easier and slower, without the hesitation of the first time. He loved her fully and completely.

Afterward, still basking in the afterglow, she laid her head on his shoulder, saying, "I dinna think my da will approve of ye, but I am too old to waste time waiting, so if ye will have me…"

He grinned. "I think I already had ye. And I, too, willna wait for yer da to give us his blessing. Will ye wed me, Mistress Leena?"

She started to speak, but he put his finger on her lips. "That might have been harder for me to say after all these years of living my life in the grave with Marjorie, but ye set me free. Nay, I set myself free. I made my choice to join the land of the living and loving because of ye. Will ye marry me?"

"Aye, I will marry ye. A priest can write my name on a proper document if we can find a priest, but as is the custom in the Highlands, we can be handfasted. 'Tis as good as a marriage." Lifting her head, she said, "Shall we be handfasted, Master Haliburton?"

"We shall. How do we do it?"

"Get dressed. 'Tis no' done naked, although naked afterward would make it official, but we've already done it in the wrong order, and done it well, so get dressed."

They put on the same clothes they'd been in for days, and Leena lifted from her saddlebag some cloth pieces she'd bought in Stirling. Tearing off a strip of blue, she tied it in her hair and draped a longer strip of green around Reid's shoulders.

Then tearing off three narrow strips of different colors, she braided them together, knotted the ends, and wrapped the braid loosely around both their wrists together. "The words we say are only for us, so we say whatever binds our hearts. I'll go first."

She began. "Before we bound our hands, ye had already bound me to ye by filling my life. When ye looked into my eyes for the first time, ye awakened me, and then ye kissed me, and ye gave me what I'd been waiting for. As long as I endure in this world, I will hold ye close within all that I am and all that I have. I promise ye this with all that God has blessed me."

Reid rubbed the handfasting tie between his fingers. "Three strands. I remember a verse from the book of Ecclesiastes that my mother often quoted to show the strength of a family, and 'tis true of the strength of this cord that binds us. 'Though one may be overpowered, two can defend themselves. A cord of three strands is no' quickly broken.' I gladly give ye my love. I gladly give ye my soul. Use them both as ye will. I pledge to stand in front of ye in times of trouble, and as my hand is now bound to yers, I will hold it with all I am and all I have, and our lives will be each other's. I love ye as truly as I live and will love ye for as long as God lets me."

After she'd absorbed his words, blinking away the tears falling slowly out of her eyes, she said, "We seal our handfasting vows with a kiss." It began as a small kiss, but it wasn't enough for either of them. Lifting her off the ground, he smothered her with his lips, and she eagerly accepted him.

"Ahem!" came a voice from under the crumbling doorway in the wall of the castle.

The newly handfasted couple separated, and Reid, quickly unwrapping the ribbon from his wrist, turned to face the intruder.

A handsome, dark-skinned man stood in the open archway. "I am Shipopi," the man said in heavily accented English. "I come for you."

Leena had heard about Africans from a place called Kush along the Nile River who had dark, reddish-tinged skin like this man. He wore a long, unbuttoned gentleman's coat that flared out behind him with the wind, and his close-fitting pants tugged below his knees and fitted over scuffed and worn leather boots. Dangling across his bare chest hung a wide-bladed dirk, and another hung from the purple sash around his waist.

"I ken who ye are. Ye gave me this." Reid pointed to a greenish bruise still lingering on his jaw and a cut over his left eye while bracing himself for an attack. He pulled Leena behind him with his left hand.

"No my want," said Shipopi. "Captain say beat man with gun. Come now to son called Willie."

"Willie! What do ye ken about Willie? Where is he? Tell me!"

Shipopi's raspy voice remained without a trace of malice. "I no like Captain steal boy. I want give back to you. Come with me." He smiled, baring two gold teeth among his other crooked white ones. "I help you get Willie." Shipopi raised his hands as if in surrender. "I promise. I help you get Willie."

"Why would ye help me?"

Circling each other, the pirate moved into the courtyard, and Reid, with Leena behind him, moved around until his back was to the doorway. "I said *why?*"

"Captain say look for you. Make you hurry. You too slow. I no like how he take care of boy. Not enough to eat. No blanket to sleep. Shipopi a slave, run away be pirate. I get food and a blanket, not boy. I no like."

"McDever would kill ye if he kenned ye were here."

Shipopi gave a curt nod. "Aye. I take you to boy."

Suddenly Reid became aware of a stiff breeze from the open doorway across his back and realized Leena no longer stood behind him, blocking the wind. Still, he didn't dare take his eyes off the pirate to look for her. Shipopi's round brown eyes and Reid's blue ones stayed locked on each other.

"How do I ken I can trust ye?" asked Reid.

In a lightning-fast move, Shipopi drew his sword out of his belt and held it out toward Reid. "I kill you and you never find boy. Boy live as pirate. You never see again." The tip of his sword edged toward Reid's neck. Reid, with no weapon, put out his hands, crouched, and prepared to duck under the sword to charge at Shipopi when Leena's voice echoed against the crumbling walls.

"Have ye ever seen a man die after being gut-shot?"

She pointed Reid's gun directly at Shipopi's midsection, holding it with both hands, her finger on the trigger.

"Have ye seen one die that way?" she demanded. The pirate didn't answer.

"It takes a long time to die a verra painful death. I'm certain pirates throw all men shot in the gut into the sea to ease their misery, but here, on land, ye will no' be so lucky. This gun is loaded, so I tell ye to put yer sword on the ground, the other one, too, and step back."

Shipopi hesitated, so she ordered, "Put yer swords on the ground and step back!"

The pirate obeyed and took three steps back into the courtyard. As he did, Reid dashed over to Leena and took the gun from her now-trembling hands, aiming it at Shipopi. "She's a verra good shot. I've seen her shoot an oak from one hundred yards."

"She have courage to shoot a man? No like a target."

"She has the courage. Now lie on the ground on yer stomach, and put yer hands behind yer back." The pirate stretched out on the ground with his hands behind him.

Leena hurriedly scooped up Shipopi's two swords and put them beside the saddlebags. Reid kept his gun aimed at the pirate until Reid handed her the twisted cloth that was their handfasting ribbon. "Here, tie his wrists with this. Three strands will be strong enough to hold him."

Shipopi's coat shrugged off his shoulders as Leena wrapped the cloth around the man's wrists and knotted it, and she ran her fingers along the exposed scars on his back. "This man has been whipped," she said. "Many times."

Leena had seen a man flogged only once, and the sight had made her sick at her stomach. Shipopi had suffered such a flogging more than once, maybe more than ten times.

The Moor spoke. "Shipopi a slave. No obey. I run away. Captain make me sailor. Better than slave. The boy, Willie, he give something for you. In my sack on horse. I get?"

"What is it?" asked Reid.

"I get."

"Nay, Leena will get it. Which bag?"

As the men waited for her inside the broken walls of the castle, the silent sun made sweat pop out on their foreheads while the wind rushed in and around the deteriorating walls.

Leena returned with a brown cloth vest with brass buttons, two of them missing, and asked Shipopi, "Is this it?" After he nodded, she said to Reid, " 'Tis Willie's vest."

Reid grabbed it out of her hand. "Aye, 'tis Willie's. How did ye get it from him, ye murderous thief?"

"The boy give me. He say take it home. He no want. He say you keep. He say over and over, take it home."

"I dinna understand," said Reid. "Why would he give me his vest and say to take it home?"

"I do," said Leena, stepping in front of Reid, blocking Shipopi's view. She ran her fingers along the hem of the vest. Taking Reid's fingers, she did the same with them. All at once his eyes lit up with understanding that Willie had threaded the wheel wire through the hem, but then his face fell. Willie wanted him to go home and leave him with the pirates.

"Hold the vest," he said to Leena as he moved her to one side.

The next time he looked at their prisoner, Shipopi stood on his feet, and taking a quick step, he swung his still-tied wrists around Leena's neck.

"Put gun on bench. Put saddle on top," said Shipopi. "I let her go."

"Let her go now," said Reid. "And I winna shoot ye."

Shipopi tightened his grip on her throat. Leena gagged.

"All right," said Reid as he laid the gun on the bench and dragged one of the saddles over on top of it. "Now let her go."

Lifting his arms over Leena's head, Shipopi twisted the strands on his wrists until they popped open, and his wrists slid free. Tossing the ribbon to Reid, who caught it with one hand and stuffed it inside his sark, Shipopi said, "Want to see how I stand up?"

Dropping to his stomach, Shipopi laced his fingers behind his back. Spreading his legs wide on either side of his body, he swung them around until he sat up with his legs straight out in front of him. Lifting his hips, he slid his arms underneath and then under his legs to get his hands in front. Then it only took one fast motion to be on his feet.

"How did ye do that?" asked Reid.

"I do since child. For me easy. Now you come with me. See Willie."

Reid and Leena gave each other questioning looks.

"Can we trust him?" asked Leena.

"I dinna ken, but he can take us to Willie faster."

Walking over to Shipopi, she took his hand in hers and rubbed her fingers over it. "This hand is rough in places and smooth in others. 'Tis a hand that has seen hard work, but ye didna try to kill me with these hands, just hold me in place."

She turned back to Reid. " 'Tis our only choice. He kens the way, and we must go where the Devil drives us. We have no choice. What do ye think, Reid Haliburton?"

Reid rubbed his hand over his chin and studied Shipopi's face for a long while. "We will find out soon enough if a pirate thief can be trusted." Picking up the saddles to take to the horses, he tucked his gun into his waistband. "We'll follow at a safe distance. Lead the way, Shipopi."

Chapter Eighteen

Shipopi led the trio along a road heading east toward the coast until sunset. The terrain, which had been hilly and grassy, gradually turned rocky and treeless as they moved closer to the sea.

"Where are we headed?" asked Reid after they stopped for the night beneath a rocky cliff.

"Call place Arbroath. Where ship is now," said Shipopi, taking a big bite from the roasted chicken they had purchased from a farmer on the way. "Captain get gun, sail away fast. All he want is gun." He swallowed the mouthful of chicken and wiped his lips with his fingertips. "I get boy for you."

Tossing the shell of a hardboiled egg bought from the same farmer onto the fire, Reid asked, "Why are ye doing this for us? McDever will kill ye if he finds out."

"He try, but I say it right give boy to you."

"Where does McDever think ye are now?" asked Leena.

"He send me get you. Say you too slow. He say bring you fast. He no give you boy, but Shipopi give you boy."

"Why?"

"I want to go home. I sold as slave from my village. I escape and go with Captain. But Captain do bad things. I ashamed. If I get you boy, I go home with honor. Important I go home with honor. You understand?"

"But 'tis still verra dangerous," said Reid. "The closer we get to McDever, the worse it gets for ye and for Willie and for ye, Leena."

"I'll go with ye no matter what happens," said Leena.

"But ye shouldna," answered Reid. "Ye shouldna be here. Now I have both ye and Willie to worry about. I willingly risk my life, but no' yers. Why did I allow ye to come this far with me? Why didn't I tie ye up and let the first honest face I found take ye home? Or, better yet, left ye at the inn until I could come back for ye?"

Laying her hand on his chest, she said, "I am the reason we are here. I let McDever take Willie. If I had just told him where we hid the wire, we'd be free of him, and all of us would be safe at Makgullane."

He started to speak, but she stopped him. "Aye, I ken if he has the gun, the evil he might do with it, but trying to control the whole world is God's job, no' yers, and ye have to stop regretting that I am with ye. No matter what happens, I dinna want there to be guilt or remorse for ye. I have enough of my own, but we will do our best to rescue Willie, and if all goes awry, and we pray it doesna, but if it does, 'twill be no blame for ye to take. Ye're no' to blame for my stubborn soul in coming with ye. Besides, together is where we should be."

He pulled her into his arms, and they sat silently for a long time before Reid said, "My life has been one of surprise and confusion ever since I met ye, but remember that, for all time, I take ye just the way ye are and am grateful for it."

Closing her eyes, Leena rested peacefully against

his shoulder.

"No fear," said Shipopi. "I have plan. All be well."

Neither Reid nor Leena answered him.

Two days later, the three of them stopped at a cliff overlooking the sea as the smell of salt air surrounded them.

Shipopi pointed to the *Scarlet Lion* floating in the deeper water offshore. "I get boy. Bring him to you. Wait here."

"Is Willie on the ship?"

"Nay, but I know where. I bring boy here."

"Wait," said Reid. "How do we ken ye will bring Willie and no' bring McDever to capture us?"

After lowering his eyes, Shipopi raised them to Reid and knelt down on one knee. "I give you my word. My honor so I can go home. I give my word. Wait here. I come with boy. Then you give me wire and tool. Fair trade."

Shipopi started down the narrow, rock-strewn path from the upper trail toward the shore.

Leena and Reid kept their eyes on the Moor until he disappeared out of sight under the ledge overhanging the beach.

"Over here," said Reid, indicating a cluster of rocks casting a shadow across the path. They huddled in the shade, and Reid pulled her onto his lap, gently pushing her head against his shoulder. "I wish it could always be like this," he said.

Her head jerked up. "Like this? Waiting for an evil man to return our son?"

"Nay, the two of us together, close like this." Again he moved her head under his neck, and his pulse beat against her cheek. "We havena had much time together, and I want to spend every minute of it telling ye how much ye mean to me. Ye've been my life since I lifted ye out of the street, but I couldna tell ye then. I couldna touch ye the way I wanted to. I may have been in a muddle, but believe me when I say my heart ne'er was. 'Twas ye from the verra beginning."

Wrapping her arms around his waist, she hugged him closer as she lifted her mouth to his and kissed him in a way that mere words could never explain.

"If I cherished ye more, my heart would explode," she purred. "No matter what happens here, ye are the keeper of all my dreams and my hopes. No need to say the words. Our love has its own powerful voice."

He reached to untie her trews and tugged them down. "I'll always want ye."

Twisting until she straddled him, she opened his trews, freeing him, and lifted herself over him. Their joining was brief but powerful, and after it ended, both lay against the other, panting and satisfied. Afterward they adjusted their clothing and dozed in the safety of each other's arms until two figures on the far side of the ledge came toward them. A tall one and a smaller one.

"Willie!" said Reid, leaping to his feet. He started toward his son, but Leena put her hand on his arm to stop him.

"Something's wrong," she whispered. "Willie's gait is off. He lists to one side, stumbling when he walks."

Suddenly she understood the problem. Willie had his hands tied behind his back. He also shook his head and mouthed something, but she couldn't understand the words.

Reid started forward, but he'd taken only two steps

when a knife with a thick carved handle landed in the dirt at his feet. Another one bit into the dirt in front of Leena.

Now Willie came close enough for Leena to read his lips. "They're behind me," he mouthed. "Stay back."

"Far enough!" sounded a voice from higher up on the cliff. "Take another step, and my next throw will be in the boy's gut!"

"The gun is yers," shouted Reid. "All we want is the lad."

Jonas McDever and five others of his men stepped out from behind the rocks and into the open to stand beside Shipopi and Willie.

"Shipopi," said Leena, "ye gave us yer word, yer honor."

Laughing, Shipopi said between guffaws, "My word, my honor is to my captain. Not to one who stand in way. Aye, Captain?"

"Aye, Shipopi, a man loyal to the bone. Now, the lad stays with us until I get the wheel lock wire, and you put it into place. Properly! And until I hold the rifling bore. After it's all done and mine, you can have the boy. He's a most disagreeable one, stubborn even when we took a strap to him."

Reid lunged forward, but Leena wrapped her arms around him to hold him back. Stepping in front to face him, she whispered, "Willie is alive. 'Tis all we care about. The wire is threaded into the hem of Willie's vest, and both it and the rifling bore are in my pack. Let me try to negotiate."

"Ye canna!"

"I can try." Turning around to face McDever, she

said, " 'Tis a one-sided bargain and all in yer favor. We dinna agree to it."

"What are ye doing?" growled Reid into her ear. "Ye canna haggle with a pirate like McDever."

Under her breath, she said, "The longer I keep him talking, the longer we have to figure a way out of this."

"McDever has evil in his soul, and Willie is my son. No' for ye to risk."

"He is my son, too." Her solemn tone made him drop his head before balling his hands into fists.

Shouting to McDever again, Leena said, "What are our choices in this matter?"

McDever crossed his arms. "Well, let me see. You have a gun in your waistband, but we outnumber you, so we can kill all three of you anytime we wish. Or we can merely wound you and leave you here to die slowly."

"Those options might leave ye with the rifling tool, if ye can find it, but ye still willna have the wire."

A sly smile crept over McDever's face. "You do have a third choice. You can cooperate completely and give me everything I want. If you do, we will let you leave here unharmed."

"I dinna believe ye."

"I am being quite generous. The choice is yours."

Leena put her arms akimbo. "Here's what we propose, something that will benefit all of us. I will get the rifling bore tool, and Reid will toss it over Willie's head to ye. At the same time Willie will run to me."

"What about the wire?"

"First, one thing and then the other. Give us Willie, and let us go behind this ridge out of yer sight, and we will leave the wire where ye can find it. Any gunsmith worth his salt can figure out where it goes. Do we have a bargain?"

McDever pulled a face, but after moving behind Willie, gave hand signals to his men until they fanned out in a wide semicircle in front of their captives. "You have a bargain."

"We canna trust him," said Reid under his breath. "Pray the good Lord intervenes for us. 'Tis our only hope."

"I ken," said Leena. She sucked in a deep breath, closed her eyes, and prayed for help and guidance. *Keep McDever fixed on the gun while I do my best for Willie.* "I'm going to get my pack. 'Tis on the ground over there." She pointed.

McDever waved his hand in the air, and Leena walked over to the pack, her heart nearly beating out of her chest. Lifting the flap, she drew out the rifling bore. After tying the pack around her waist, she held up the bore and walked back to Reid, handing it to him.

"If this turns out to be a foolish plan, will ye forgive me?" she asked.

"There is naught to forgive. My plan would have us all dead by now." He stroked his thumb along her cheek. "If I ne'er get a chance to tell ye again that I love ye, remember that I do." Kissing her quickly on the lips, he turned to face his enemy.

"I'll count to three and toss this to ye," said Reid. "Willie, get ready to run to Leena."

"I am counting on a true throw," said McDever. "Magnus will have his knife, and the others their guns, aimed at your son the whole time."

"Do we have yer word that we can leave after we have Willie?"

"My word is as good as yours."

"Willie, are ye ready?" Out of the corner of his mouth, he said to Leena, "If I hit McDever square between the eyes with this, will it help us?"

Shaking her head slowly, she said, "We're outnumbered. The only way we can escape all these men is if he lets us. If he is satisfied, he just might. He is the Devil driving us."

"Get ready, lad."

Willie nodded.

"One, two, three," shouted Reid as he threw the bore directly at McDever. Willie ran as best he could with his hands tied behind his back, and as soon as he reached Leena, she dragged both of them to the ground.

"Are ye all right, Willie?" asked Leena. He nodded.

"Ye have the bore," said Reid. "We're going to back up to where we left our horses. After we're mounted, we'll toss the pack with the trigger wire behind a tree. Agreed?"

Narrowing his eyes, McDever said, "Agreed." He motioned to his men. "Let them pass."

Reid directed Leena and Willie ahead of him in a quick trot while he backed up, keeping his eyes on the pirates. Deep scowls crossed all their faces, and two of them spit at Reid's feet, but he kept moving.

As soon as the trio stepped behind the tall rocks out of sight of the ledge, Reid said, "Run!"

Leena and Reid each took Willie by an arm to help him keep up until their horses were in sight. "We're almost there!" cried Leena.

The words were barely out of her mouth when Shipopi and four other pirates stepped into the open in front of them.

"You no leave," said Shipopi, jerking Willie out of Leena's arms, while the others pushed Reid to the ground and lashed his hands behind his back.

McDever came around the rocks from the ledge, laughing, while Leena shouted, "Liar!"

Lifting his shoulders in a mock shrug, he grinned. "Did you think me an honest man? Surely not!"

"Leave them be," said Reid. "Ye betrayed our agreement. I'm the one ye want. I winna fight ye if ye let them go."

This time McDever rolled his eyes and shook his head. "Brave words, but you won't fight us as long as we have them."

Leena resisted the hands trying to force her arms behind her back by collapsing on the ground and refusing to stand on her own. The pirate dragged her upright, but she stayed as limp as a rag doll.

"Leena!" said Reid, and for his trouble received a sharp blow to the gut.

Willie said, "Leave her alone!"

"Boy, haven't we beat you enough? Shut your mouth."

She struggled against Magnus as he yanked her again to her feet and started to wrap the rope around her wrists until McDever said, "Leave her be. She has courage, but she'll behave herself as long as we have the boy. Won't you?"

Leena nodded very slowly as she waited for Magnus to release her before brushing the sand off her trews.

"Now where is the wire?"

Leena hesitated until Shipopi thrust his curved

sword under Willie's throat. The boy leaned back as far as he could away from the blade.

" 'Tis in my pack." She patted her pack at her waist. "We would have left it on this side of the rocks, if ye had been true to yer word." Smacking Magnus's hands aside, she untied the pack and handed it to him.

Magnus dumped out the contents, watching two hard boiled eggs and Willie's vest fall out.

"Where is it?" growled McDever. "Tell me or the boy loses his throat."

"Ye have it in yer hand," said Leena. " 'Tis in the vest."

After Magnus handed the vest to McDever, the captain shook it and ran his fingers over the cloth. When he came to the hem, he gave a sideways look to Leena. "So, I had it all the time. Boy, this will cost you."

"Dinna touch him!" said Reid, struggling against the ropes and the arms that held him.

"The captain winna punish Willie," said Leena.

"But it will be my pleasure to do so," said McDever. Grabbing the necklace she wore and jerking her closer, he added with a salacious grin, "And I might take my pleasure in other ways."

"Nay, ye willna," said Leena, her nose nearly touching McDever's. "Ye willna brutalize the woman who is the only one who can convince Reid and Willie to cooperate. Ye hurt me, and they winna ever help ye. The gun will ne'er work right again."

McDever released the necklace.

Leena went on. "And ye willna punish Willie either. 'Twas yer mistake ye couldna find the wire. He ne'er lied to ye. He only remained silent. Even under the code of pirates such as yers, ye have to admire such bravery."

"I do not listen to women."

"Aye, but do ye listen to yer men?" She scanned the faces of the pirates standing around McDever. "Would yer men follow a man who would punish them for having bravery like that?" Every man turned to look at their captain and then to each other with questioning glances. The pirate code may be brutal, but every man fiercely followed it.

"My men follow my every command."

"Willie Haliburton isna one of yer men."

Shaking the vest in the air, McDever said, "I'd rather be haunted by a succubus than a nagging woman. If you vow to follow my every order from now on, I will not punish the boy. Do I have your word?"

After a quick nod, Leena said, "Ye do. Do I have yers, as much as 'tis worth?"

With a ferocious frown, he said, "You make a hard bargain, but it is the last one. I will keep my word about the boy only as long as you give me no trouble. And yours, Haliburton?"

"If I put yer gun together properly and teach ye how to use it, will ye release Leena and Willie? Set them free. I'll stay and no' give ye any trouble. My pledge for their freedom."

McDever gave another cruel laugh. "You are a foolish man, Haliburton. I don't need your pledge. Now that I have the weapon, the wire, and the boring tool, I don't need you. You are only still alive out of the kindness of my heart."

"But I'm the one who can put the gun together."

"You forget. So can the boy."

"I willna!" shouted Willie.

"I think you will…to save your da's life."

Willie hung his head. "Let them go, and I'll do what ye want."

Straining against his ropes, Reid said, "Ye only need one of us to finish the gun. Take me. Let the lad and the woman go free."

McDever snorted.

"I'm sorry," said Leena to Reid under her breath. "I did hope the man might make a true bargain with us, that he might have some scrap of decency."

"Ye got him to agree in front of his men to no' punish Willie. That is more than either of us could have hoped for."

To Magnus, McDever said, "If Haliburton opens his mouth again, shut it for him."

"Aye, aye, Captain!" said Magnus with a bit too much glee in his voice.

McDever led the group down a path on the cliff leading to the shore, with Leena and Willie directly behind him. Two pirates followed them, then Shipopi, and lastly, Magnus and another man dragged Reid.

Reid struggled against the men forcing him down the path, but his eyes never left Shipopi until he said, "A man without honor is no man at all. Even a lying, thieving pirate's honor is better than no honor at all, and ye have no honor."

Magnus cocked his arm to hit Reid, but Shipopi put his hand on Magnus's chest and shook his head, giving Reid a malevolent glance.

Reid spit at his feet. Shipopi stopped, looked at the glob on the ground, picked up the spittle along with some surrounding sand, and tossed it into Reid's face.

Laughing cruelly, the rest of the crew assured Shipopi that he had avenged the insult without the need for Magnus to bloody his hands.

They finally reached the shore where the warm, thick sand made walking slow. It became especially difficult for Willie, who couldn't keep his balance with his hands tied behind his back. Leena kept him on his feet as best she could.

Along the cliff that rose behind the beach, the water had carved out several stony caves as the water rushed in and out with the tides. Years of waving water had also etched out another smaller cave deep in the back wall of one of them. Two rowboats, anchored just outside the smaller cave opening, banged in an eerie rhythm against the stone with each wave.

The pirate men forced their captives through the knee-deep seawater to the back wall beside the rowboats. McDever pointed to Leena and Willie. "Put them in. Take them to the ship. Bring the man here."

Two of the pirates hesitated, one of them saying in a low voice, "A woman on shipboard is the worst bad luck."

The other members of the crew nodded and murmured their agreement until McDever said, "The only bad luck you will have is if you don't do as I say right now. We take the woman and the boy and sell them to the highest bidder. And all of their price will be yours."

Reid cried out, "Nay! Take me, no' them!"

McDever whirled around. "I dislike having captives on board. They are usually nothing but trouble, but I'm taking these two only because I can. I leave you knowing that I have them, hoping that thought torments you." He gave Reid a sinister smirk.

Reid lurched toward him, but Magnus grabbed Reid by the hair and slammed his head against the stony wall of the inlet.

"Besides, a comely wench is in demand by every stewholder along the coast, and a boy with a strong back worth nearly as much. Any of my crew who don't want to share in the coin these two will bring can stay here on shore."

The murmuring changed to reluctant consent to take the woman onboard.

"Leena," said Reid as Magnus and another pirate dragged him toward the entrance to the cave, "stay alive. Whatever it takes, stay alive. I'll come for ye. I'll come for ye!"

Falling to his knees in the water, Reid gasped, "Willie, I give Leena to yer care. Be her warrior."

"I will!" cried Willie. "Da!"

As the men dragged Reid to the opening of the cave and shoved him inside, he called out, "Nay!" as his head and legs folded through the small opening. Once inside, he got to his knees and tried to force his way out, shouting, "Stay alive, Leena, Willie. No matter what…"

Shipopi's fist found his jaw, and Reid fell silent on the cave floor.

As Shipopi lifted her into one of the rowboats, Leena kicked her feet wildly, and one of her heels caught him in the knee. Suddenly he grabbed Leena around the waist and shook her. "Obey!"

After he tossed her in a heap on the floor of the boat, Leena said, "Yer village is dishonored. Ye are no man at all."

He reached for her, but Willie shouted, "Leave her alone!" For his outburst, Shipopi grabbed him by the hair and flung him to the floor of the rowboat beside Leena. Two pirates started to take the boat out of the inlet toward the *Scarlet Lion* floating offshore.

"Stop!" called Leena. "Bring him with us. We'll do what ye ask. Bring Reid with us."

"Shut your mouth, woman!"

Realizing the hopelessness of their situation, she wrapped her arm around Willie as tears ran down her cheeks.

The second rowboat, filled with brush, branches, and leaves, sat still anchored inside the inlet. McDever ordered the kindling stuffed into the narrow entrance to the cave, and despite Reid's efforts to kick it out, it didn't take them long to completely pack the cave opening.

McDever said, "Light it."

Leena gasped and turned Willie's head into her shoulder as the pile started to blaze and smoke filled the low walls of the inlet.

She had let this happen! If she had only turned over the gun to McDever on the road and told him where to find the wire hidden in Willie's vest, they wouldn't be here. They would be home safe and in the loving arms of family at Makgullane. Now Reid would suffer and soon be dead. She had lost the man she cherished, Willie had lost his father, and she'd live with her shame and her broken heart for the rest of her life.

"Reid, Reid," said Leena as Willie cried, "Da. Da. I'm sorry. 'Tis my fault."

The smoke stung her eyes, and she remembered what Dillon had told her about where the real fault lay.

"Nay 'tis no'," she said. " 'Tis this foul pirate's fault, and we willna forget that. No' ever."

She made up her mind and wiped the tears off her cheeks. She would not let Reid's death be in vain. She and Willie would survive, one way or another, find their way home, and spend the rest of their days making certain that everyone remembered Reid as a strong, courageous, loving man. He would not be forgotten!

Shouting over the crackling fire and the roaring waves, she called out, hoping Reid could still hear her, "I love ye, Reid, for as long as..." The kindling caught with a loud crack as the flames scorched the stones outside the cave. She fell silent.

While pungent smoke billowed out of the inlet across the water to the sea, the rowboat reached the *Scarlet Lion* anchored offshore, and the pirates lifted Leena and Willie onboard.

Chapter Nineteen

The crew of the *Scarlet Lion* scurried like squirrels up the two large masts and the smaller one at the bow to unfurl the sails. The cloth billowed in the wind, moving the ship slightly in order to raise the heavy anchor more easily. After the creaking sound of the iron chain stopped, the ship shifted away from the coast with the breeze and the current. Magnus, at the helm, pulled the wheel and directed the rudder to take the ship out to sea.

Everyone ignored Leena and Willie left standing under the mainmast in the center of the deck. They were the only ones watching the smoke from the inlet as it disappeared into the clouds, knowing the man they both loved suffered a painful death.

After a few minutes, Leena said to Shipopi as he strode by, "Untie his hands."

The man grunted, but Leena repeated in a sterner voice, "Untie his hands." Turning Willie so his hands faced Shipopi, she said for the third time, "Untie his hands. Are ye thinking us two wee folk can overpower a big beast like ye?"

After glancing around to see if anyone might be watching, Shipopi pulled out a small knife, sliced the ropes around Willie's wrists, and without a word, headed to the stern of the ship.

Rubbing the raw marks on his wrists, Willie asked,

"What do we do now?"

"We wait here and see what opportunities come to us."

Willie sniffed loudly. "I willna cry," he said, scrubbing the tears away. "I ne'er cried no matter what they did to me. I winna let them see me cry." He bit his lip and sucked in a jagged breath.

Reid's last promise to come for her and Willie repeated in her head, and while those words gave her courage, they did not bring hope. He would not be coming to rescue them. They were on their own, and even in this dire situation, she would not let Willie fall into despair. They were together, and together they would survive.

Leaning her mouth close to his ear, she whispered, "When we are alone, we will grieve for yer da and my husband."

"Husband?"

"Aye. I will love yer father for the rest of my life, and I will ne'er forget the way he loved me, even if 'twas for only a short time. Nothing else matters except the remembering."

The edges of Willie's mouth turned up. "If Da trusted ye to take care of us, then so will I. Ramy and Hendrie need someone now that Da is…gone."

"When we're alone, Willie, we'll mourn, but ye need a brave face now. As long as these men are within sight, we'll do what they say. They'll think we're behaving ourselves, but ye and I will work together to escape. 'Twill no' be easy, but we will get away somehow. We'll also remember what yer da said. 'Stay alive no matter what.' Can ye do that with me, Willie? Can ye do that, William Haliburton, son of Reid

Haliburton, the best gunsmith in all of Scotland?"

"What are you two blathering about?" snarled Captain McDever as he came close. "No talking!"

In unison Leena and Willie said, "Aye, Captain."

McDever gave the pair a curious look before walking away.

Leena scanned the deck. She had to keep Willie's mind occupied, and hers, too. Dwelling on Reid's heinous death or the cruelty of the men who held them captive would only break their hearts and their spirits. For Reid's sake, she and Willie would get back to Ramy and Hendrie, someday, somehow.

"Here's what we have to do. Study everything on this deck, how far up to the helm, the locations of the rigging and the masts, the mainmast, and the mizzenmast. Check where all the ropes are, the gates, and where the rowboats are. Especially learn the positions of the cannons and who carries a gun and who has only a sword or knife."

Willie nodded.

"Memorize the place of everything on this ship from the bow to the stern. If we get any freedom to move around, we'll start counting steps so we can walk the deck in the dark. We have to ken the exact distance from the port side to the starboard." At Willie's confused look, she said, "That's the left to the right. Port is always on yer left as ye face the bow or the front of the ship. 'Tis called port because a ship anchors on that side in the port, and starboard is from two other words that mean to steer and the side of a boat."

"How do ye ken about ships?" said Willie.

"My grandfather had a book on ships in his library. And even though Makgullane is far from an ocean, and

I'd ne'er get to the sea, I read it over and over.

"Think of the ship as a small town on the water. This deck is, let's say the town close, and the helm up there in the bow is city hall, and under that is the captain's quarters, which is like the town mayor's office. Look over this front half of the deck, and in a minute, I'll ask ye questions to find out what ye remember. Later we'll try the back half."

Willie did quite well on Leena's quiz.

"We'll do this as often as we can until we've got it all memorized. Now I want ye to watch the men and what they do. Magnus is the first mate and is like the constable and can take over for the captain. Each man has a job, and ye have to match the man with the job. Some are above deck, and some are below. They dinna change their clothes, so that makes it easier for us."

"Shut yer mouths," said McDever as he came past them again.

"Aye, aye, Captain."

Willie quickly followed suit.

Stopping, and stepping closer, McDever grabbed both of them by the arm. "You will do as I say, just as I say it, or it'll be a flogging for the boy."

Leena struggled to keep her expression calm. "Ye said ye wouldna punish him."

Squeezing Leena's chin between his fingers, he said, "I won't punish him for not telling me about the wire in his vest, but I didn't include anything else in that promise. You will stay in line to save the boy, won't you, my pretty miss? If you aren't any trouble, I might sell you to a stewhouse and make him a powder monkey. Either way it would be an easier life than as a slave on the African coast. Just ask Shipopi. He can tell you all about being a slave."

"We winna be any trouble, Captain," said Leena, "will we, lad?"

"Nay, Captain," said Willie. Only Leena saw his knees quaking.

After cruelly wrenching his hand off Leena's face and leaving scratches from his jagged fingernails, McDever strode to the helm, barking orders at each man as he passed him.

"What's a powder monkey?" asked Willie.

"He helps the gunners." She didn't tell him that a powder monkey carried the gunpowder to the cannons during a battle or that the danger involved often made a powder monkey's life very short.

Whispering in Willie's ear again, she said, "And we will be brave. Yer da showed us how to be brave, and we will do the same."

"Da ne'er made us a promise he didna keep." His lip quivered. "If Da says he'll come, he'll come." He leaned over and buried his head at Leena's waist, smothering his face.

Leena stroked his back and said a silent prayer that Willie would continue to have such faith in his father. It would make him stronger for the possibly futile tasks ahead.

The sun edged its way under the horizon as it started to rain, no lightning or thunder or strong winds, just steady, cold rain. By this time, Leena and Willie had sat down and curled up under the mast. It didn't give them much protection, and soon the rain drenched them to the skin.

Magnus lit three covered lanterns near the wheel helm before he pointed at Leena and Willie, saying to

Shipopi, "Take them below. Lock them in the brig. I cannot stand to look at them anymore."

Not speaking, Shipopi came over to the mainmast and jerked his hand for them to follow him along the deck to the hatch leading to the stairs below. Just as he leaned down to lift it, one of the other pirates with shaggy black hair and missing teeth stepped out of the shadows, grabbed Leena by the arm, tore open her sark, and squeezed her breast. His breath nearly caused her to gag. She cried out and swung her hand at his face, but he gave her a hard hit to her jaw, and she collapsed into his arms.

"Five minutes with her," said the pirate, pawing at her clothing. "You can watch if you want."

Without saying a word, Shipopi snatched Leena away from the pirate, tossing her roughly onto the deck. Pulling the man to him, Shipopi covered his mouth with one hand while twisting his neck with the other until a loud crack sounded. Then he dragged the lifeless body to the side rail and threw him overboard headfirst. The man quickly sank into the black water as the ship sailed past him.

"Thank ye," said a gasping Leena.

"Quiet," said Shipopi. "Give me more trouble, I tie your mouth shut. You want?"

"Nay," said Leena as she let Shipopi heft her up by the arm and drag her stumbling down two sets of stairs into a damp, smelly iron cell at the stern of the ship. Willie followed.

After a hard shove into the cell for both Leena and Willie, Shipopi slammed the cell door shut with a loud clank and turned the key in the lock. The three glared at each other as he put the key chain around his neck and left them alone in the darkness.

Stretching out together on the narrow wooden shelf, Leena and Willie tried to get some sleep. When it became clear that neither of them would, she said, "Crying helps, and we have to do it verra quietly. Tears, but no noise."

They both let hot tears wash over their faces. She wiped off his cheeks, and he did the same for her.

"Now we'll sleep," she said. "We've shed our tears, but tomorrow we'll be strong, and we'll watch and listen and learn, and one day we'll go home. We will ne'er give up the fight."

Willie said very softly, "Aye, aye, mistress."

After a restless sleep, they awoke to find two wooden bowls of mashed turnips and a mug of fresh water sitting just inside the bars of the cell.

"Eat as much as ye can. We winna get fresh food much longer while we're at sea, or fresh water either."

Stomping her foot hard as a rat scurried near the bench, heading for their food, she said, "Fewer rats up top, so we have to get out of this cell as often as we can."

They ate the mush hungrily with their fingers and shared the water.

At midday, Shipopi appeared with two bowls of a vegetable stew with tiny bits of salted pork in it and another mug of water. He laid the bowls and mug just outside the cell and picked up the empty bowls and mug from the morning, giving the captives a long, hard look before leaving them in the darkness again.

Before they had time to finish their food, Magnus came to unlock the cell. "The captain wants you alive and healthy so you'll fetch a good price. Out and up on the deck. Move!" They scrambled to obey while stuffing the rest of the food into their mouths.

As the big man pushed them toward the stairs leading up, they passed a man stirring a pot on the fogón, the wooden box filled with sand with a low fire in it, and another man using seawater from a barrel to scrub out an even bigger pot.

"We thank ye for the food," said Leena in a loud voice. "We are grateful for ye making it for us."

The confused looks on the sailors' faces satisfied Leena that she had complimented men who had never before heard a kind word about their food. And they would remember who said it, and every friend she and Willie made took them closer to freedom.

"Move along," said Magnus, giving Willie a sharp shove in the back.

They stretched their arms and legs as the bright sun lifted their spirits after being in the musty underdeck. Even though Magnus restricted Leena and Willie to a space between two barrels, they had room to move and stretch their aching muscles.

"Which side of the ship are we on?" asked Leena.

"Port."

"Close yer eyes. Tell me how many crew members are on deck."

His eyes flew open. "I dinna ken."

"Eleven. Check if I'm right."

Eleven exactly. "Ye dinna come up top without taking note of as many things as ye can."

And so the lessons continued until nightfall when Shipopi locked them in the cell once again.

This time he brought bowls with chunks of cheese floating in a soup of cabbage and carrots. Pulling two apples out of his waistband, he said, "From cook."

Convinced the apples served as a small repayment for her compliment earlier today, Leena took a big bite and chewed noisily. Willie followed her lead, and both of them smiled at Shipopi, who scowled and left them alone again.

"We canna trust him," said Leena, "even though he saved me from that pirate, and he's no' mistreating us, we have to protect ourselves first."

They both slept better that night, and in the morning they awoke to find a torn blanket covering them.

Chapter Twenty

Magnus came early the next morning to take them on deck. "Keep walking," he ordered when they reached the spot between the barrels where he had confined them yesterday. "Captain says you are to get exercise. Keep walking."

Magnus followed Leena and Willie around the deck for two laps from the bow to the stern and back again. At the start of the third lap, Magnus growled, "You know where you can walk now, so keep moving and don't take one step anywhere else. I'll be watching you. Understand?"

"Aye," said Leena.

"Aye, aye," said Willie.

Magnus headed for the helm, only looking back once to give them a stern glare.

"This is good for us," said Leena quietly. "We can get a closer look at everything on deck and learn where it is and how the men use it. The lesson today begins with everything on the port side, its exact location, how many steps, and anything else we can learn."

"Aye, aye, mistress!" said Willie with a salute.

Leena quickly pulled his hand down. "Dinna do that. We're no' pirates, and we canna act like one. Now, how many steps between the rope coil here and the next one?"

At midday, Shipopi tossed the captives two dry,

crunchy sea oatcakes and walked away again without saying a word. As the sun started to set, the Moor jerked both of them by the arm and led them down the steps, but instead of going below to the cell, he shoved them into a small cabin on the second level.

Two hammocks swung along one wall, one atop the other, and the only light came from a small round window on the starboard side. Attached to the wall at the front hung a small table and two crude stools, and on the table were two plates with the night's evening meal of salted pork, boiled potatoes, and an apple.

"I dinna understand," said Leena. "We're grateful for better accommodations, but still…"

Crossing his arms across his chest, the Moor said, "In three days we stop at MacCummings. We anchor in bay. Captain to marry. Big party. You put gun together tomorrow."

"Tomorrow?" squeaked out Willie.

"Aye. Gun is bride prize. It work good for bride." He tugged the door closed and locked it from the outside.

Sitting opposite each other at the table, Leena put her spoon down and smiled at Willie as he ate. He would grow into a man so much like his father. Rich sapphire eyes, an easy smile, and broad shoulders along with a quick mind and steady disposition. Despite everything Willie had been through, he never whined or pouted about it. He would be quite a man. Like the one lost to both of them.

"Why do ye think the captain did this for us?" asked Willie between mouthfuls.

"I dinna ken. Mayhap he has a soft heart."

Willie snickered. "Whatever he has in that chest of

his isna a heart."

Just then the door to the cabin opened, and Shipopi carried in a bucket of seawater with a small slab of soap tied to the side. He placed it on the floor and tossed two squares of heavy, rough cloth and two sets of clean clothing into the corner. Then he locked the door behind him again.

"Well, I guess the captain wants us to wash up," said Willie. "I've been in these clothes ever since we left Stirling." Lifting his sark, he showed her a red, scaly rash around his waist. "Itches from me being so dirty." Leena also saw several red welts from the beatings the boy had taken.

With as much modesty as they could manage, Leena and Willie rinsed, washed, and scrubbed themselves clean from head to foot.

They dressed in the clean clothing, obviously hand-me-downs from other sailors, all of it too big, but by tying the excess cloth into knots and holding it all together with the rope belts, they were finally dressed.

Willie wore trousers of a faded blue, with an oversized, pale brown sark held in place with a belt that looped around his waist three times. The gray wool stockings came up to his midthigh, but he held them up with two smaller ropes, and he squeezed the thick stockings into his own boots. Tying a green bandana over his curls, he let the ties hang down his back.

"How do I look?" he asked Leena as he spread out his arms and twirled.

"We're quite a pair!" She danced around the room, showing off her own outfit. She, too, wore faded blue pants, patched at the knees—or what would have been the knees on a taller man—a green sark, and black stockings. Her leather belt cinched in at her waist kept the clothes from sliding off, and she pushed her feet into her own boots, tucking the wooden teardrop necklace under her sark.

One more long piece of thin cloth still lay in the corner. "What's this for?" asked Willie.

Leena stared at the cloth dangling from his hand, and suddenly its purpose came to her. " 'Tis to bind my breasts."

"Why?"

"Ye can pass for a cabin boy, but if anyone saw a woman onboard… Hand it to me and turn around."

The cloth wound around her chest six times, crushing her breasts and holding them firmly in place after she ripped the end and tied it into a knot.

"I also have to hide my hair."

Together they wound Leena's thick hair around her head and covered it completely with a tightly tied green bandana just like Willie's.

Later that night, as they swung in their hammocks, Leena below and Willie above, Leena let her mind wander, and it always came back to the gunsmith she'd met such a short time ago. A year and a week with Johnnie. Two weeks with Reid. Both might as well have been lifetimes.

Both men were a part of her soul now. Johnnie rested in a comfortable spot in her heart while Reid blazed, wounding her with his pain. Determined to keep Reid's flame bright, she renewed her pledge. She would stay alive, and she'd make certain Willie did, too. Together they would honor Reid's memory by making their way back home to tell everyone about how Reid Haliburton had lived and loved.

She choked back a sob before falling into a restless sleep.

Chapter Twenty-One

In the predawn dark, McDever burst through the door to Leena and Willie's cabin, a lantern swinging from his hand. With his free hand, he twisted the ropes on the hammocks and tossed both captives onto the floor.

"You're not here for your comfort, so on your feet! On your feet!" he shouted. "Today you will put this gun to rights."

Behind him stood Shipopi holding Reid's gun and Willie's vest. He thrust both at Willie, still on his knees from landing on the floor.

"I dinna have the tools," said the boy.

Reaching out, McDever grabbed Leena by the neck, lifting her up until only her tiptoes touched the floor. Holding her out in front of him, he snarled, "You can make do with what we have onboard or you can make do without her. Your choice, but you will do it now."

"Do it," croaked Leena as she clung to McDever's arm. "We…can…wait."

Hesitating only a moment, Willie said, "Give me the gun and my vest. What tools do ye have?"

McDever released Leena, leaving her gasping, while Shipopi handed Willie the gun, the vest, and two narrow screwdrivers.

Sitting at the table against the wall, Willie went to

work. "Move the lantern closer. I canna see what I'm doing."

Shipopi held the light over Willie's head as it swung back and forth with the motion of the ship.

Handing back the gun, Willie said, "I canna say how well 'twill fire. I didna have the right tools. The trigger and the flash pan may be loose."

McDever grabbed the gun, and then Willie, and dragged him out of the cabin and up the stairs to the deck. "You fire it."

Willie loaded the gun with ammunition and powder, set the flint pan, and pulled the wheel lock trigger. " 'Tis no' as tight as it should be. Hand me that little tool again." After he made his adjustments, he pulled back the wheel lock trigger again, cocked the gun, aimed off the starboard side, and fired as smoke from the barrel plumed up around his face. " 'Tis as good as I can get it without the proper tools."

" 'Twill do," said McDever. "Take him below and lock him in. I must be well skilled with this weapon if I'm to get the highest price."

The *Scarlet Lion* often sat becalmed with no wind in the sails over the next six days, making slow progress north. During that time some of the crew began to accept the presence of Leena and Willie. Most ignored them, but on occasion a few engaged in friendly conversation.

According to some of the more talkative pirates, *The Scarlet Lion* sailed for John O'Groats, a former Dutch settlement, where the people called Groaters, Dutch for *de groot* or "the large," made their home. Authorities rarely bothered to investigate so far north, making it a perfect place for pirates and outlaws to hide. The ship would anchor in the harbor to sell or trade cargo to men who wouldn't ask questions or care about its origin.

One of the men living at John O'Groats happened to be an old friend of Captain Jonas McDever, an outlaw named Barker MacCummings, but besides renewing old friendships, McDever had agreed to marry MacCummings's daughter, thus binding their future business arrangements.

"Who would wed Captain McDever?" asked an incredulous Willie.

Thomas, a young sailor on his first voyage on the *Scarlet Lion*, answered, "Many of us think the same thing, but we dare not ask. All we know is we're heading to John O'Groats with the gun."

Kieran, one of the older sailors, said, "MacCummings will take the gun as part of the bride price and pay Captain a finder's fee. Captain wanted to go to London to sell it, but you made so much trouble for him, he didn't have time. He didn't want to miss his wedding."

Thomas spoke in a whisper. "Being in the good graces of MacCummings will earn him more in the long run, and Captain says we'll each get a bigger share of the bounty we already have onboard if we let him sell the gun here. 'Tis a'right with me."

"Me, too," said Kieran. "I can sell goods like the spices, Indian hides, and pieces of silver plate, and…" He leaned in closer. "And the box of gold coins, but I can't do nothing with a gun."

Willie interrupted. "Captain shares the cargo with ye?"

"Aye. 'Tis our pay. Ours ain't what you'd call

steady work."

"Now I ken why I had to look like a man," said Leena after Shipopi locked them back in the cabin again.

Willie gave her a confused look.

"McDever canna let anyone ken he has a woman on board. It might make this MacCummings suspicious about how McDever came to have the gun or what he might be up to with a woman captive, and he canna have MacCummings get suspicious, no' before the wedding. The marriage is a business arrangement, and if the man thinks the gun is in any less than perfect condition, the deal falls through. If we can pass for crew members, McDever can get away with it."

Willie nodded his understanding.

The *Scarlet Lion* sailed into the narrow harbor off the shore of the settlement of John O'Groats, anchored, and a small contingent readied to go ashore to greet their hosts.

As Captain McDever made his way across the deck to the smaller craft to take him ashore, he passed Leena and Willie watching near the starboard side. He suddenly stopped and turned around.

"Who brought them up here?" he bellowed. "Take them below afore someone figures out they're not part of the crew! I want them kept locked up while I handle MacCummings."

Shipopi stood steady until McDever shouted, "Move!"

Shipopi grabbed Leena and Willie by their necks and led them down the stairs to the cabin, shoved them inside, and locked the door behind them.

Chapter Twenty-Two

For the next sennight, from what Leena and Willie could see through their window or when Shipopi took them up top to walk around the deck, the lavish wedding preparations between Jonas McDever and his bride-to-be, Galvyn MacCummings, would take precedence over any other business during the visit. No one had off-loaded any of the cargo from the *Scarlet Lion*, and so far no one from shore had come aboard to even look over what the ship carried.

The wedding festivities on the rocky beach lasted for six days before the actual marriage ceremony. The centerpiece of the celebration featured a huge bonfire, burning day and night, around which everyone gathered to eat, dance, and sing.

Everyone flocked around the bonfire. That included the regular inhabitants of this far north community of John O'Groats, the MacCummings crew, and the entire McDever crew except for Shipopi, Leena, and Willie.

Pointing to shore from the ship, Leena said, "Look at the show of presents. The bride's father will get most of them, but I'm certain his daughter kens this marriage is only a business bargain." With a laugh, she added, "At least she'll get gifts every time the *Scarlet Lion* sails this far north, and she doesna have to put up with the captain in between times."

On the day of the wedding, the bride, dressed in a fancy dark blue dress trimmed with white lace, and the groom, wearing an equally fancy captain's uniform, stood before the priest in front of the fire while the rest of the guests gathered nearby. Leena, Willie, and Shipopi couldn't hear the words, but after the bride and groom shared a drink of whiskey from a silver chalice, the short ceremony ended. At the encouragement of the priest, McDever tugged Galvyn close and kissed her roughly on the mouth. Releasing her quickly, he walked over to her father to shake his hand, but did not return to his new wife's side. However, the women of the community soon surrounded her and ushered her away before bringing out food while the men carried in crates of whiskey and barrels of ale from which everyone imbibed copiously well into the night.

The smell of the smoke from the bonfire raised horrible memories of the inlet where Reid died, and it took all of Leena's resolve to hold back the tears. She did it for Willie's sake. She could not pile her grief onto his. The wedding also brought back Leena's memories of handfasting with Reid, and the heartache she'd put aside. It threatened to engulf her now. If she didn't find a place soon to cry and pound her fists at her heartbreak and grief, she'd burst wide open.

"Shipopi," she said, barely keeping the trembling out of her voice, "may I go to our cabin, alone, for a while? Ye can lock the door behind me."

"I'll go with ye," said Willie.

"Nay, I need time alone, just for a while." By now the tears had started to push their way out of her eyes. "Please, for a little while, please."

Shipopi said, "Come," and led both prisoners to the

cabin, locked Leena inside, and took Willie back up on deck.

Leena heard the click of the lock behind her, releasing her from the need to put on a courageous face, and all her thoughts were of the man from Stirling and how her chest ached so badly for him her heart might burst. She could almost feel his arms around her waist when he saved her from that fall in the mud, and those eyes, those incredible blue eyes and the way they sparkled when he looked at her. She remembered how he tossed his head to shake his soft gray and white-tinged curls out of those eyes, and she heard his mellow, throaty voice and sensed his warm hands on her arm. His lips on hers, the kisses she would never forget. Slowly licking her lips, she still tasted him. And felt him holding her, loving her, and keeping her safe. She sank to the floor. She could smell his masculine aroma, unique to him, so unique that in any group of men, she could find him with her eyes closed. She did close her eyes and inhaled his memory.

Going to the porthole, she waited for the flood of tears to come, but it didn't.

Where are the tears?

Didn't she grieve? She did, but tears weren't the release she needed. She needed to live for Reid, for his memory, to keep him alive inside her. The same way she had kept Johnnie's memory alive through his chapbooks and his music, Reid would live through his sons. They would grow into men their father could be proud of, and she'd make certain they never forgot him.

She heard another click of the lock, and the door burst open as Willie ran in and fell at her feet. Shipopi filled the doorway, but when she looked up at him, he pulled the door shut.

"I kenned ye came here to cry for Da," said Willie, "and I couldna let ye be alone."

He threw his arms around her, and she held him close while his tears soaked her sark.

Here are the tears. They are Willie's tears.

"I ne'er let them see me cry," he wailed. "Shipopi said to leave ye alone, but I couldna. I ran away from him and came to ye, but I ne'er let him see me cry. Only ye will ken I cried."

After Willie's sobs dried up into sniffles, she turned his face to hers. "What would yer da say to ye if he were here?"

Willie shrugged.

"Picture him sitting right over there against the wall. Is he there?"

Willie shook his head.

"Try harder. He's right there."

And there he sat with his long legs folded against his chest and his arms resting on his knees. Those eyes, those rich cobalt eyes looked back at her, and she reached out as if to ruffle his hair. Closing her eyes, she tried to feel him beside her, to remember his kiss. When she opened her eyes fully again, Reid's image had vanished.

Willie, wiping his nose with his forearm, said, "He'd say to get home to Ramy and Hendrie. That he wants his sons to be together, to be a family."

"He'd say the same thing to me, so that's what we're going to do. I didna hear Shipopi lock the door. Mayhap now is our chance."

Together they crouched behind the door and turned the handle. The door opened.

Leena peered into the dark passageway. All quiet. Stretching out of the opening a little farther, she looked up the stairs to the deck. "All clear. Now's our chance."

Taking Willie's hand, she led him up the stairs to the deserted deck and into the moonless night. No noise drifted over from the shore. The men had drunk their fill, fallen to the ground, and slept where they lay while the bonfire faded to ashes.

"Now is where all we learned helps us," she whispered and pointed toward the starboard side and peeked over the railing. "I can hear the rowboat hitting against the side."

"Fifteen steps to where the only boat they left here is tied," said Willie. "One, two, three. Here's the barrel. Four, five, six, seven. Here's a rope coil and one of the mast sails. Eight, nine, ten, eleven, twelve. The rain barrel. Thirteen, fourteen." He looked over the side. "Here it is."

Still crouching in the blackness, they both scanned the deck and listened. No sounds, no movement except the gentle rocking of the ship with the flow of the sea into the harbor.

Climbing over the side, they dropped as quietly as they could into the boat and lowered it to the water. Willie untied the small boat from the ship while Leena used an oar to push it away.

As quickly as possible, Willie and Leena sat on the seat together and started to row. It took all their strength to get through the currents where the ocean pushed into the harbor, but they made it and were soon out on the open sea.

"We stay within sight of the shore, and we keep moving. The farther away we get, the better. 'Twill be daylight afore Shipopi brings us food and finds out we're gone. Ye were verra brave. Ye would make yer father proud."

Willie let out his breath slowly. "I'm still verra frightened." He pulled on the oar.

"Bravery doesna mean ye are no' afraid. It means that despite being afraid, ye do what needs to be done. I'm verra afraid, too."

"Ye ne'er act like ye're frightened."

"Yer da once said to me that only a lunatic who has lost all his senses is ne'er afraid. And we are no' lunatics. Dig into that oar. We have a long way to go tonight."

The only sounds they heard were the oars dropping into the water and then the swish as the boat moved forward. The peaceful silence of the ocean eased and calmed their heartbeats, despite the strain of pulling on the oars. They had found a way to get home.

With the next pull on her oar, it caught on something, and she couldn't drag the oar through the water. Mayhap a rock or a large clump of seaweed held the oar firm. Struggling, she tried to lift it out of whatever held it by standing and pressing her entire weight on the handle, but it wouldn't budge.

"We're caught on something. Help me."

Willie lifted his oar into the boat and heaved all his weight onto Leena's oar. The paddle let loose a little, but then sank back in the water. A second later, the oar freed itself, rocking the rowboat until it almost turned over as seawater sloshed over the sides. When the boat stopped rocking and righted itself, Shipopi sat on the seat across from them.

After she got over the shock of the Moor in the

boat, she said, "Ye swam all that way?"

"It no very far."

"We're no' going back."

"I throw in ocean," said Shipopi. Reaching out, he grabbed Willie by the sark and lifted him off the seat.

"Nay!" shouted Leena, latching onto Willie's arm. "We'll go with ye."

Shipopi shoved the boy back on the seat, took the oars, and rowed the boat back toward the harbor.

After a long silence, Leena said, "Ye have no honor. Yer village is ashamed of ye."

Shipopi pulled even harder on the oars. "Shipopi give food. Clean clothes. I take care of you. You do wrong thing."

"Ye have treated us kindly while we've been held captive, but ye killed my husband, Willie's father. Ye lied to us, and ye keep us prisoners. Ye are as evil as yer captain."

Snarling, Shipopi splashed the water with his oars, soaking Leena and Willie. "No more talk!"

After Shipopi locked the prisoners back inside their cabin, he kept guard just outside the door as Leena and Willie lay in their hammocks, wanting to sleep but unable to.

" 'Tis for Reid that we must keep being brave," said Leena. "Yer da is part of ye, and no one can take that away. They can try, but he is inside every part of us. 'Tis more than remembering. 'Tis that caring, his and ours, is for always and forever, and nothing else matters."

"I'll remember," said Willie.

" 'Tis more than three sennights since we left yer da at the cave, and we have many more days to remember him, and more importantly to live for him…and yer brothers…and my brothers. Ne'er forget what is ahead of us. We will hold onto our dreams. 'Tis only us now, and we are strong!"

"I'll remember. I'll remember."

Chapter Twenty-Three

Coughing and choking on the smoke filling the small cave, Reid forced his mind to think. The flames licked at his neck as he crouched in the small space. *I have to get my hands untied!*

He twisted his long legs until his wrists faced the fire, and closing his eyes against the pain, he reached backward until the flames touched the ropes. Gasping as the fire burned his skin, he pulled his hands away. But knowing what he had to do, he reached out again, determined to bear the hurt. When he tugged against the knots, the rope gave way a little. Bracing himself one last time, he endured the flames and, using the strength left in his arms, split the rope and his hands were free.

Putting his arm up against his mouth and nose, he inhaled what tiny bit of air remained in the thickening smoke. Through the flames, he saw the cool water of the inlet. *Can I make it through the fire to reach the water before the smoke chokes me to death?*

He closed his eyes, and a vision of Leena came to him. He saw her out on the water, calling to him, waving her arm for him to come. Her mouth moved, but he couldn't hear her voice. He had to do whatever he could to get to her!

He struggled up on his knees and, with a nearly suffocating breath, sprang through the blaze despite his cramped legs. He landed with his face and chest in the water, but his left foot wedged between stones at the base of the opening, so close that the flames whipped around his stockings and made their way up his trews to his knee. Churning his arms, he kept his face above the waves and sucked in the fresh air still floating above the water and under the smoke.

Leena called to him. This time he heard her. "Come to me! I need ye!" He had to save himself and her. He promised he would come to her.

Bracing his right foot against the stone wall, he kicked. The first kick tore his boot off his left foot, but the rock held his foot fast. She called to him again, this time more desperate. He had to get to her. He had to!

The second, more determined kick, pushed him free of the rock and all the way under the water. Now he had to make his way out of the cavern before he drowned.

The cold water eased some of the pain from his burns, but the salt stung all the raw places on his skin. Even so, nothing lessened the scalding sensation in his lungs. He struggled with each breath. *Too much smoke! I have to get more air!*

He took a breath as best he could, coughed, and put his face in the water to wash away the sting and tears in his eyes. Lifting his head, he reached out for the stone wall of the inlet.

Inch by inch, foot by foot, he edged his way along the wall toward the opening to the sea. Halfway there, he found a ledge big enough for him to sit on and rest. Exhaustion nearly overwhelmed him. Although still shivering from the cold seawater, he plunged in again and gradually made his way to the entrance of the cave that opened to the sea. Here the smoke floated out, making the air fresher and a little more soothing on his lungs.

Jagged rocks lined the opening of the cave and reached upward. Reid stretched with his left hand to pull himself up and out of the inlet, only to scream in pain when his palm touched the small ledge. Gripping the stones with his right hand, he pulled his left in front of his smoke-tinged eyes. A blister of burned skin bubbled over the palm. Quickly, he thrust his hand into the icy water. The pain lessened, but he couldn't stay here without freezing to death. He had to get out of the ocean.

Using his right hand and his left elbow, he dragged himself onto the first rock and braced himself with his unburned right foot. He desperately wanted to rest, he needed to rest, but he had to get higher up, all the way to the ledge above the beach.

He closed his eyes again, and this time both Willie and Leena stood above him on the ledge. They beckoned him, giving him the courage to pull himself up, bit by bit until he reached the upper shelf. Once he swung his legs up and over the side, he lay on his stomach, drained. He didn't know if he slept or if he fell unconscious, but either way he didn't suffer the hurt that throbbed over his left side from his neck to his foot.

****

The sound of footsteps pounded on the deck above.

As the door to the cabin flung open, Shipopi raced in, his sword drawn. "Quiet," he said. "Men of MacCummings' crew. *Lion* crew captured. Too drunk to fight back. Stay quiet. Captain is betrayed."

Shipopi braced himself against the door as several men rammed into it from the outside, trying to get it open.

"Door jammed," one shouted. "Get to the hold. We can get this open after we get the cargo on shore!"

Willie and Leena hunkered down in the corner behind Shipopi as the men from MacCumming's crew ran up and down the stairs carrying the boxes from the ship's hold. All at once a roaring cheer sounded.

"They found the gold," whispered Willie.

Another hour passed until there were no more pounding footsteps, no more crates dragged up top, no more hollering voices.

Shipopi didn't move from his position at the door until the blade of an axe ripped through the wood, cutting into his shoulder. Seconds later, the next blow of the axe opened a hole large enough for three grim-faced pirates to step through the splintered wood.

"Look, prisoners," said one of them with an eye patch. Grabbing Leena's bandana, he tried to jerk her to her feet. The bandana came off in his hand, and her hair fell out across her shoulders. "Hey, mates! This one's a woman. A good-looking one."

Leena's skin crawled.

****

Very slowly, Reid opened his eyes. Everything moved in waves around him like some giant dirty thumb had smudged the world. He closed his eyes again.

A voice penetrated his fog.

"He opened his eyes," said a woman. "Has been three days. At last."

Suddenly more voices echoed in his head along with one familiar one that said, "Do ye think ye can come back to us now? Well, *a'dhuine*, will ye join the land of the living?"

"Is that ye, Taran?" croaked out Reid. He opened his eyes all the way, blinking through the fog. " 'Tis ye!" The blurry shapes around him cleared, but surging pain sped through his chin and shoulder.

"Quiet now," said a woman wearing a dark green kirtle and a faded gray apron. "I just finished changing yer dressings and tying the cloths on. Dinna tear them off. Lie still."

A wide strip of cloth bound his neck. He tried to reach for it, but the woman gently pressed his arm down. "Careful."

Barely moving his lips, Reid asked, "What happened? Where am I?"

Pulling a stool up to the bed, Taran chuckled. "Every time I meet ye, ye're lying abed. Ye're the same cumberworld ye've always been. Useless, doing naught but taking up space."

"I remember being in water." His lungs hurt with each breath.

"I found ye lying on the ledge that runs along the coast here near Peterhead. Pure luck! Ye'd probably been there for a day in the sun. Ye were a mess, worse than when I found ye in yer bed in Stirling. I wrapped ye in my horse blanket and got ye here. Mistress Cope has fixed ye up right well. She kenned the ointment for yer burns."

"Aye," said the woman with weathered features. "I mixed an egg with vinegar, rose oil, and my secret blend of herbs so yer burns winna dry out. When they crust over, I'll change the recipe, and the scars will be less noticeable."

"Yer left side is burned pretty badly," said Taran.

"What did they do to ye?"

"Tied me up in a cave and set it on fire," said Reid. "I remember Leena calling to me."

The woman and Taran exchanged a look that Reid recognized as pity, and suddenly, in one enormous gust, everything that had happened since he left Stirling came back to him. "Leena! Willie!" He tried to sit up, but Taran gently pushed him back down, and Reid hadn't the strength to protest.

"If ye stay still, I'll tell ye what I ken. Ye have burns all down yer left side. They'll eventually heal, and probably no one will much notice them, except for the ones on yer neck."

The woman added, "Ye have the Lord to thank that the fire didna reach yer pretty face. I gave ye a potion to make ye sleep through the pain. 'Tis why ye're so groggy."

"Why did ye no' go home?" slurred Reid. A rabbit on his tongue made it hard to form the words.

"It's been nearly two sennights since ye left us on the road. We got Dillon, Brother Thaddeus, and yer lads to the abbey, and two monks volunteered to take them on to Makgullane. I came back to where we'd left the cart on the road to see if we could salvage anything. Most of it was gone. All picked over. That's when I decided I'd have to find ye and my sister and bring ye home myself."

Reid found it hard to stay awake. "How did ye ken where we were?"

"I started east, and people at every place I stopped told me about a man with graying hair and a woman with gold streaks in hers heading to the sea. Ye left an impression everywhere ye went, especially at the inn where the horrified innkeeper told me a tale about a cheating husband and the wife who followed him. Only my sister could weave a story like that one. I kenned it had to be ye and Leena. As I got closer to the shore, the gossip changed to how McDever and his pirates had been stealing and ransacking all along the coast. Then I nearly stumbled over ye on the path. We've been with Mistress Cope for three days."

"We have to go after McDever," said Reid. "He took Leena and Willie aboard his ship."

"He's headed to John O'Groats," said Mistress Cope, "an outpost on the far north shore. He goes there to hide from the law and rest a bit. I hate to tell ye this, laddie, but yer woman and yer son will be sold along with whatever else he has onboard."

"Nay!" cried Reid, trying again to sit up.

"Rest easy, *a'dhuine*," said Taran, putting his hands on Reid's shoulders. "As soon as ye're stronger, we'll go after them."

"When?"

"I told ye he'd be pestering us to leave right away," Taran said to the woman. To Reid he added, "Ye have to give us at least a week so the burns on yer leg can be nearly healed. They'll be scabbed over, but no' raw like they are now. Mistress Cope's ointments work wonders. Everything is much improved in only the three days we've been here."

"I thank ye, Mistress," rasped out Reid.

"The ones on yer hand and yer ankle will take longer, but if ye keep them propped up on the pillows now, and ye drink as much water as Mistress Cope can give ye, ye can manage when we leave. She can also give ye something to ease the pain, and even if we take it slow, she says we can make it to John O'Groats in less than a week. We'll ride some of the way. That'll be the hardest on ye, but we can get a boat at Baniff and take it across the bay to Wick. Then 'tis only about sixteen miles to John O'Groats. I dinna ken what we'll find when we get there, but if ye're a good lad, we'll go after my sister and Willie as soon as we can."

"My wife," said Reid before his head rolled to the side and he fell asleep.

Chapter Twenty-Four

The MacCummings pirates dragged Leena and Willie out of the cabin and up to the deck while the two men holding Leena groped her breasts and her legs every chance they got. Once in the rowboat, they rode across the harbor to the shore in silence, and once on dry land, the pirates dragged their captives over to where the surviving members of the crew of the *Scarlet Lion* sat in the sand, their hands tied in a line to a single rope.

A second rowboat followed with Shipopi, bound, gagged, and bleeding. On shore they lashed him to a pole with his hands over his head. His shoulder dripped blood from the blow with the ax, as did other cuts and scrapes on his face and body from the beating he'd obviously endured for protecting the hostages.

The pirate with the gold tooth jerked Willie to his feet and tied him at the end of the rope with the crew. When Leena stretched out her hands to be bound, he said, "I'll take care of this one," and started pulling her away.

Willie cried out, "Nay!" and received a hard punch to his gut that knocked him to the ground. The young crew member, Thomas, lifted him back to his feet while Willie continued to shout, "Leave her alone!"

Leena had a good idea what Gold Tooth had in mind for her, and she determined to bear it and never cry or beg for mercy.

All at once, someone snatched her out of Gold Tooth's hands and pushed her into the middle of a group of women.

"She isna yers!" said one of the older women. " 'Tis the MacCummings law. No man can have a woman without her first saying 'aye,' or he is hanged."

Gold Tooth barked, "She's part of the spoils. I get my share, and I choose her."

Stepping out of the mass of men came Captain Barker MacCummings. Waving his hand for quiet, MacCummings said, "My law remains. The woman is no' yers. She stays with my daughter, Galvyn, as part of the bride price."

"Ye scoundrel, Barker MacCummings!" shouted Jonas McDever, tied hand and foot. "Ye betrayed me. I wed yer daughter and when we celebrated, ye took my men and my ship. Ye'll pay for this!"

MacCummings, a robust man with a shaved head, laughed. "We're both thieves to the core, and a thieves' law is every man for himself. I'll take ye to Edinburgh and turn ye in to be hanged, and as a reward I'll earn a pardon for myself from the king."

"What about Galvyn? As my wife, she's as guilty as I am," said McDever. "I'll say she helped me get rid of my stolen goods."

"Hah! Ye think anyone will believe ye just because ye have a fine-looking face? 'Twill no' be so fine-looking when we're done with ye. Galvyn, come here."

The tall, slender woman with her black hair tied in a loose bun on top of her head came to his side.

"Is this man yer husband?"

Glaring at McDever, she said, "I ne'er saw this

man in my life. I would ne'er wed him."

Gently pushing her back toward the women, MacCummings said, "Go back inside and tend to this woman who now belongs to ye."

"What about the lad?" called Leena as Galvyn took her by the arm and led her away.

Pinching Leena's cheeks with her fingers, Galvyn said, "Tell me true. Is the lad yer son? Or is he one of the crew? Is he yers?"

Leena nodded her head as best she could despite Galvyn's hard grip on her face, saying, "He is my son."

Locking her fingers around Leena's teardrop necklace, Galvyn tore it off her neck.

"Nay!" said Leena, reaching for the necklace. "My husband gave it to me. Give it back."

Galvyn held it out of Leena's reach. "Which do ye want, yer necklace or yer son?"

Without hesitation, Leena answered, " 'Tis yers. Give me the lad."

Galvyn motioned to the pirate in charge of the prisoners, who untied Willie and gave him a stumbling shove in the direction of the women. Wrapping her arms around him, Leena moved him with the group of women toward a stone building back from the shore.

"I thank ye," said Leena to Galvyn.

"We will see how thankful ye are after ye've been here for a while."

****

Two days later, the still celebrating and now drunken MacCummings pirates were unaware of two men crouching and watching them from behind a bluff.

"Do ye see them?" asked Reid in a low voice. "I canna find any women or bairns, only men, and some of them are tied up. 'Tis Shipopi on the stake."

"Ye told me how he tricked ye into getting captured," said Taran. "I ne'er heard of a wedding like this one either, a party with so much bloodshed. Ye stay here, and I'll go around and find out what I can."

"We should both go."

"Nay. My cap will cover my hair, and if I'm spotted, from a distance I can pass for one of the crew, but they'd remember a man with bandages on his hand and neck and ken ye were no' one of them. I'll get back here afore dark, but if I dinna make it, ye're on yer own, *a'dhuine*."

"*Beannachd leat, a'dhuine*," said Reid, knowing they needed more than luck to find Leena and Willie and get away from here alive.

"The same to ye," said Taran.

The day passed slowly for Reid. The nearly healed burns on his leg and back itched something fierce, and he struggled, failing quite often, to keep from scratching the sections of burned skin that stung when the bandages shifted over them every time he moved. Mistress Cope had begged him to stay a few days more, but for Reid, not knowing what had happened to Leena or Willie exceeded any physical pain he'd have to endure.

The day before he and Taran left, Mistress Cope had said to him, "Ye barely ken her. I understand yer need to get to yer son, but the woman?"

"Time has little to do with it. I tried to be content with only her friendship, but I couldna. Every minute with her made me feel happy for the first time in a verra long time. I tried to stop loving her, but I couldna. I told myself she would ne'er be mine, but it did no good."

The woman swept the dust from under his bed as she talked. "Some folks wed after only a short courtship, and some wed having ne'er seen the other until they get to the church, but ye've been wed afore. Ye ken what a marriage is all about. Some men want what they canna have. Were ye drawn to her because she wouldna be staying in Stirling?"

Reid shifted his weight to ease the stiffness in his back. "She could have gone back home and out of my life, leaving me with a broken heart, but after McDever threatened my sons...to save them I had to give them to her, and I kenned she'd take good care of them. McDever is evil. One look in his eyes and ye ken it."

A vision came into his mind of his three lads laughing and chasing each other until they tumbled to the grass. "I had to come after them, and as soon as I saw her again, I kenned my sons and Leena had melded together in my heart. We were family, and nothing else mattered."

" 'Tis strange to hear a man talk about feelings in his heart."

" 'Tis no' strange for a man to have feelings. Did yer man have feelings for ye afore he died?"

With a deep sigh, she said, "Aye. He spoke of them only when we were alone, but when he did, I kenned the good Lord had a hand in sending him to me. And I ne'er doubt the Lord's good hand."

Days after Reid left the warmth of the Copes' croft, he moved around the bluff surrounding the pirate village to get a better look, but he never saw even a glimpse of his wife or his son.

Lying on his back, he stared at the sky at sunset until Taran slid next to him, out of breath. "I almost got caught," he said. "They may be the worst pirates, but they are no' doitit. I managed to talk my way out of trouble, but I dinna ken how."

"Did ye learn anything that can help us?"

"I did. 'Tis the McDever crew held prisoner. Jonas wed the MacCummings daughter, and afterwards, in celebration, the father of the bride got all the men from the *Scarlet Lion* drunk, verra drunk, with his crew only pretending to keep up with them. Then around midnight, MacCummings' men rounded up the McDever pirates, boarded the *Scarlet Lion*, and stole all the cargo."

"That's one way to get out of paying."

"That's no' all. MacCummings intends to turn McDever, and any of his men who are still alive, over to the authorities in Edinburgh for hanging in order to earn a pardon for himself. The wedding was only a ruse to get McDever up here, and the priest who said the words over the happy couple was no' a priest at all."

"But where are Leena and Willie? Did McDever turn them over to MacCummings to sell as slaves or worse?" Reid struggled to control his quavering voice.

"Dinna worry, *a'dhuine*. They are both safe with the MacCummings women in that stone building. The women protect their own."

Reid's shoulders slumped in relief. " 'Tis one thing in our favor, mayhap the only thing."

"We should try to get some rest here tonight. I can tell by yer face that yer burns are hurting ye."

"They're better, and 'tis naught I canna bear. 'Twill be better when I hold Leena and Willie again. We have to try and find out exactly where they are."

Reaching into his pouch, Taran said, "I stole some

meat off the spit at the bonfire. 'Tis a little burnt but will still put something in yer belly. Here. We can go looking after ye eat."

Taking a bite, Reid mumbled while chewing, "Why is Shipopi hanging from the post instead of tied up with the others on the ground?"

"The talk is that he tried to protect Leena and Willie from the MacCummings men when they came aboard the *Scarlet Lion*. Hid them in a cabin and blocked the door. The pirates broke through with an axe, but Shipopi still tried to stop them. Cut one of them pretty bad. Now they're taking turns hitting him with whatever they can get their hands on. He may no' survive the night."

Reid caught a glimpse of Shipopi hanging from the pole, his eyes swollen shut.

Chapter Twenty-Five

Despite their confinement in the women's house, Leena and Willie were thankful not to be outside and tied with the men. At least they were out of the rain and had food to eat, even if it was only leftovers. Galvyn and the other women were harsh taskmasters, and the captives worked from dawn to late at night, scrubbing floors and emptying smelly, waste-filled chamber pots so the women didn't have to go outside and use a cluster of bushes cordoned off as a makeshift privy area. They washed bedding and clothing in pots of boiling water and hauled the wet laundry up to the fourth floor attic where they hung it to dry. They also carried in firewood and kept the fires burning day and night.

The first night Willie spilled a few drops of stew as he filled the bowls for the evening meal, and a woman beat him with a wooden spoon until Galvyn grabbed the woman's hand to stop her. "These two were stolen from their homes and have already suffered at the hands of the ones who stole them. They were given to me, and I will be the only one who decides if they are to be punished."

"Thank ye," said Leena to Galvyn as she lifted Willie from his knees.

"Ye will work, and we will feed ye, but do not expect us to be yer friends. Now clean up the stew and serve the others. Lad, ye will get only a half portion tonight."

"Aye, mistress," said Willie, reaching for a rag.

The women came to accept the prisoners in their midst, but they were prisoners just the same. When they found a few moments alone, they talked of how to escape, but they might have to wait until summer for less harsh weather.

****

Unknown to them, Reid caught his first glimpse of Leena and Willie in the moonlight from the bluff. "Look!" he said as he pointed toward the women's house. "There they are. They're alive."

Willie and Leena each carried a heavy chamber pot, sloshing with waste, toward a cluster of bushes. After dumping the contents and covering it over with loose dirt, they returned to the house.

"I have to go to them," said Reid, standing up.

Quickly, Taran latched onto his arm and pulled him down. "Ye canna run in there like a pig to the trough." He looked skyward. " 'Tis clouding up. When they hide the moon, we'll go down and find out exactly where they're being kept. Then we can make a plan to rescue them, but *a'dhuine*, we have to have a plan."

Reid sat back down on the sand of the bluff. "Why are ye always right?"

"Runs in the family."

A thick layer of clouds drifted over the moon before Taran and Reid made their way to the women's house. The only light came from the fading glow of the fireplace, but Reid mouthed, "I see them," as he pointed through the wavy glass pane of the window at Leena and Willie sleeping on a pile of blankets beside the hearth. He raised his hand to knock and get their attention when Taran pulled his arm down again.

"Tomorrow, *a'dhuine*, when we have a plan."

Reid nodded, and the two men crept back to their hiding place on the bluff.

****

Leena stirred with a dream of Reid lying next to her, holding her. She awoke with a jerk and started to lean in to kiss him, only to discover that Willie had flung his arm over her. Flopping back on the blankets, she nearly cried. *I could feel him, and I could smell him, the scent that is his alone.* With a sigh she tried to recreate that wonderful dream, but she could not.

****

They came up with a variety of plans, rejecting them all until they decided they'd do whatever they could to create chaos on the shore in the morning. It would cover whatever they did to free the ones they had come here for. Through the night they worked tirelessly, giving themselves their best chance to rescue Leena and Willie.

At dawn, Reid took two guns out of his pack, along with two horns of powder and two pouches of ammunition, handing one of each to Taran. "Reloading will be slow with both of these, but 'twill be the same for the pirates. The only gun we have to worry about is the one MacCummings holds."

"Do ye have yer two knives in yer belt?" asked Taran as he poured the powder and rammed the ball into the barrel of his weapon. "Are ye no' afraid to get bloody when ye stick a knife into someone?"

Turning a cold eye toward his brother-in-law, Reid said, "I've suffered at the hands of the Devil on Earth, and I've got the scars to prove it. I am no' afraid of anything, except that Leena and Willie will be hurt. I will do whate'er it takes for their sake."

"We dinna have much of a plan, but whate'er happens, we will find them and get back to the boat dock in Wick. We sheltered our horses two miles from here. Get to them and ride to Wick. We willna wait for each other. We take the next boat across the water and head for home. We can meet at Mistress Cope's. Agreed?"

Reid shoved the gun into his belt and wrapped his cloak over it. "Taran, I am no' verra good at…finding the words…but ye have been… I…I—"

"I ken," interrupted Taran. "Ye have vexed me since the moment I met ye. Ye have brought me naught but trouble, and the same to my sister, and I may ne'er forgive ye for that, but…I'd do it again. Ye're worth it."

Reid lowered his eyes.

"I ken Leena loves ye. I dinna understand it, but then I've ne'er been able to understand most of the things she does."

Reid raised his head.

"Bring her home," Taran said solemnly.

Reaching out his hand, Reid clasped Taran's shoulder. "With ye and the Lord on my side, I will do that."

Taran patted Reid's arm.

"But Taran, ye should ken that if I have to sacrifice ye to save her and my son, *a'dhuine*, I will."

"And I will do the same to ye, *a'dhuine*," said Taran.

****

That morning, the sun shone bright, but it struggled to warm the air. A blustery wind blew into the shore from the sea, and everyone at John O'Groats bundled up in heavy cloaks, hoods, and caps, everyone except the crew from the *Scarlet Lion*, who sat shivering on the ground.

At first light, Captain Barker MacCummings ordered his men to rouse and take all their prisoners onto the *Scarlet Lion* for delivery to Edinburgh to be hanged. What began as a semi-orderly transfer of prisoners soon degenerated into pandemonium because of two strangers who had crept into the crowd during the night.

One by one, the strangers cut through the crew's ropes around their wrists while ordering them to pretend to stay tied. Then everyone waited patiently until daylight to make their escape. The guards, assured their captives were secure, ignored the quiet stirring among them.

At the first sign of moving the prisoners, they attacked the two nearest guards, beat them to the ground, stole their weapons, and took off running toward the bluff. The others soon followed.

"After them!" shouted MacCummings as his hopes of earning his own pardon disappeared in the mist.

After the first round of gunfire from the MacCummings' pistols, and with no time to reload, the McDever crew attacked, and victory would soon be theirs. Throats were slashed, bellies split open, and heads bashed in.

As soon as the noise from the fighting reached the house, the women quickly prepared to defend their home. Galvyn MacCummings thrust sharp kitchen knives into the hands of both Leena and Willie. "Ye are entitled to defend yerselves against any of yer enemies, no matter who they be."

"Even a MacCummings man?" asked Leena.

"Any man. No matter who wins this, ye and the lad will suffer for it, and 'tis a woman's duty to protect herself and those who belong to her above all else. Get over there by the window and watch who comes."

Taran shouted over the din as he and Reid raced toward the women's house, " 'Tis now or ne'er for my sister and yer lad. Both sides are our enemies."

"Then now it is," answered Reid. "Pull yer cap down over yer head, and I'll use my hood to cover as much of my face as I can." The pirates, too busy fighting for their lives, ignored them.

The only ones who recognized the strangers running toward them were a dark-haired woman with yellow streaks in her hair and a nearly grown boy watching out a window of the women's quarters.

Leena saw them first. Both men had their faces nearly covered, but the tall, lanky one loped toward the house just like her brother might, and long strands of blond hair flew out from under his wool cap.

But it couldna be. No one kens we're here.

The other one in the heavy cloak also looked familiar, but as he came closer and the wind blew his cloak off his head, his eyes glittered in the early sunlight.

He's dead! A ghost! She'd seen the horrid flames and the black smoke. Her breath came raw in her throat, and her knees shook so much she nearly fell to the floor.

"Do ye see him?" she said, grabbing Willie for

support. "Is it…?"

"Who?" said Willie.

She pointed out the window with her finger. "There."

Willie squinted and rubbed the wavy glass windowpane with his sleeve. "I canna see who it is."

Out in the yard, the tide of the fighting turned in McDever's favor. With knives and pistols stolen from fallen men, the crew of the *Scarlet Lion* fought for their lives. Soon most of the MacCummings men were either dead or severely wounded, and many others lay very still hoping to be thought dead or wounded.

"To the house!" shouted someone. "Women!"

The McDever men rushed the house, hoping to enjoy the spoils of war with defenseless women, only to discover that the MacCummings women, often left alone for long periods of time while their men were at sea, had found ways to protect themselves. Galvyn, learning the techniques of warfare at her father's side, proved a strong and capable leader and teacher.

The first wave of McDever men knocked down the wide double doors and pushed their way inside, only to be shot by six women standing in a row. While these women stepped aside to reload, another line of women threw daggers at any of the attackers foolish enough to keep coming. One by one the men fell. The others, unaware of the fate of their comrades, kept moving into the house until a third row of women armed with daggers left only ten of McDever's men standing and able to fight. They retreated. By this time, the women had reloaded their guns and were ready for the next wave, should any man be foolish enough to attack again.

In the noisy confusion, Leena grabbed a wooden bowl from the table and flung it at the window, breaking several panes and scattering the shards on the ground. "Reid, Taran, this way. 'Tis a trap!"

The MacCummings women, too busy defending themselves, ignored Leena's screams.

"This way! This way!" Willie, having finally recognized his father, kicked out the rest of the window, leaned out, and shouted, "Da! Da! This way!" Using his knife, he scraped away the shards of glass from the frame and put his foot on the sill to step out.

Reid, hearing them first, grabbed Taran by the sleeve and pulled him toward the shouts coming from the window. As they reached the side of the house, Willie leaped out and ran into his father's arms, nearly knocking him to the ground as Taran lifted his sister through the opening.

Meanwhile, inside the house, Galvyn saw her prisoners escaping. Confident the rest of her women could stop the attacking McDever men, she turned her gun at the strangers outside the window who held the lad and the woman in their arms.

"Nay, Galvyn! Stop!" cried Leena, standing in front of her men with her hands out. "Stop! They're here to help!"

"Da! Da!" called Willie. "Dinna shoot him!"

The last wave of McDever men fell or ran off as Galvyn crossed to the window. "Who are you?" she demanded.

"Reid Haliburton. Taran Cullane. We came for my wife and my son."

"Do you know them?" Galvyn asked her prisoners in a rough voice.

"Da!' said Willie as he clung to Reid's waist. "I kenned ye would come!"

"Aye! Aye!" said Leena. Unable to stay standing on her trembling legs, she sank to her knees.

"Are ye alive?"Taran boosted his sister to her feet. "No time for that now. We're taking ye home." Passing Leena off to Reid, Taran took Willie beside him, saying to Galvyn, "McDever and the rest of his men are heading for their ship. They'll be gone soon, and ye'll be safe. Ye better help yer own wounded. We intend no harm. We just want to get away."

"Galvyn," said Leena as she stepped across the shattered glass on the ground to face the woman. "Ye have been naught but kind. We thank ye, and we will ne'er forget what ye did for us."

Galvyn grunted and shrugged. "Be off. We have work to do for our own men."

Leena took a step back toward Reid just as Galvyn reached out the window and grabbed her by the hair. "Wait." Taking the necklace with the mahogany teardrop off her own neck, she handed it to Leena. The two women exchanged knowing looks before Leena ran toward the bluff hand in hand with Reid. Taran and Willie followed.

Taran checked behind them to make certain no one followed while Reid led Leena and Willie toward the bluff.

"How?" gasped Leena. "I ne'er thought I'd see ye again."

"Neither did I," said Reid. "This way. After we're out of sight, we have about two miles to our horses. Dinna stop. We winna be safe until we reach the boat at Wick."

"How did ye escape?"

Reid held up his left hand with the bandages nearly torn off, and Leena gasped. "How did it happen?"

" 'Tis of no matter now. I'll tell ye all later. Keep moving. We have to get away from here."

"No one is following us," said Taran after he caught up. "They all got on the ship and are readying it to sail."

Reid made his own quick glance back. "The post is empty. They took Shipopi with them."

The four reached the top of the bluff and slid down the sandy slope out of sight of the beach, first Leena and Reid, followed by Willie, with Taran at the last.

"This way," said Reid. "The horses are about two miles away."

"Two miles too far," said a voice from behind them.

Turning, they saw Jonas McDever with Reid's gun pressed against Willie's head. A battered and bruised Shipopi stood beside his captain, his sword drawn as he held it out toward Taran.

The next instant became a blur as Taran raised his own gun and shot at Shipopi, wounding the Moor in the shoulder. Despite this injury, Shipopi whirled around and the tip of his sword sliced the skin open on Taran's chest. Taran faltered as Shipopi pushed him to the ground, pressing his foot and his blade at Taran's throat.

In the confusion, Willie jerked his elbow into McDever's stomach, causing the man to stumble, and in doing so the gun flew out of his hand and slid down the hill toward Leena, who picked it up. McDever grabbed a startled Willie and held the boy around the neck, nearly choking him. Drawing a dagger out of his sleeve, he pressed it into Willie's throat.

McDever, flashing a superior grin, spoke in a cruel voice. "The Moor and I have this boy and your friend while you have the gun. You want these two alive, and I want the gun. Who will surrender first?"

Chapter Twenty-Six

McDever jabbed the edge of his knife against Willie's throat so when the boy swallowed, the blade scraped his skin, leaving a bloody trail.

"What will it be, lass?" jeered McDever. "Are you sure enough of your aim to hit me instead of the boy?" He jerked Willie up and off his feet. "Shipopi tells me you're a good shot, but are you good enough?"

Leena held her aim steady.

"The gun is yers," said Reid. "Take it and get on yer ship with what's left of yer crew and leave us here. The tide is going out, and ye dinna have much time to sail away. All we want is for ye to leave us here...alive."

"*Alive* is not a word I'm fond of when it comes to you, gunsmith. My biggest mistake was not killing all of you when I had the chance. I tried to be rid of you again, but if a fire couldn't stop you, I will do it now. You defied me, and your son has been naught but a thorn in my side." He shook Willie and dropped him to the ground before yanking him up by his hair again.

Spittle dripped from the side of his mouth. "If you think I'll leave any of you here alive, you're wrong!"

"Then what do we have to gain by doing what ye want?"

"In exchange for the gun, I'll make your deaths as quick and painless as possible. I won't take the woman to the ship, strip her naked, and give her to the crew. And I won't make you watch while I do it. I'll have Shipopi slit your throats, quick and easy. That is the best bargain you can hope for."

Reid took a step toward him, his fists clenched. At the same time, McDever drew the tip of his knife along Willie's cheek, opening a jagged cut as Willie squirmed. "Defy me again, and he will die in pieces, slowly bit by bit."

Reid stood still. "Let Taran take Leena and Willie away from here. How many times do I have to swear I winna fight ye? I'll surrender completely. Let them go, and Shipopi can take me in their place." Reid fell to his knees and put his hands up.

Laughing again, the pirate said, "No greater love hath a man than this, that he lay down his life for a friend. John 15, verse 13." At Reid's incredulous look, he said, "Did you think I never had a proper upbringing? Aye, I was taught the Bible, but it is so much rubbish. A man hath no greater love than for himself."

Turning his attention to Leena, McDever said, "Your arm is starting to shake, Mistress Adair. How long can you hold it? Think about how long I can hold on to this boy before my arms grow weary, and I will still have the strength to slice his neck one last time. A shame to end such a short life."

"I'm no' afraid," said Willie in short bursts as McDever tightened his arm around him.

A crooked smile spread over McDever's handsome face. "Are you willing to take a chance? His life for a gun? Will that be a fair trade? Will your aim be true, or will you murder the boy you call your son?"

Leena shot a pleading look at Reid.

Reid dropped his arms. "Leena, whate'er ye decide, 'twill be the right choice. Either take yer aim or surrender the gun to him. I trust ye with my…our son's life. Either way…McDever can take our lives, but naught else. Aye, Willie?"

"Aye. I trust ye, Leena. Take yer aim," said Willie.

"If we all die today," said Reid, " 'twill be together, kenning we loved each other and were loved in return. It doesna matter about the pirate or the gun, only us." He stood and stepped toward Leena. "Only us."

Taran, still on the ground, reached out his arm toward his sister. "I stand with ye and Reid. We are family and…" Before he could finish, Shipopi kicked him in the jaw, knocking him senseless.

She held her arm out toward McDever for a minute more before, with a heavy sigh, she slowly lowered it and rested the gun against her leg. "I'm sorry, Reid. I canna do it. I canna risk Willie's life with my shot. The beast has won."

McDever ordered, "Shipopi, take the weapon from her…and kill her quickly."

The Moor gripped his sword and in slow, measured strides moved in a wide arc from beside his captain over to Leena and Reid who kept their eyes fixed on his every step.

"Nay, Shipopi," said Leena. "If ye have any self-respect left in ye, ye will no' do this. We trusted ye once at the castle ruins. Show us we can trust ye again."

Reid stepped away from Leena and toward Shipopi. "Ye will need to kill me first." Shipopi stopped moving forward as Reid said, "Dinna be a man like yer captain. Be a man of honor."

Shipopi growled, and crouching down, scooped up a handful of sand and threw it in Reid's face. As Reid staggered back, blinded, Shipopi charged at Leena.

She covered her head with her arms.

"Nay!" cried Reid.

In one quick motion, Shipopi grabbed Leena by her arm, wrenched the gun from her grip, and batted her to the ground with the hilt of his sword.

Raising the gun toward the sky, he gave a shout of victory…before he aimed and fired in the direction of his captain.

A deafening explosion sounded as smoke from the pistol filled the air.

Willie's voice echoed, "Da! Da!"

Reid, his sight still obscured by the sand, crawled over to Willie, the lad's whole body racked with sobs. Reid lifted him into his arms, and still holding his son tightly to his chest, called out, "Leena! Leena! Are ye all right?"

No reply.

As the smoke cleared and tears washed the sand out of his eyes, he saw Leena lying face down, not moving, with Shipopi standing over her, his sword and the gun dangling from his hands. "Nay, Shipopi, let her go."

Willie pushed himself away from his father and crawled over to Leena. "Please, nay, Leena, please, wake up!" Lifting her head, he cradled it on his lap. "Please, Leena!"

Shipopi stood motionless until his knees buckled out from under him, and he collapsed in the sand.

Following his son over to Leena, Reid gently

rubbed her back, all the while praying that his weapon had not caused the death of the woman he and his son loved so desperately.

Suddenly she coughed and stretched up. Opening her eyes, she shook her head and looked at both of them beside her.

"Are ye all right?" asked Reid.

"I thought he killed ye," said Willie.

Helping Leena into a sitting position, Reid repeated, "Are ye all right?"

Falling into him, she smiled, and he kissed her. "Ye're alive! Willie, look, she's alive. Stop crying, lad, she's all right."

Willie slowed his tears and threw his arms around both Leena and his father.

After a lingering moment, Reid crawled over to the Moor sprawled on the sand and put his ear on Shipopi's chest, listening, but he could barely make out a slow, faint heartbeat. Carefully, Reid ran his hands over Shipopi's chest and neck where deep bruises and cuts covered him. Taran's gunshot had left a bleeding gash on his upper arm, but as Reid's hand pressed into the Moor's belly, Shipopi cried out.

"His belly is distended. He has internal injuries, bad ones, from the beating he took from the other men."

Shipopi opened his eyes and, in a gasping breath, said, "Shipopi have honor." His breathing slowed.

"Aye, Shipopi has honor," said Reid. "Yer village is proud of ye, proud of such a man."

The big man took in one more shallow breath. His last.

Reid, Leena, Willie, and Taran, whose bleeding from the cut on his chest had slowed, sat with Shipopi for a long time before Reid said, "We have to get Taran bandaged up. Then we'll bury Shipopi. 'Tis time to go home."

McDever lay in a heap on the back side of the bluff with the top of his head nearly blown off.

Chapter Twenty-Seven

On the road in the southern Highlands

Reid and Leena stood at the edge of the cliff overlooking the valley and the lake where two monks had died, a picturesque view despite their deaths. He held her tightly against him as the wind buffeted around them.

"We're almost home," said Leena. "I'm glad we sent Taran and Willie on ahead. We can rest at the abbey before heading to Makgullane. Yer body's been through a lot these past weeks, and we can stay there as long as we like. Give ye all the time ye need to heal."

"I winna lie to ye. I ache all over, some places worse than others, but if ye're beside me, ye're all the comfort I need. Ye're what matters, ye and my lads, my family."

"Do ye think we'll make a good family?"

" 'Twill take time to adjust to each other, but the lads love ye, and ye them, and ye ken how much I love ye, so all will be well soon enough. The worst is behind us. Only the best is ahead." He kissed the top of her head. "All I need is to make love to ye every night, which I intend to do in the first soft bed we find."

He wanted to prove his love physically, even though he'd begged off making love since escaping from the pirates nearly a month ago. He told her that he needed more time to recover from his injuries, and Leena had agreed, lying quietly beside him every night, pretending to be unaware of how his body reacted to her nearness and of his need to claim her.

But every time, the idea of standing before her naked made him cringe from revealing his terrible burns and scars, at how the fingers of rough tissue crawled over his skin. He had no doubt she would ignore, or pretend to ignore for his sake, the hideous appearance of his entire left side and his back, but could he ignore it? She deserved better than the gruesome man he had become. Clothes hid his scars from other people, but alone and naked, Leena would know the awful truth.

McDever had taken a lot from him, physically and emotionally, but by not loving Leena as she deserved, could he let that evil man take even more?

Reaching over, she took his burned left hand in hers and massaged it, just as she had every night on the road. It helped him sleep.

Clearing his throat, he said, "There is something I want to tell ye. A decision I've made."

"Aye?"

He looked out over the loch as he spoke. "I willna be a gunsmith anymore. No' ever again will I make a weapon."

"Reid, are ye certain? Ye worked hard to become an expert at yer craft, and ye have a fine reputation, one of the finest in Scotland."

"I dinna care about any of that. Making that gun almost cost me ye and the lads. If ye had died…if McDever had… I… The gun began it all, and I winna ever do it again. I'll no' risk ye. Ne'er! Do ye understand? Say ye understand."

Hugging him even closer, she said, "I understand. My life begins and ends with ye, no' the gun. Ye hold all my dreams, and all I want is ye, so whate'er ye decide is my decision as well."

Picking up his pack from the ground, Reid opened it and withdrew the gun and the rifling tool. Gripping the rifling tool, he moved away from Leena, took a step back, and threw it fast and hard into the glen. It flew through the air and dropped into the lake, sinking immediately.

"I canna stop progress. Someday someone will invent a tool like that, but it winna be me."

He settled the gun in his hand. "I ken that sometime, somewhere, someone will put together a weapon even more effective than this one, but I will no' be responsible for that, no' after what has happened. After this gun is gone, I can focus my attention on my family, their happiness, and their safety. I dinna ken what I will do next, but it will no' be making weapons."

Again he took a step back, cocked his arm, and heaved the gun even farther than he had the rifling tool. The gun floated in the air until it fell into the middle of the lake. It sank, leaving only vanishing circles in the water.

Taking her in his arms, he murmured, "Ye're all I want."

She stretched up to meet his lips, and he wanted to swallow her into himself. His hands roamed over her back and tugged her bottom, nearly lifting her off the ground. He wanted her desperately. His mouth and tongue took hers over and over as he fell to his knees, taking her with him. Reaching under her kirtle, he caressed the smooth skin of her leg and slid his hand up to her bottom. His kiss moved to her neck, and she moaned. That sweet sound he'd heard before, the sound that drove all his senses to a peak.

Her hands roamed up and down his back until she tugged his sark out of his trews with one hand and touched his scarred back with the other.

His whole body stiffened. He could ignore the cold wind that blew over them across the valley, but he could not ignore the cold wind inside himself when she touched those ugly reminders of the fire in the cave. He pulled away and stood up, helping her to her feet with his right hand.

"It will be dark afore we get to the abbey if we dinna leave now," he said, leading her toward the horses.

She didn't answer.

****

The small room in the abbey did indeed have a soft bed and a warm fire.

She shifted under the quilts, her clothes draped over a chair while Reid stood at the foot of the bed, still dressed in his sark and trews. Patting the side of the bed next to her, she purred, "I want ye near me."

He hesitated, biting his lower lip.

"I want to see ye, all of ye."

Again he hesitated. " 'Tis no' a pretty sight."

"I've touched the scars under yer clothes."

"Seeing them is worse."

"I am no' a weak woman."

He didn't answer.

"I want to make love with the man I love, but if ye only want to lie beside me and keep me warm, I will be glad for that, too."

She waited as he paced along the side of the bed until, after a slow, deep sigh, he stripped off his sark that exposed the scars on his neck and on his back near his waist.

"Turn around," she said.

After another sigh, he did, exposing ripples of scar tissue covering the lower half of his back. "The ones on my leg are worse." He raked his hand through his hair. "I ken I shouldna be, but I am ashamed. They're a sign I couldna save ye from danger, and they are no' part of who I want to be."

Her heart ached at how he suffered still. "But ye did save me. Ye came for me, and ye endured those burns for me. I cry whenever I think of how it happened. If I could, I'd share those burns with ye. If ye could give them to me, I'd take them. But all I can do is love ye and make love with ye to prove it."

He gazed at her face for a minute before he slowly untied his trews and dropped them to the floor. Quickly climbing beside her in the bed, he tugged the quilts over him.

"Nay," she said, pulling them back. Coming up to her knees, she lightly passed her fingers over the nearly healed scars on his neck. "I've seen these, and they will fade away until I am the only one who kens they are there."

Her fingers moved gently along the burns on his leg. Even though most had closed, a few of the deeper ones still seeped, and she dabbed the edge of the quilt against them. "Does that hurt?"

"Nay." He kept his eyes on the ceiling.

Stroking her hands down his leg, she reached his

burned left foot. As soon as they got home, he would have new boots made to ease the rubbing of the leather against the scars, but right now he made do with a sliced open boot tied on with a rope around his ankle.

" 'Tis ugly," he said. "Ye dinna have to look at it."

"I want to look at it. 'Tis part of ye now, and there is no' single part of ye I dinna love. I am so sorry it gives ye pain, but it will ne'er change my heart."

She leaned over him and kissed him as he lifted his arms around her neck and pulled her on top of him. Covering him with her warm body, she kept kissing him as he stroked her from her neck to her bottom, using the fingers on his right hand.

"Use the left one," she said. "I want to ken how it feels against me."

"I canna feel much with the scars on the fingertips and palm."

"But I can."

His left hand with its bumpy scars massaged her body, bringing her new sensations. He touched her in a deeper, heavier, rougher way, and she wanted more of it. She sat up, and gripping his burned hand, she moved it between her legs. "Touch me lower. Touch me here."

And he did. She moaned and pressed her body into his hand. Reaching behind her, she grasped his erection, and he took in a long deep breath. Bending down again, she pressed her body into his hand and moved against it while she kissed the scars on his neck. With the soft touch of her fingers, she closed his eyes while her mouth and tongue caressed every scar down the side of his body.

"I can feel the wetness and the pressure even on the burned spots," he said.

"I will do whatever gives ye pleasure." And she continued the luxurious journey over his entire body.

"Leena, ye are a woman like no other," he muttered when her lips reached his straight and stiff length. As her mouth encircled him, he sighed with pleasure until she lifted up on her knees on either side of him and took all of him inside her.

"I give ye my whole heart," he said as they both moved in unison.

"And I will ne'er let ye have it back."

They made love all night long and slept through the day until the next night when they loved each other again.

Chapter Twenty-Eight

One month later, family and guests crowded into the manor house at Makgullane for the wedding of Reid and Leena. Although they had already handfasted, the couple wanted an official ceremony for the benefit of all the people on the estate who cared about Leena and wanted to get to know Reid. Leena's father, Robin, declared it "any excuse for a party!"

The guests nibbled on tasty tidbits prepared by Marta and drank from Robin's collection of whiskey and wine as they gathered inside the hall and waited for Colin McDunn to begin the ceremony with his bagpipes. Among the guests were Brother Thaddeus, still using a cane and looking rather wan and pale, but smiling as bright as the shiny cross around his neck. Father John had journeyed with him and now stood at the altar ready to marry the two who had saved Thaddeus's life.

Colin first played a merry tune designed to scare away evil spirits and protect the bride and groom as they entered into this marriage. However, if the couple neglected to toast the piper or pay him with a dram of whiskey and gold coins after the ceremony, any protection his music offered became invalidated, dooming the marriage.

Since Reid said he could not afford any more bad luck, he double-checked before the ceremony for the piper's whiskey and that he'd tucked a generous payment for Colin under his plate. Unbeknownst to him, Leena did the same!

The first of the wedding party to enter the gathering room were Willie, Ramy, and Hendrie, all dressed for the first time in breacans in the Cullane plaid with linen sarks. Willie led the way, stood next to the priest at the head of the room, and directed his brothers into their proper places beside him. The scar on his cheek had faded, but he wore it proudly as his testimony that he had escaped the pirates.

Escorting the groom, a custom to ensure he showed up, were Leena's brothers, all six of them, Hugh, Fergus, Bran, Dillon, Taran, and Quinn. They, too, were in their finest Highland dress.

As the men stood at the front by the altar in a line according to height, Reid reached over to touch Taran and Dillon on the shoulder one at a time, saying each man's name correctly. He held out his hand palm up. "Yer dirk, *a'dhuine*."

He didn't tell them that Leena had pointed out Taran's small mole in the middle of his eyebrow, something Dillon didn't have. It took careful study to find the pale mole under the thick hair of his eyebrow, but Reid would do whatever he had to in order to get Taran to pay up.

Taran laughed and clapped Reid on the shoulder. "Aye! I'll pay what I owe ye. The dirk is yers, and I'll ne'er call ye *a'dhuine* again. From now on 'tis *a'bhràthair*."

Reid pulled a face.

"Gaelic for 'brother,' " said Dillon.

"I'll settle for *a'bhràthair*, and ye can keep yer

dirk," Reid said, giving Taran a light shove.

"Now get back where ye belong to wed our sister," said Dillon, stepping between them. "Both of ye."

The last two members of the wedding party, Leena's mother, Suannoch, and her younger sister, Meara, came down the aisle wearing deep green gowns with sashes of the Cullane tartan draped over their shoulders and around their waists. They acknowledged the oohs and aahs of the guests with smiles and nods of their heads.

As soon as Leena, escorted by Robin, appeared at the hallway door, Colin changed the tune on his pipes.

"Look!" shouted Hendrie, running toward her. "There she is!" Reid stepped out to stop him, but Hendrie dashed down the aisle and stood in front of Leena, taking a deep bow. "Ye look most beautiful!" he said. After some of the guests laughed, he said indignantly, "She does!"

Her lacy, light blue gown sparkled with embroidered flowers and leaves from her waist to her hem. The same needlework highlighted her wide sleeves and her square neckline. Around her narrow waist, she wore a finely knitted tie in the same reds and greens as the embroidery, and as a tribute to the family she loved, she carried a handkerchief in Makgullane plaid tucked into her waistband.

Deciding against a veil, she had braided her hair across the top of her head in a way that highlighted the blond streaks. Clipping the braid back, she pulled strands of hair out of it to frame her face and wove flowers that complemented the trimmings on her dress into her long tresses down her back.

She caressed Hendrie's cheek. "I thank ye. Now

back to yer spot in the front."

As she looked up, the other people in the room vanished. She only saw Reid watching her with his exquisite sapphire eyes. He had gained back some of the weight he'd lost, and the color in his cheeks had returned, but nothing compared to those eyes. He wore his hair, now more white than gray, long and loose, covering the scars on his neck. Keeping his injured left hand behind his back, he made a deep, sweeping bow and held out his right hand for her to take.

He held her hand through the whole ceremony, of which neither of them heard very much, so enamored were they with each other. To the titters of the guests, Father John had to nudge each one every time their turn came to say their vows, but right before he pronounced them man and wife, Reid interrupted. "I have something more to say."

"Of course," said the priest.

Reid began, gazing at his bride. "For a long time, I couldna say the words I wanted ye to hear, but I have them now. I mean, I have some of them." He cleared his throat. "I want ye to ken, Kathleen Cullane Adair Haliburton, that I honor each of those names because they are yers. Ye belong to yerself, just as I belong to myself. Ye are no' mine to own, but I will pledge that yer name will be the last I say each night, and the first I speak in the morn. I take ye into my care, and the first of all I have is yers. I pledge ye my living, and my dying, for as long as ye'll have it. Ye have my heart, my life, and all my dreams." A tear fell out of the corner of his eye. "Love ne'er dies. People do, but ne'er love, and ye have my love in this life and the next."

"Us, too!" piped up Hendrie, with Willie and Ramy

joining in. "We pledge the same!"

"Da told us what he wanted to say," said Willie, "and we decided we wanted to promise the same." After a pause, he said very loudly, "Meena."

Ramy added, " 'Tis Mum and Leena together. Is that all right with ye?"

" 'Tis perfect," answered Leena.

Without letting go of Reid's hand, she smoothed her other palm over each lad's face, saying, "My son."

Stepping back to face Reid, she threw both arms around his neck, kissing and kissing him as he lifted her off her feet and twirled her around, their lips never parting.

Applause filled the room.

Peering around the kissing couple, Father John shouted, "I now pronounce ye husband and wife."

Immediately, Colin's bagpipes started up as Dillon and Taran tugged the wedded couple apart, pushed them into the dining room, and sat them down at the head of the long table.

"Where's the quaich?" called Taran.

Ramy, taking the two-handled cup off the altar, handed it to his uncle. Pouring the dram of whiskey into it, Taran held it out to Reid and Leena, saying, "Drink!" After the bride and groom each had a swallow, he handed the quaich to Colin as his "payment" while Reid slid the coins under his plate into the piper's hand. He grinned as Leena did the same with the coins under her own plate.

The celebration began and lasted well into the night.

****

In the wee hours of the morning, Reid and Leena

lay in each other's arms deep in the soft bed in the master bedroom that Robin and Suannoch had given them for the night.

"Do ye think we'll be this happy for always?" asked Leena, nuzzling his shoulder.

"Nay."

She sat up straight. "What? Ye dinna think we'll be happy?"

"Nay, no' every day," said Reid. "There will be days when ye will vex me until I want to tear out my hair."

She smacked him on the chest. "Me vex ye?"

"Ouch, but even if I am as bald as a stone in the yard, I will ne'er regret a day I had with ye. Ye can have all my hair, and I will try to grow more because I love ye as much as the flowers love the sun." He pushed her onto her back. "Do ye hear me, wife? As much as the flowers love the sun." Leaning in, he kissed her soundly.

She finally let his lips leave hers, and she whispered, "I'll stitch ye a hat to cover yer bald head. I'll stitch ye as many hats as ye need since I'll enjoy vexing ye as many times as there is heather on the hills." Sliding her hand across his chest, she said, "The sun is coming up. Everyone will be waiting for us."

"Let them wait. I promised that yer name would be the first thing I say every morn. Leena!" He rolled over on top of her and entered her warm and ready core.

"Leena! Leena!" he shouted with each thrust, and as he came inside her, she cried out, "Reid!"

Chapter Twenty-Nine

Fifteen years later, 1601

Leaving the carriage on the road, Leena walked unhurriedly down the slope into the Makgullane yard with her four Haliburton men behind her. She and Reid had come back alone for Suannoch's funeral. Then she had brought the whole family for the funeral of her father, Robin, and today they had all made the long journey from Edinburgh to Makgullane for yet another funeral, that of her oldest brother, Hugh.

Each time she came, the yard and the surrounding buildings looked so much the same, and yet so different. Nothing had fallen into disrepair, but it had a weather-worn look to it, maybe more like a well-loved look.

"Meena, where is everyone?" asked Hendrie, a slim, light-haired man of twenty-one years who worked with his brothers in the shipbuilding trade in Edinburgh. Hendrie labored as a skilled carpenter, Ramy as the lead supervisor and foreman over all the builds, and Willie as the ship designer and shipwright. The WRH ships were in great demand and offered all three Haliburtons a comfortable income.

The lads never said as much, but Leena always believed they chose to build ships because of their encounters with Jonas McDever and his crew. Mayhap in some way to assuage their fears, and in other ways to make amends for the pirates' cruel deeds.

Reid had the same reason for giving up gunsmithing and now working within the Scottish legal system. Generally, the king chose lawyers, justices, and other officials from the nobles and landowners, but Reid's powerful arguments for strengthening maritime laws and practices led to his appointment to the Royal College of Justice where he now taught and lectured.

Leena answered Hendrie, " 'Tis the middle of the afternoon. Most likely they are all out and about doing chores. They'll make their way back in time for the evening meal. The funeral is tomorrow, and there'll be no work that day."

Reid stepped beside her. "A lot of memories here," he said. His scarred left hand fell loosely across her shoulder, and she reached up to hold it.

"Aye, and all of them will always be a part of who I am along with all of ye. Since no one is about, would ye go with me to the family cemetery? I want to pay my respects afore they lay Hugh in the ground. His stone has stood over an empty grave beside the graves of my parents, Suannoch and Robin, for all these years. Authorities reported him dead, but until last month no one had identified his body. 'Twill be a relief to finally set him in his place."

"What happened to him?" asked Ramy.

"Yer Uncle Hugh cared verra strongly for Queen Mary of Scotland. He near lost his life protecting her when she was a small child, and no one could stop him from trying to rescue the true queen from her imprisonment by Queen Elizabeth of England. He died in a failed attempt to free her, betrayed by men determined to have the former queen beheaded for the sake of their own power. Yer uncle always had a fighting spirit."

Reid faced his sons. "Sometimes ye have to fight, and mayhap die, for what ye believe in. To some it sounds foolish, but to the man doing the fighting, 'tis no'. I hope it ne'er comes to it, but someday ye may have to choose between yer life and yer values, and I pray ye will choose wisely."

Rubbing her fingers over Reid's hand, Leena said, "The years we've had together mean everything to me, and I'm certain Hugh's wife, Kit, feels the same way about the years she had with him. And now she's glad to have him back home."

"We'll go with ye to pay our respects. Yer family is our family. Lead the way."

As soon as Leena came within sight of the family stones in the Makgullane graveyard, warm memories washed over her. "Cemeteries are no' to honor the bones in the dirt, but to remember the people we loved who also loved us."

Willie touched each letter of Suannoch's name carved on her stone. "Someday I'll bring my daughter here so she can learn about the woman who gave her her name."

"I'll do the same with my lad, Robin," said Ramy proudly, "as soon as he's old enough to remember his great-grandfather. He took his first steps right before we left to come here."

"This is Johnnie's stone, and over there is Hugh's," said Leena. "The grave will be dug tomorrow. All my brothers will help."

"The lads and I will be honored to help dig as

well," said Reid.

That night, Leena snuggled against Reid in one of the small upstairs bedrooms while her sons shared a room next to theirs.

"Does it feel comfortable to be back home?" Reid asked in the pleasurable aftermath of their lovemaking. He brushed gold strands of hair off her forehead. "Do ye ever wish ye were living back here instead of in Edinburgh?"

She paused for a long time before answering. "Do ye understand why 'twas so hard for me to cross the street the day we met?"

He chuckled.

"Now I cross the streets in Edinburgh like I've lived there all my life." She tugged the quilt higher around her. "I remember living here as a child and as a young wife, and I often think about what's happening when I'm no' here, but do I wish my life were here instead of with ye and the lads? Nay. My life is with ye. Ye could live in a swamp, and I'd still want to be with ye." Coming up on her elbow, she said, "Keep in mind that I'd nag ye every day to leave that wretched swamp, but if ye're there, then so am I."

Laying back, he tugged her into him and kissed her forehead. He lifted his burned left hand. "I do regret this."

Pulling that hand to her lips, she kissed it. "I regret that ye suffer with it, but it reminds me that we survived. Together we survived. We've had these years together, and I wouldna give them up for anything. Neither would Willie, Ramy, or Hendrie."

"To many more years of loving ye, no matter where we are." He closed his eyes and held her close all night long.

The wake began the next day.

Taking her sons and husband aside, Leena explained, "A funeral here in the Highlands may be different from ones ye have seen in Stirling or Edinburgh. There has only been the occasional visiting priest on the estate for many years, so traditions have evolved. In some places in Scotland, women are forbidden to participate in the wake or even go with the body to the graveyard, but no' so at Makgullane. Watch the others around ye and follow their lead.

"Oh, and mourning is saved for private times. If anyone sheds tears, they will be happy tears, so share the happy memories with them."

Dish after dish of food covered the table in the gathering room while a piper played traditional tunes on his bagpipes accompanied by a woman on a flute. Many of the neighbors and friends of Makgullane joined the entire clan that had begun with Grandfather, Laird Bretane, and now covered four generations. They all came to eat, sing, and share memories of Hugh along with those who had passed on before.

As the mourners walked to the cemetery, Ramy touched Leena's arm. "Meena, why does Hugh's widow, Kit, wear two silver chains with dice on them around her neck?"

"Yer Uncle Hugh was a gambler in his youth. His die on his necklace had one pip because he was one. Kit's has two pips for the two of them, and if ye look at Cousin Mary's chain, her die has three pips showing for the three of them.

"Uncle Fergus, as a history scholar at the University of Glasgow, joined the identification group at the grave site and recognized Hugh from the chain around his neck. Other families received body parts only because the man's name appeared on a list, no' because they were certain of who it was."

Hugh's body returned to his family wrapped in a stitched closed bag of heavy cloth, and as the men took turns shoveling the dirt over the body, each one told a memory of their brother, or friend, Hugh Cullane. Some stories were sad while others brought laughter to everyone.

Reid whispered to his sons, "These Makgullane and Cullane stories are yer heritage. Mayhap no' yers from birth, but yers from the gift of family. Ye will keep their dreams as yer own…and ye will pass them on to yer children. A family is created by love, and nothing else matters."

The Haliburtons stayed on the estate for two more weeks, listening, learning, and enjoying the family that claimed Makgullane as their own for all these years.

Every five years thereafter they journeyed back to Makgullane, bringing with them their children and then their children's children to see and hear about the heritage that had become theirs because of a gaggle of noisy geese.

Gu'n deanadh Dia maille riut. May God be with you.

Historical Information

The discovery of gunpowder by the Chinese around 850 AD began as a search for a life-lengthening elixir until, much to the scientists' surprise, the resulting compound burned their hands, and then burned down their houses. Although the use of gunpowder in firearms dates back to the 1200s in China, it wasn't until the 1400s and 1500s in Europe that gunsmithing grew rapidly.

As soon as gunsmiths began experimenting with gunpowder's use in smaller handheld firearms, the demand for such guns grew, and governments throughout the continent began to maintain extensive storehouses of weapons. England lagged behind until King Henry VIII asked the leading gunsmiths to come to London to work for him, which many did. Earliest civilian gun ownership was restricted to the wealthy and noblemen, but before long such ownership became widespread.

The making of a gun required considerable patience and knowledge, sometimes taking as long as four hundred hours to complete a single weapon. Gunsmiths needed to be skilled in both wood and metal work and to be experts in precision craftsmanship.

I fictionalized the weapon designed by my fictional character, Reid Haliburton. I researched how guns of that time operated, and I created an improvement that worked only for the purposes of my story.

The character of Jonas McDever is loosely based on a real life pirate, Peter Love. Born in Lewes, Sussex, England, Love captained the *Priam*, and for a time used the Isle of Lewis in the Outer Hebrides of Scotland as his base. There he met and befriended another outlaw named Neil MacLeod.

Love hid the *Priam* full of stolen cargo in a cove held by MacLeod, a cargo consisting of cinnamon, ginger, pepper, cochineal, sugar, seven hundred Indian hides, twenty-nine pieces of silver plate, a box of various precious stones, and a large amount of cash. MacLeod, seeing a way to expand his own coffers, invited Love to attend a feast during which Love married MacLeod's daughter, although some sources say it was MacLeod's aunt.

By distracting Love with the festivities, MacLeod's men attacked the ship and seized it. They also intended to turn Love over to the authorities in Edinburgh and thus earn MacLeod a pardon for his own illegal activities. The spices, etc., on board the *Priam* were of little value to MacLeod and his men, but they quickly divided the cash, leaving no record of money in the governmental reports.

Love and nine of his crew were subsequently tried in Edinburgh on December 8, 1610, and sentenced to hang at Leith, northeast of Edinburgh. *"To be tane to ane Gibbet ypone the Sandis of Levth, within the fflodes-mark, and their be hangit quhill thay be deid."* The only words needing translation from the Old English are the last seven—"there be hanged until they be dead."

In an ironic turn of events, three years later Neil MacLeod's own kinsman, Rory Mor MacLeod, betrayed him. Arrested and found guilty of high treason, Neil MacLeod was hanged in April of 1613.

Another true story gave me the idea to have the pirates try to kill Reid by trapping him in a cave and setting a fire in the entrance. Clan feuds were frequent, and the one between the MacLeods and the MacDonalds was particularly brutal. One nasty act of revenge after another led to a MacLeod invasion of MacDonald territory. Aware of the coming attack, the entire MacDonald clan hid in a cave. They would have escaped detection except for a careless lookout who left footprints leading to the cave entrance in which the MacLeods lit a smoky bonfire that suffocated all 400 of the MacDonald clan inside.

The connection between Hugh and Queen Mary of Scots as a child is a key plot point in my second book about the Cullane family, *By Promise Made*. Although this connection is entirely fictional, it gives Hugh the motivation years later to try to rescue Mary from her cousin, Queen Elizabeth I of England. This subsequently led to his death and brought Leena to Makgullane for his burial in the last chapter of *Keeper of My Dreams*.

A word about the author...

Susan Leigh Furlong is the author of numerous articles, plays, and novels, none of which will ever be published, but she is the published author of a play about the Last Supper, two nonfiction books about the history and people of her small town in Ohio, and two romantic adventures, *Steadfast Will I Be* and *By Promise Made*.

While her life with her husband, two curious cats, and assorted relatives and friends is full and rich, she still gets lost in the lives of her characters. She lives with them, fights with them, and eventually rescues them.

A former teacher and writing coach, actor and director, and now a practicing grandmother, she hopes you enjoy the lives she creates—just for you!

Thank you for purchasing
this publication of The Wild Rose Press, Inc.

For questions or more information
contact us at
info@thewildrosepress.com.

The Wild Rose Press, Inc.
www.thewildrosepress.com